misTRUSTful

never play with a womans emotions...

Also By C.R. Jackson

"Rain Dancing: when you're ready to release the guilt"

misTRUSTful

never play with a womans emotions...

C.R. Jackson

Published by

K.D. Publishing

Published by K.D. Publishing
Distributed
A&B Distributors
1000 Atlantic Avenue
Brooklyn, New York, 11238
(718) 783-7808

Cover Design and layout: Joi Jackson for MMI, Inc.
Cover Models: Trayce Toles and Frank Gailor.
Photography: Rod Hollimon for MMI, Inc. All rights reserved

Media Management International, Inc.
875 Crew St.
Suite 117
Atlanta, GA 30315
(770) 842-3841

This is a work of fiction. Names, characters, places, and incidents either are the product of the author's imagination or are used fictitiously, and any resemblance to actual persons, living or dead, business establishments, events or locales are entirely coincidental.

Manufactured in Canada

03 04 05 06   4 5 6 7 8 9 10 11 12

In Loving Memory of Mrs. Nezzie "Nell"

Thomas, Mrs. Margie

Jackson, Keith Daniel Magby, June

Thomas, and "Tweety" Jackson

one

"So how old are you?" the woman asked as she downed the olive from her Martini. The question caused the young man to cock his head from left to right as he attempted to make sense of it. She chewed slowly and deliberately while attempting to focus on the eyes of the young man standing in front of her. The dim light of the club provided a relaxing atmosphere, and made it difficult for each of them to see each other. However, the confident and brisk tunes flowing from the saxophone ushered her last question directly to his ears. She placed her drink on the bar in a way that insisted he answer the question before it was repeated. The young man took a deep breath as he finally took the seat next to her. He was now sitting between her and the woman who came in with her.

He looked at her. She never flinched while waiting for a response. Feeling a bit defeated, he placed both elbows on the bar. His face rested in both of his large hands. He rubbed his head a few times then pivoted his barstool to face her. His hands dropped to his lap as he began to speak. "Ya' know Dee, I knew when I saw you walking in here that you had a whole lot of trouble behind you. But, I never thought that you would be bringing all of this with you," he said as he looked

1

in a corner of the club where two gorgeous women sat in idle chit-chat. If he didn't tell the truth to the two women in the corner, the woman sitting in front of him would.

"Uh-huh," she said taking another drink from her glass. She placed seven dollars on the counter, finished the drink, then stood to her feet. "Well I'm sorry you see it as trouble son. But believe me," she continued, "I didn't drive all this way to bring you some trouble." She paused for a moment before continuing. "Before I go let me answer the question for you. You are nineteen years old," she said leaning in front of him to grab under his chin.

"And the way I understand it, yo' young ass ain't even supposed to be in here. Now with you being nineteen and all, I won't even embarrass you. Truth be told, I want to smack the shit out of you right here and now. But since I was the one to raise you over all of these years, I know that I don't have to do that. I know that I can turn around and walk out of here and not even have to worry about whether or not you did the right thing." She looked straight into his eyes and continued. "So you're about to give me a big kiss and a huge hug; and the same for your godmother. You're gonna watch both of us walk out of here and in two hours you'll call to make sure Mama made it home okay," she concluded.

"But Dee," Davis attempted to explain. His mother would have none of it. She raised her right index finger to her lips to signal him to hush. He did exactly that as he began hugging and kissing them both. Soon they disappeared from the club.

He took another deep breath as he looked once again at the two women sitting in the corner. "Shit," he thought aloud as he began his trek to the other side of the club. "How in the hell did I end up in this," he said once again as he searched his memory for an answer to his question.

10 MONTHS EARLIER

It seemed as if a long gray sea had been coming at him for the last hour and a half. Fatigue was setting in. He was on Interstate 20 West, the only way to reach that majestic city of Atlanta. Although he was only 19, Davis wondered if he would ever see the infamous city he had heard so much about. He had friends who had been traveling there since they had been ableto drive legally.

One of those friends was 21 year old Michael Cain. He and Davis first became friends in the first grade. In spite of his lack of book sense, he still was Davis' best friend. No one could ever understand the combination.

Davis was a young man who seemed to have his head on straight. Not only was he respectful, but he was extremely smart. In fact, he graduated in the top five percent of his class. This was unheard of for someone from Sunset Homes. Also known as "The Set," a low-income housing development in Augusta, GA, it was surprising when any young black male graduated at all.

Big Mike fell into the category of non-graduates. As a matter of fact, he fell into a lot of categories that were looked upon with angry eyes by most of the elders of Sunset Homes. He was fearless and always looking for respect and praise. He would do anything to gain this respect. Usually, fighting fit the bill. It was also his favorite. His 22-inch arms could deliver a blow that would leave his opponent out of breath. His ego and high success rate created many opportunities to fight anyone at anytime. That's what Davis loved about him; at first, he didn't know why. Surely, he didn't enjoy watching people get humiliated.

Not until Davis was a senior in high school did he realize why he enjoyed Mike's acts of violence. The class was English; the assignment was an essay; and the topic was "My Hero." There were no role models in the Set. Only people who partied too much all of their lives and were now regretting it. For such a simple topic, Davis caught hell trying to think of a hero. His teacher, a white female, suggested he write about his father. It took all the strength he had to stop from laughing in her face. He knew his father was a sorry ass, but was too proud to let anyone else know, especially someone white.

After getting the definition of a hero from a dictionary, he had a revelation. His hero was the same guy who always treated him to dinner at the local buffet and a movie at the local dollar theater. He was the same guy with whom he had many useless debates with, such as who had more money: Run D.M.C. or the FAT BOYS .

"Whoa," he thought. "Big Mike is my hero. That's why I love to see him fight." It was like someone who enjoyed watching Superman save a child from a burning building. That's what heroes do, and they do it well. It wasn't that he closed someone's eyes or opened someone's head, but it was the proficiency with which he did it. It was pure art watching him fight. He was the best.

Big Mike was the one who first brought back word about this great city that Davis and his friends later deemed "Phatlanta." He took the trip with his friends who sold herb. He began hangin' with this crowd when Davis started playing high school basketball. Big Mike told him about the huge skyscrapers, the six lane highways, and the exceptionally attractive and intelligent women. Although Davis couldn't understand why Big Mike would be interested in an intelligent girl, he at least made an attempt to envision such a female. A very poor attempt it was, considering all of the women Davis saw were either unattractive or had some noticeable flaw. Whether that flaw came in the form of a bad complexion, a huge butt, long feet, or obesity, it turned him off. He was like any other young man his age that looks for the perfect woman. He would learn later that no such thing existed.

Visions of beautiful women would dance in his head for

the duration of the trip. He was making the trip with the love of his life: his mother. He stole a look over at her. She was sleeping with a proud smile on her face. He stared at her for a second before he was thrown back into reality by the red sports car that came whizzing by. As he regained his concentration of the road, he wondered how he had managed to drive safely for the last 15 minutes while daydreaming so much. He decided to check the

dashboard controls. The car needed gas. He pulled off at an exit in Conyers, Georgia and came to a stop at the Amoco gas station. His mother woke up.

"Where are we?" she asked in a voice that was muffled with sleep and thirst.

"I think the sign said Conyers," Davis responded. "We need some gas. Do you want something to drink?" he asked walking towards the store.

"Nah. That's all right. I just gotta use the rest room." He walked to the counter and waited to give his money to the attendant.

"May I hap ya?" the clerk asked. The bad English and uneducated accent didn't surprise him at all. Behind the counter was an overweight black female who had a gold tooth in the front of her mouth that blended with some very synthetic-looking gold tracks in her hair. The bangles around her wrist jingled noisily. She twisted one of the tracks in her hair around her forefinger.

"Yeah. I would like $10 on pump number 3," he responded.

"Dat'sall? " she asked.

"Excuse me?" Davis asked, after losing her last two words somewhere in the laziness with which her mouth spoke them.

"I said will dat be all?" she repeated.

"Yeah, thanks," he said as he walked out of the door.

As he began pumping the gas, his mind focused on Atlanta again and the possibility that there probably wouldn't be any uneducated-sounding women like that where he was going. That's all he had grown up around. He was definitely looking for something different.

But what exactly was it he was looking for? How did he know he wanted something different? He had so many questions about women. It really bothered him that he didn't have any credible men around to answer his questions. Every man in the Set acted as if he were God's gift to women. The only positive thing they had to say was that "she has a big ass," or "she surely knows how to fuck." They never commented on a woman's intellect; nor did they ever discuss how to deal with a female's emotions. He had no idea of what made a virtuous woman.

His thoughts were interrupted as his mother thrust a scented handy-wipe in his face, implying that his hands smelled like gasoline. She hopped in the driver's seat.

"It won't be long now," she said with a much clearer voice. It was evident that she had taken a sip of her diet cola. She was a recent fan of diet sodas since being instructed to moderate her fat intake by her doctor. As he stared at the large cup in her hand, he thought, "This diet cola business must be the greatest marketing ploy ever. Weight loss in a bottle? C'mon. So it had a few less calories? It also had a high sugar content and a whole lot of some type of acid that couldn't be too good for the bladder."

Davis and his mother often joked about her inconsistent eating habits. Every Sunday she would make something like macaroni and cheese, country fried steak with gravy, rice, corn bread, and string beans made in fatback. As she would prepare the plates, Davis would set the table and prepare the drinks. Each time before he had an opportunity to finish pouring, she would ask the same thing: "Ya' sure mine's diet? Ya' know I don't mess with that other stuff no mo'." Davis would always respond the same way: "Yeah Dee. Um' sure yours is diet."

Delois Virginia, or Dee, as everyone affectionately called

her, was the inspiration of his life. She got off of welfare, started working and stopped smoking. Dee was a fair-skinned, middle-aged woman with a great smile that was backed up by an extraordinary set of teeth. For the most part, she was a jolly woman. She loved to laugh, and she loved to debate; no matter the topic. She would get so involved in her discussions that her voice would rise, and her opponents would usually find themselves wondering, "Why is this lady getting so upset?" She would then break the atmosphere with one of her deep penetrating laughs. Standing 5' 10", she was a fairly large woman.

Dee had huge hands. Davis often thanked the Lord for whippings with belts instead of a smack across the head, as was the case with most of his friends and their mothers.

Since his mother was driving, he decided to get a little sleep. When he opened his eyes, his mother was pulling off of I-20's Lee Street exit. As they drove down Lee Street, he saw the Morehouse School of Medicine on his right. He wondered to himself just how much did it look like a college. Before he could form an opinion, he noticed a building, which did look like a college in the distance. Actually it was a group of buildings surrounded by a gate. It was Spelman College.

"Look Davis," his mother exclaimed excitedly. When he followed her pointing finger his eyes landed on a large metal statue of Martin Luther King, Jr.

"Wow," he exclaimed. "This is Morehouse!"

He was at the Atlanta University Center. The AUC, as it is more commonly known, consists of the Inter-denominational Theological Seminary, Morehouse School of Medicine, Morris Brown College, Spelman College, Morehouse College, and Clark Atlanta University. Delois was escorting her only child to his first year at Clark Atlanta.

Before he knew it, Davis was in front of Brawley Hall. This was to be his home for the next year. It was the only male dorm on campus. "The only male dorm," he thought to himself. Those words rang almost silently from his lips. He couldn't say it too loud because he didn't want his mother to hear him. Oh no, he couldn't have his mother thinking that her baby was there to become some sort of womanizer. To him, womanizer was too strong of a word. But it wasn't too far off because he was definitely there to get acquainted with a better class of females.

Dee spent the next hour getting his room straightened out. She knew that it wouldn't stay that way for too long, but her motherly guise obligated her to do it. She was careful to place her favorite picture on his desk. It was the picture she took with him the minute he came off the stage with his high school diploma. Her eyes puffed up as she thought about it, and a single tear ran down her face. She thought about how much their lives had changed. Four years ago, she was on welfare, and they lived in a roach infested apartment in Sunset Homes. It was her baby that gave her the strength to make a change in her life. After getting off public assistance and working a steady job for three years at the local hotel, they were finally able to move out of the projects and into a decent apartment. She was also able to buy a used car and say good-bye to public transportation.

Davis opened the door, and she quickly wiped the tears from her eyes. He had gone downstairs to pay his room deposit. He met some fellow freshmen in the process.

"Well are you ready for the tour?" he said, pretending not to see her cry.

"Yeah I guess so," she said as she headed towards the door. The two of them headed down stairs.

The campus was absolutely beautiful. The smell of fresh cut grass and the sight of the water fountains in the center of the yard were breathtaking. Dee and her son even stopped to take a picture in front of it. As they snapped the picture and started to walk off, they both heard a voice chase them down from behind.

"Yeah, snap your pictures now because the water will

stop running just as soon as all of the parents leave."

Davis turned in the direction of the voice. He and his mother turned to see a tall, wiry fella dressed in a pimpish fashion, including a Kangol.

"They just turned the water on yesterday. They did it just to impress all the parents who were coming today. Man, that fountain is only on 10 days out of the year. By the way, I'm Tyrone."

As Davis shook his hand, he introduced himself and his mother. Dee shook her head at the slickster but never spoke. Davis knew what that meant. She was quietly using her supermom intuition to check out this character.

"Listen folks, you can follow that tour and get that proud institution babble that the guide will give you or you can follow me and get the truth from a guy who has spent a year here already," Tyrone offered. Davis couldn't understand why this guy was making such an attempt to get to know them, but it made him cautious. He looked over at his mother to see what she thought. She had a sour look on her face as her eyes looked Tyrone up and down. She didn't like this young man, and Davis knew it.

"Thanks anyway man but we'll finish this one out," Davis declined as he grabbed his mother's hand and headed towards the rest of the group.

The tour lasted another 30 minutes. Later, Davis and his mom found themselves enjoying a bagged lunch prepared by the University.

"Davis this is a nice looking campus, huh?" Dee commented.

"Yeah," he replied.

The truth is that he really didn't know what the campus looked like because he spent all of his time looking at the girls near the front of the tour group. He couldn't believe it. Damn near every girl was flawless. His mouth began to water just thinking about them. After lunch Davis walked his mother to the car. Much to his surprise, their good-bye was short and simple. He thought Dee would get all mushy. The truth was her mind was on the drive back home. Her son wasn't going to be on her side for the trip back. She was naturally worried since she had never taken a road trip by herself. Although the drive was only two hours, she figured she'd better make use of all of the daylight left. As she drove outof the parking lot, she yelled to Davis.

"I'll call you when I get home." Tears fell from his eyes as the 77' Nova turned the corner and drove out of sight. He was still in the same spot.

The time was now 6:04 p.m., and Davis had about two hours before his dorm meeting. He started back to his room. Maybe he could get a nap before the meeting. As he opened the door he was startled; his roommate had arrived. The guy was about 5' 9" tall. He rushed to Davis with his hand fully extended to introduce himself.

"Hey man, h' ya' doin'? My name is Holly Johnson from Orangeburg, South Carolina." Davis was speechless. Surely he knew people who were country, but he never knew anyone who flaunted it. Holly flaunted it with much pride. Davis couldn't help but notice his ungroomed head. This was odd considering it was the middle of the day. Next he spotted the huge ring around the collar of a very much-tattered Panama Jack shirt. He hadn't seen one of those shirts since seventh grade. At this point, Davis was nervous about dropping his eyes down to the jeans. Just as he suspected, Holly was wearing Wranglers. He didn't have on boots. Instead, he was sporting a pair of Asahi tennis shoes.

After this brief overview of his roommate's outfit, Davis looked the boy in his eyes. Holly was one of those people that looked startled all the time. He was extremely bug-eyed, yet his teeth were incredibly white. Davis reached out to shake his hand and introduce himself. Holly even had the firm handshake of a country boy.

After the two finished unpacking, they both headed downstairs for their first dormitory meeting. They were early. There was only one other person in the lounge, and the TV was blaring. Davis sat down and started twiddling his thumbs. He really wasn't in the mood for talking. He just wanted to get this meeting over with so he could call his mother to make sure she made it in . He raised his head to get a view of whomever was coming into the lounge when he heard a female's voice on the television. He was overwhelmed when he finally focused in on the woman on the screen. He couldn't help but gawk at her beauty. It wasn't just her face that caught his attention, but it was her mannerisms and voice as well. Her hair draped the top of her head like a black velvet handkerchief. Her eyebrows were full and flowing, and her eyelashes were short and bold. Her eyes were a rich chocolate brown and twinkled with life. Her nose was flawless and covered in the same rich caramel coating that covered all of her body as far as he could see. Her mouth was the best of all. Her lips were puffy and moist, and his only regret was that she didn't have on a deep red lipstick to highlight them.

As he slowly came back to reality, he noticed that she had some type of object in front of her face. What the hell was she doing. As his eyes focused, he was able to discern the object as a microphone. "Oh, she's a reporter," he thought aloud. He was not going to let this report end without learning this lady's name. It suddenly flashed, iKia Brent." He would fall asleep with the vision in front of him for many nights to come.

Needless to say, he didn't pay much attention to the meeting. The guy he met earlier, Tyrone, was a resident assistant (RA). Tyrone looked strangely at Davis throughout the meeting; as if he were sizing him up. Once after breaking off the stare with Tyrone, he turned his head to Holly, who had taken his shoes halfway off. As if that wasn't bad enough, his ankles and heels were white with ash. "I need a shower and some sleep," Davis thought to himself.

As the meeting ended, Davis dashed for the phone.

Dee's voice was soothing to him. They were both tired so they didn't talk much. After about five minutes, Davis told his mother to take good care of herself before he hung up the phone. He was off to the wonderful world of community bathrooms. The last thing he remembered before his eyes closed was a small conversation with Holly.

2

The next morning, Davis' eyes were greeted to confusion about his whereabouts. The bed beneath him felt different. "Now where am I?" he wondered. He could smell the morning air. It was definitely an August morning in the south. He wanted to get his mental calendar together before getting out of bed. There was so much for him to do today.

"Let's see. I have to go to financial aid, the scholarship office, the admissions office, and the bookstore. Now when I finish..." His thoughts were cut off by a humming noise. It was coming from Holly. Davis dismissed it as snoring. He was about to finish planning his day when he heard the same sound again - only louder. He looked over at his roommate. He couldn't see his face. Holly was totally engulfed by the covers. But Davis noticed the covers shaking violently. He became alarmed. "Oh my God! He's having a seizure!" Davis exclaimed. It was too early for anyone to be awake to help him. He had to regain his composure. "Ok ok. I need to calm down." He quickly paced across the room. "I've seen this done before. Raise his head," he thought.

Davis quickly ran to Holly's bedside, leaned over his bed and simultaneously reached for the desk lamp and the sheets covering his head. At almost the same instant he pulled the covers off of the bed, he heard Holly moan intensely. A wad of saliva came flying at Davis' head. Davis attempted to duck, but part of the wad caught him on the cheek. This didn't bother him. He had to make sure his roommate was okay.

Holly was no longer shaking. He was just lying there motionless. He stared at Davis with his huge eyes, but he didn't stir. Davis' mind started to get the best of him.

"Damn! Is he dead?" he asked himself. That's when Holly blinked and Davis knew everything was okay. Davis was about to smile with relief when he noticed something odd. "Why is this guy butt naked and why is he holding his penis?" Holly's eyes followed Davis' eyes to where they were looking. Holly saw his hand wrapped around his penis. He could only curse himself at that point. By now, it had hit Davis like a train.

"This muthafucka was masturbating!" he said to himself. Then Davis thought about the wad of saliva on his cheek. It wasn't saliva. He tried to get himself together before he said anything to Holly, but he just couldn't.

"You nasty bastard!" he yelled as he stormed out of the room. He headed for the bathroom. As he walked down the hall he reached for his face and with a vicious swipe pulled the disgusting gunk from the side of his cheek. It hit the hallway floor with a vicious thud.

He only spent a few seconds wiping his face. He had to get back and "cuss the fucka' out." As he started back to his room, Holly was already dressed. He started running towards the bathroom. While Davis watched his roommate running full speed coming his way, he suddenly remembered the wad on the floor. But before he could warn him, Holly reached the spot. His foot made contact with the slippery substance on the newly waxed floor, and his feet came out from under him. The rest of his body followed his feet. His eyes widened. It seemed like he was in the air a full ten seconds - eight seconds of which was spent yelling and bracing for impact. "Blam!" Holly hit the floor. It was unlike any noise Davis had ever heard. Holding his mouth like it was on fire, Davis turned around and ran back into the bathroom.

Once inside, he let out a laugh that was so loud, it caused a nearby shaver to nick himself. After regaining his composure, he went back out into the hallway to make sure Holly was okay. A crowd of guys formed around his body. Once Davis saw Holly struggle to his feet with the help of the wall, He returned to apologize to the shaver.

"Yo man, I'm sorry about that," he offered.

"That's all right chief. Don't sweat it," the shaver responded in a raspy voice.

"I'm Davis man. I live in 204," he said as he extended his hand in friendship.

"Oh for real? I live in 205 man. I'm Lester."

Davis stood quietly against the wall as he giggled inside. He could not believe how laid-back this guy was. And the way he talked was so slow and confident.

Lester asked Davis for some shampoo. Davis couldn't understand where this question was coming from. He didn't have anything in his hands. He didn't see any sitting around in the bathroom either.

"Why ya' asking me for shampoo?" he finally asked Lester.

"Oh um sorry, that must be your last lil' bit," Lester responded. "That what's in ya' head now." He pointed at Davis' head.

Davis started running his hand through his head nervously. His hand felt something cold and sticky. "What the hell is this?" he thought aloud. Then he remembered the scene of himself ducking from the wad that came towards his face when he was checking on Holly. His face winced with repulsion, and he made a b-line for the shower.

He quickly jumped into the hot shower and immediately began to relax. He was truly hoping that the incident this morning would not be a sign of the rest of his day. When he got back to his room to get dressed, he refused to talk to his roommate. Holly continuously tried to explain, but his efforts were in vain. Ironically, in Davis' mind, it was funnier than anything else. It was Holly's problem. Davis thought to himself, "I hope he never has a seizure for real because he may have to die."

Shortly thereafter, he was out of the door and ready to start his day. He ran into Tyrone. The two ended up having an interesting walk across campus. Tyrone seemed to be a real womanizer. Davis deduced this from all of the lovely young ladies that came up to give him welcome-back hugs. However, Davis thought it was bizarre how Tyrone kept introducing him to others as his boy or partner. They barely knew each other. There was definitely something strange about this guy, but Davis figured since he was new on the campus scene, he could definitely use someone to show him around, and more importantly, introduce him to the females.

Soon the two split up. Davis headed to the scholarship office. The rest of the walk was pretty interesting. He was able to notice a lot more since no one was talking in his ear.

The scenery was beautiful. "Damn, black folk every-where!" Davis was overwhelmed. In the distance, he heard music blasting from the rooms of students who were just waking up in the dorms. He heard all types of music: N.W.A., Eric B and Rakim, Ghetto Boys, Al B. Sure. It was awesome.

As he got closer to his destination he noticed more people on the scene. The guys seemed different from those in Augusta. They didn't appear to be thugs. They weren't dressed in argyle sweaters, wearing glasses or anything like that. They weren't carrying a bunch of books either. Actually, they wore jeans that were too big for them, untucked shirts, and Timberlands. They spent half their time pulling their pants up on their behinds, as his mother would say. They talked differently; they were able to express themselves. They didn't spend half their conversation repeating that idiotic phrase; "ya know what um sayin'?" Their conversation wasn't just about some girl they were trying to screw or who they beat up last night. The conversations actually had substance. Of course they still talked about girls but most of it was tasteful.

The guys definitely were not the only ones he noticed. The young females he had seen up to this point were all attractive in some shape or form: from the tall, dark ones to the short light ones. The physiques varied from thin to plump and sexy. He was so enticed that when he reached his destination, he found himself longing to stay outside and enjoy the view. How could he leave all of this? But it was time to get down to business and make his mother proud.

Once he got upstairs to the office, he walked into two women who carried a distinctive southern flair. "Hello, my name is Davis Virginia, and I'm here to sign in," Davis said in a childish voice. He was definitely intimidated by the presence of the women. Keeping their silence, the two women looked him over with probing and penetrating eyes. He was nervous for a second. What was it? Had he done or said something to offend them? Did he not knock before entering? Why wouldn't they say anything? Whatever the problem was, he was sure he didn't deserve the look he was getting from them. He couldn't decide which was worse. One was peering at him with a pair of beady eyes that looked straight through him. The other had the old, familiar look over the rim of her glasses. He would have quickly apologized if he knew the problem. It seemed as if an eternity had passed. He wished they would just speak. "Well hey baby, how you doing?" The woman with the glasses finally broke the silence. "I'm Ms. Nebby and this is Ms. Holman." Davis spoke to the other woman in a very nervous tone.

"Sweetheart, where's your mother?" asked Ms. Holman.

"She left yesterday ma'am," he replied.

"Oh, that's a shame," replied Ms. Holman.

He began to get more comfortable as it hit him that they weren't intentionally trying to make him feel uncomfortable. They were simply trying to size him up. He didn't want to get ahead of himself, but in retrospect, he could tell their looks were of adoration. They were happy to see any young black male walking in the door on a campus where the ratio of females to males was 11 to 1.

"Come on into my office Davis and let me get you all signed up," Ms. Nebby said.

He followed the short robust woman into an office filled with file cabinets, graduation pictures, and plaques all over the wall. He looked on the desk. It was cluttered with papers. The desk's nameplate read Rhonda L. Nesbitt. He concluded "Nebby" was an affectionate derivative that she acquired over the years. She engaged herself in some loose conversation with Davis and he responded to each comment very politely. As she talked to him, she diligently worked up his paperwork. From her expensive skirt and blouse complete with an elephant broach, to the expensive perfume she wore, he could tell she was truly a professional. She smelled like she had taken a shower in her perfume. It always amazed him how older men and women always went heavy on the cologne and perfume. Did they just over do it or had they just been wearing it so long that it was in their skin for life?

She continued with the small talk. She glanced at Davis and noticed how he was loosing interest. Then like the professional she was, she suddenly threw the conversation into overdrive. She wanted to get his ears early because she knew that he was a walking piece of sirloin around a campus filled with female canines. As she turned her swivel chair towards him, she raised her eyes to look over the rim of her glasses again. She had his complete attention.

"Now let me tell you something baby. College, especially a black college, can make or break a young African-American male such as yourself. Now I know you didn't come down here to waste anybody's money. I'm telling you that time management is the secret to handling college. In short, you're not going to have any time to chase any young tails around here."

He smiled and listened intently. She really had his confidence now. He had never heard anyone but southern women, like his mom, refer to young girls as a piece of tail.

She continued. "You can smile if you want to, but I'll tell you now that there are over 1,000 people walking around the AUC right now with some type of venereal disease."

This really caught his attention. That statistic was all he could think about for the rest of the conversation. Towards the end, she offered him advice and her ears to listen if he ever needed it. With that, he was on his way.

As he walked out of the building, the sunlight hit him like a prizefighter. With squinted his eyes, he noticed a lot more people roaming about on campus for one reason or another. Everyone was now out of bed and trying to register for the fall semester. They were not the only ones up and about. The hot Atlanta sun was making its appearance as well. The sun highlighted the women he passed on campus that stepped lively and with a purpose. They already looked like professional women with their sunglasses on and their bags draped across their shoulders. They all had finely pedicured toes peeping from the top of their sandals.

There was one young lady in particular walking towards him who caught his eye. She had a fair complexion and wore a white cotton summer dress that polished the curves of her 5' 9" frame. On her feet she wore a pair of thong sandals, which exposed the flaming candy red nail polish on her toes. Her feet, like her legs, were so finely lotioned they were shining. As she got closer to him he was able to notice her lips. The gloss she wore was as succulent as a morning rose covered in dew. Her hair was short with brown highlights that complimented her eyes that were covered by a pair of black sunglasses. When she passed him, his nose was fortunate enough to partake in the fresh scent that enveloped her body and was as pure as a bar of Ivory soap and some designer lotion. He didn't want to seem like a masculine oaf, so he turned around when she passed. But after five seconds, his neck would have nothing less. His head turned back around, and he watched her backside. Her calf muscles were lustrous, protracted, and seductive. He wanted to bite one of them. While his eyes were centered in that direction, he decided to look for the all too common ash on the back of the heels. There was nothing but beautiful brown, glossy skin. He then decided to travel up a bit. There it was. One of the most perfect asses he had ever seen. It was what the boys back in Sunset would refer to as an "onion." It was taut and rounded. When his vision moved up even further, the semi-backless sundress gave him a little treat. The back of any infant couldn't have been any smoother than the back on which he now gazed. As his sights rose above her shoulders, his whole body jerked as his mouth released an "Oh my God." The young lady's neck was twisted in such a fashion as to give her eyes the optimum angle to gaze back into his. She took off her shades and turned to look at him.

He started to think about the embarrassment when he suddenly heard the words, "Her name is Keandra Dixon." Davis turned in the direction from which the words were spoken. He found a smirk on the face of Tyrone. He started to wonder if this guy was following him. "Everybody calls her Kee-Kee," Tyrone continued. "Don't sweat it. I'll be sure to introduce you." After exchanging pleasantries and having one last look at Kee-Kee, the two guys decided to get some breakfast.

As they entered the cafeteria, the sounds and sights of people conversing and hugging greeted them. Obviously, they were upper-classmen who missed each other over the summer. That's when Davis really started to appreciate the presence of Tyrone. He did not want to look lonely and even more, he did not want to look like a freshman. With Tyrone being a sophomore, he was killing two birds with one stone. As Davis waited in line, he looked out over the crowd of people. It was varied in geographical representation, as was evident by their dress and dialects.

The two grabbed their food and took their seats at a table facing the door so they could see everyone who entered. Tyrone gave Davis the lowdown on everyone he knew who came in. During that time, a couple of girls made their way to the table and embraced Tyrone. One of the hugs suggested the two had been intimate at one point in time. He made it a point to introduce Davis to all of the young ladies. While Tyrone was getting reacquainted with them, Davis watched the door. He noticed three guys walk in who looked as if they were from Pakistan. He wondered a little more about their origin when he noticed his roommate waddling in with a look of sheer hunger on his face. Davis used his hand to cover his forehead as his head dropped and slowly turned from side to side as if to say, "oh no!" Holly had no idea what type of social gathering this was.

Davis continued to watch him as he made his way to the serving counter and engaged himself in a conversation with the lady on the other side of the counter. He looked at Holly's hair. Surprisingly, it was combed. His face wasn't even ashy. His clothes were neatly pressed, and he was wearing new tennis shoes. Davis' eyes focused on his roommates lips at the exact same moment his voice went up an octave and uttered the words, "Anything we want?" Davis shrugged in his seat, looked towards the ceiling and covered his eyes with both of his hands. "What is he doing?" Davis uttered under his breath. When he took his hands from his face, Holly's pudgy little finger pointed through the glass to the food on the other side. Holly was licking his lips so intensely that he didn't see half the cafeteria now looking at him. "Man what is your roommate doing with his lil' country ass?" Tyrone asked. Davis didn't like the tone of his voice. He told Tyrone that he would catch him later and he got up and left. He was hell bent on getting out of there before Holly saw him.

He managed to exit without being seen. As he left the

cafeteria, he bumped into the same awesome creature he saw forty-five minutes ago: Kee-Kee. "I guess you didn't see me coming this time?" she said to Davis, who literally glowed with a smile. "Ah, ah,...um sorry," escaped from his mouth. He couldn't believe he was talking to her.

Her pearly whites were exposed as her mouth released the words, "Oh don't worry. It's okay." He and his dumbfounded, yet innocent, stare amused her.

"Well I guess I'll c'ya."

"Yeah," Davis replied as she continued walking to the cafeteria. He went to his room and fell into a coma-like sleep. It had truly been a long and exciting morning.

He awoke hours later to the ringing of a phone and the same confusion he had earlier that morning. There was still a strange mattress beneath him that prompted him to find his bearings. By the time he had done so, he noticed that someone else was in the room.

"Phone for ya' roomy," Holly said as he shoved the receiver into Davis' face.

He sat up on his elbows, rubbed the sleep out of his eyes and finally reached for the phone. It was Tyrone on the other end. Tyrone began to explain how he had run into Kee-Kee in the cafeteria, and how she invited him to a party her sorority was throwing. She told him to bring a friend. After the call, it took Davis 45 minutes to shower and get dressed.

Davis waited where Tyrone told him for at least ten minutes. During that time, his thoughts drifted to his mother. What was she doing? Was she used to him not being in the house? He made a mental note to call her tomorrow. Then his thoughts turned to his roommate. While he was ironing his clothes for the party, he kept exchanging eye contact with Holly. He knew Holly wanted to make an attempt to explain his actions from that morning, but Davis never gave him the opportunity. Truth be told Davis didn't care what Holly did as long as he didn't do anything like that in his presence. He began to think about the task at hand.

Okay, he knew that a sorority party meant lots of girls. That made him excited and nervous. He certainly wanted to meet some girls, but these were college women. Plus Kee-Kee was going to be there. Should he approach her? Did she think he was attractive at all? What if she thought he was a doofus for almost running into her near the cafeteria like he did?

He heard a car horn coming from the nearby curb. "Hey dawg, c'mon," Tyrone yelled from the back seat of a red Nissan Sentra. Davis started walking briskly toward the car. As he got closer he noticed the young lady in the front passenger seat. He took in her splendor as she gazed into his eyes. Out of shyness, he quickly broke the stare. Then he took note of the driver. It was Kee-Kee. She was all made up for the party. She was radiant. As Davis climbed into the back seat, Tyrone began the formal introductions. But, Davis never heard him. He was too busy concentrating on the driver. The car started moving, and Tyrone continued with his bothersome conversation. Davis realized that he would have to break his concentration on the specimen in the front seat and entertain Tyrone in some chatter.

It turned out to be a short drive to the club. As the Nissan circled the club twice looking for parking, Davis couldn't help but notice the size of the crowd waiting to get inside. "Whoa, people are everywhere," he said. Everyone else in the car snickered at his naïveté. Then Tyrone spoke. "Dawg, this is the welcome back party for the AUC. Everybody from every school is here. Clark, Spelman, Mo'Brown, tha' House, hell, even the cats from the theological center are here." There was another snicker from the front seat.

Shortly thereafter, the four entered the club. It was filled with people who were dancing, yelling, and drinking. The dancing and yelling mostly came from a large group of girls on the dance floor that danced in unison, all wearing the same color jackets. "This must be the sorority", he thought.

The two young ladies they rode with scurried away to join in with the group. Afterwards, Davis found himself stranded because Tyrone started the hugging game with people he hadn't seen all summer. Davis didn't mind because it gave him a chance to explore. The club scene was new to him. There was only one club for teens in Augusta, and he didn't like the element that hung out there.

It took Davis about an hour to push through the crowd and circle the club. By then he bumped into Tyrone again, so the two made their way to the bar. The liquor was flowing freely - even though the place was filled with minors. Tyrone got hold of a cup of gin and orange juice and asked Davis if he wanted some. Davis didn't drink for two reasons. It was an expensive habit and he feared that he might become an alcoholic. So he ordered a strawberry cooler. It would keep him busy and make him look as casual as everyone else.

With drinks in hand, he and Tyrone embarked on a conversation that lasted well over an hour. As the liquor loosened Tyrone up, he made it a point to show Davis almost every girl in the club he had "screwed" and the methods he used to get closer to them. Davis was shocked that the methods worked - considering their simplicity. During their talk, a young lady approached Davis and asked him to dance. Davis was almost rude as he turned the young lady away. He couldn't dance and he wasn't ready for strangers to know it. From his mother, he would learn a couple of years later that there are two types of men in the world: those that can dance and those that can't. Dee would proceed to tell him that a woman could tell which category a man belonged to within seconds on the dance floor; he might as well try to keep a beat and have fun out there.

As their conversation grew closer to an end because of Tyrone's slurring of speech, Davis noticed Kee-Kee walking up. She looked exhausted and her hair had fallen because of her sweating. He still thought she was enchanting even as she wiped the sweat from her forehead with her forearm.

"Tyrone, Stacey is going to give you a ride to the dorm 'cause um bout to go," she shouted after noticing Tyrone's condition. She then looked at Davis. "Will you ride back with me Davis?"

"Of course!"

3

Kee-Kee's proposal to Davis caused him to have mixed emotions. On one hand he was ecstatic about being alone with her. However, she was a junior and her beauty caused him to be just a little bit nervous. It was all happening a little too fast. Even though he was nervous about going with her, he knew there was no other place he would rather be. Once in the car, it took her a while to get herself together. The "line" dancing she did with her sorority sisters was very tiring. She was at it for an hour before taking her first break. She wiped all of the sweat away from her body as if it were some irritating goo. Davis cleverly cut his eyes in her direction as she did this. The sweat made her glisten beautifully.

It seemed to be much cooler outside. The temperature inside the club must have been 20 degrees warmer. Soon the little red car started rolling and the young lady behind the wheel spoke. Davis was caught off guard.

"So how come you didn't dance with me?" she asked. He was stuck. He didn't know what to say. He surely didn't want to sound stupid. He attempted to catch his breath before he replied. "You didn't ask me."

"Did that answer sound stupid?" he thought. "She doesn't think I'm illiterate does she?" His heart raced as he waited for her to speak again. At that moment, she reached out and slapped Davis on his shoulder.

"Boy, you so crazy" she said in a laughing voice. He was totally relieved to hear her reply. It was almost as if he heard a hint of adoration in her voice but he didn't want to get ahead of himself. The car suddenly grew quiet. He turned to look out of the window as he struggled to think of more intelligent conversation. His burden was soon lifted as the car pulled into the parking lot. "This drive was even shorter than the first one," he thought. Once he closed the car door, he took a deep swallow and thought to himself, "all I have to do now is walk her twenty feet to the door and say good night." That's exactly what he was prepared to do however as his lips began to form the words, he was cut off as she began to speak.

"Davis would you mind waiting with me for a while, I forgot my key so I have to wait for my roommate," she explained. He couldn't believe his ears. The night wasn't over yet. As his eyes grew bigger at the surprise of her request, his mouth uncontrollably released his response.

"Hell yeah I'll wait with you?" His face quickly grew into a squinted position. He couldn't believe how anxious he was.

Kee-Kee giggled at his cute anxiety as she reached for his hand and led him around back to the other side of the dorm. The two sat down in an isolated spot on the grass. They were secluded from any light. He couldn't help but notice how close she sat to him. Did she like him, or was this just something that mature college students could do without obligation? "Should I put my arm around her," he thought to himself. He was sweating heavily because by now she was really sitting close. He didn't want her to think that he was trying to get fresh with her but at the same time he didn't want her to be insulted by him not returning some type of affection. At that exact moment, she slowly lowered her head into his arm pit area. He nearly fainted. He looked to the sky as if he were asking Jesus himself for instructions on what to do. After a few seconds he lowered his head, took a deep breath and looked around to make sure they were alone. He proceeded to take another deep breath. Quickly he raised his arm and guided it around her back. His hand was now able to wrap around her biceps. He gently squeezed her arm.

"What's the matter? You're not cold are ya' buddy," he managed to say. All of the words completely left his mouth before he started to think how stupid he must have sounded. Again he looked to the sky and this time he winced as if he were in pain. He wrote his "move" off as a failed attempt because of stupidity and began to lower his hand as if he would have to start all over again.

"Davis please don't take your arm away. I'm kinda' cold," His eyes grew to the size of quarters.

"Is there anything that can go wrong tonight?" he thought.

So there he was sitting with one of the most gorgeous women he had ever seen. She was closely nestled under his arm and the two were generating considerable body heat. This was turning out to be a great beginning to his college career.

He looked over towards the ground in her direction. Those same lovely legs that carried her into his sight earlier that morning were now arresting his vision and nearly his breath. His eyes then followed the legs down until they met those soft pretty feet. Each foot was capped by five of the prettiest toes ever touched by the moonlight. He envisioned himself on a couch massaging her beautiful feet while listening to soft jazz. Suddenly, he got a good whiff of her perfume. It was a voluptuous scent . The smell was intoxicating and it loosened him up some.

"You smell nice," he admitted in a slight hypnotic voice.

"Thank you," she replied, but he never heard her. His senses ran wild. His eyes were joyous at the sight of her legs. His nose was thankful for the scent of her body. And his hands were numb from the excitement of touching her hot flesh. Boy if Big Mike could only see him now. "This is the one," he thought to himself. "And to think, I met her on my first day on campus."

Her head soon popped up. He was filled with fright. "Is she ready to go in now," he thought. But she wasn't. Instead, she just looked at him. By the time he looked back at her, he noticed just how intensely she was staring at him. He tried to match the intensity but he couldn't. It was clear that she had something on her mind but he just didn't know what it was. She continued with her stare and it began to make him nervous. "What is she doing," he thought to himself. Her eyes were now doing something different. As he stared back into them, he noticed that something funny was going on. Her eyes were smiling at him. He thought it was strange and was prompted to look even closer. Her eyes were glossy and dilated. Then he noticed her luscious red lips as they parted to speak.

"Daa-vis," she sung in a sultry and mischievous voice. Then it him like a bolt of lightning. "She wants to get busy," he thought to himself. Being the young virgin that he was, he had to fight the urge to yell for his mother. At that moment she pounced on top of him. Straddling his body between her legs while pushing his upper torso toward the ground.

"Oh my God," he said to himself. He looked into her eyes. And the eyes, they changed again. They weren't smiling anymore. Now they were possessed and determined. She closed in on her prey and he knew it. He was confused. Just a few moments ago, he envisioned the two of them together in married life. Now he wasn't so sure that he wanted a wife that would behave in such a fashion. It would be years later before he realized that this was exactly the type of behavior he wanted his wife to have - a strong sex drive.

She continued with her exploration ferociously. She started unbuttoning his shirt and proceeded to run her hand across his hairy flesh. Delois Virginia's baby boy laid there in a pleasant terror with his mouth wide open. Since she straddled him, her vaginal area sat right above his penis and this caused him to have an erection. It was painful. No sooner than he could finish his thought, Kee-Kee unzipped his pants.

He could literally hear her growling. His best move was to lie there and not interrupt her. It wasn't rape because he clearly wanted it to happen. He was just so shocked that he was loosing his virginity to such a lovely and experienced woman. The feel of her hand grazing through his pubic hair quickly interrupted this thought. For about a minute she softly moved her hand back and forth like she was looking for something. This drove him crazy. He wanted her to touch it and just get it over with. This was the first time since he could remember that another hand touched his manhood besides his own.

"Davis," she moaned, "please tell me that you have a condom." Her words pierced the tense moment. She looked at his facial expression.

"Damn Davis, you're in college now. You have to be responsible enough to keep protection with you at all times," she yelled in anger. She was pissed and he could tell - even though she continued to caress him. Then came the moment he was waiting for: she moved closer and closer to "it." She deliberately engulfed it with her hand. He moaned uncontrollably. She looked closely at his genitalia. He had already unloaded. He was fading fast. The last words he heard before his eyes rolled back into his head were "Davis, why are you so excited?"

When he came to, he felt a painful but intriguing sensation on his neck. It was Kee-Kee nibbling on him. He deduced that he had been out for maybe a minute. He felt a little different. The pressure of being alone with her was gone and he wasn't as tense anymore. He felt rejuvenated. He could smell the freshly-cut grass beneath him. He noticed the star-lit sky above their heads and he could hear the insignificant chatter of people on the other side of the gate that separated the University from the surrounding neighborhood. He could feel the intense body heat and passion coming from this determined female laying on top of him. At this point he was literally aching for the passion that she was providing. He could still feel her teeth and tongue on his neck but it wasn't enough. On the other hand, Kee-Kee was really enjoying herself as she kissed around his massive neck. Now and then her hands would rub the biceps of his nineteen inch arms but apparently it still wasn't enough for him because at that moment he lunged forward, picked her up underneath her arms, and laid her softly on her back. She could hear the growl in his voice now as he parted her legs with his thighs and slowly leaned forward.

She smiled with anticipation and wrapped her arms around his neck. He began kissing her and his tongue began exploring her bridgework. Even though he had never done this before, the instructions on what to do came naturally to him although he really had to fight the urge to unleash his penis as the words of Ms. Nebby and Ms. Holman rang in his head. He ferociously sucked her succulent neck trying not to break any skin with the force he was applying. Just then another impulse came to him and he found himself doing it before he could even question it. His whole body had started moving back and forth in a smooth rhythmic motion while thrusting his midsection into hers. Kee-Kee was surprised by Davis' actions but nevertheless pleased.

By this time he had unbuttoned her blouse and uncovered a breast. He took a second to admire the splendor and perfection of it before he tore into it. He ran his tongue all over the breast while concentrating on the nipple of course. She was wailing now and even though he was new at this, he could tell that it was a sound of pleasure and that he was doing something right. In the middle of his oral expedition of her breast, he noticed that she too had now begun the rhythmic rocking. But hers was different. She wasn't rocking with him. She was rocking in a way that complimented his motion. He could feel the increased heat from her vaginal area and it made him curious. As he continued serving her breast, his hand slowly made it down to her midsection. At first he rubbed her inner thigh. The increased moaning and seemingly increased heat made him realize that there was only one thing left to do. As his hand moved closer to the inferno, he found himself wanting to thank her for wearing a skirt this evening. Just then his hand touched her undergarment and then he realized that it wasn't just heat but a hot fluid that had been guiding him because her panties were nearly soaked. Then he quickly raised up from her breast so he could use both of his hands to rescue the undergarment from around her waist. As he began pulling on her panties, she quickly raised both legs in the air to ease his struggle. As he got to her ankles, both feet suddenly relaxed and straightened in a subtle and sexy way so that he could remove the underwear with no further problems. This literally freaked him out. It was by far the sexiest move he had ever seen. He knew that his mind would replay the scene over and over again for weeks to come. At this point he took a second to look at her face. It was angelic. She seemed as if she was in a state of sheer delight. The smile on her face made her lips look even rosier as they puffed out. He had to kiss them and he slowly moved in for the kill. He kissed her passionately for a minute before he felt her hand on his. She was guiding it towards her midsection. He had gotten so involved in the kiss, that he forgot that he had just removed her underwear. Suddenly he reached another milestone. He finally made contact. She felt like a pool of lava inside, however, she felt very inviting at the same time. He used the two fingers that she had inserted to explore for a while before he naturally started the same rhythmic motion with his arm. Her moans got louder and louder and suddenly he took the side of his free hand and put it near her lips to rub them and consequently quiet her. He didn't really know what made him take this course of action but again he must have been acting out some type of genetic program because she grabbed the hand with her mouth and used it like a baby's pacifier.

He began to concentrate on the fingers inside of her. As he did, she started to move more and more violently. Her head turned crazily from side to side and her pelvis had picked up the rhythmic motion on it's own and her back arched. By the time his brain had interpreted this as some type of appreciation on her part, she started to scream even with his hand in her mouth. She placed both her hands on the base of his massive chest and pushed him off of her. He was flabbergasted at the strength. He nearly landed square-ly on his feet from that single shove. When he looked down at her, she had already began to button her blouse and read-just her skirt. She was breathing very loudly as she hopped to her feet and grabbed him by the collar around his neck. She used both hands to pull his face towards hers.

"Next time, bring a fuckin' condom so I won't have to go through this shit again," she said in a beastly voice and let him go. She began rubbing her eyes as if she had a headache. While her head was down Davis heard her say softly, "Now get out of here before you get hurt." He smiled. He knew he had done a good job as a beginner.

"Don't you want me to walk you around front?" he said as he tried to wipe the smile off of his face before she looked up. She raised her head before responding to his question.

"No, I'll be okay, I have to cool down before I go in. Just go." He didn't hesitate as he turned and walked off swiftly.

Davis started a light jog across campus to his dorm room. His body was totally numb from the experience he had just encountered. He was still mad at himself for not having a condom but it was okay. He knew that based on tonight, he and Kee-Kee would be getting very intimate, very soon. The key now was not to loose focus of his mis-sion. Registration would officially end in a few days and classes would begin.

As for right now, he was dying to tell someone about

tonight's escapades. What good was all of that fun if you couldn't tell anyone about it. But whom would he tell? It was past 1:00 a.m. Tyrone was either at the club or passed out somewhere. "Oh well, it would have to wait," he concluded.

4

The next few days were very uneventful. Classes had finally begun and Davis had a chance to meet all of his professors and see what the semester had in store for him. He felt very comfortable, too. He had already been instructed by Ms. Holman to take one major class and the rest electives. This way he could start off with a strong G.P.A.

After the first day of classes, he went to the scholarship office to give a report to the two ladies who seemed so interested in his success. During his visit, he mentioned his Calculus III class may give him a little trouble, since this was the only class where the professor gave a quiz on the first day. The truth however was that Davis made the second highest grade on the quiz and wasn't really worried about it. However, he felt compelled to manufacture some type of trouble area for the ladies. He didn't want them to think that he was some type of cocky teenager who was set to breeze through college. It's just that Davis had been preparing for college, since his freshman year in high school, and he was committed to making it a success. He knew that outside of the poverty that he had been born into, education was the only true equalizer. However due to his relentless pursuit for a college scholarship, he didn't have much time for fun, nor for female companionship while in high school.

None of this mattered because the instant he mentioned

calculus as a potential trouble spot, Ms. Nebby offered the services of a niece who had just graduated from Northwestern and moved to Atlanta. Starting next week, Davis would meet with this new tutor for an hour every Tuesday and Thursday at 12: 30 p.m. "What have I done?" he thought to himself as Ms. Nebby hung the phone up after verifying the date and time with her niece.

The following day was pretty uneventful as well except for his run in with Kee-Kee. It was the first time he had seen her in about forty hours, and he counted every hour. He was at dinner in the cafeteria with Holly. The two of them had started to bond as they talked about insignificant things. Besides Davis figured he always needed someone to go to lunch with. In college, it was so embarrassing to eat by yourself. It was one of those teenage social things. As Holly went back to bother his favorite cafeteria worker for seconds, Davis noticed Kee-Kee walk in. At first their eyes were drawn together, but after an intense stare at him, she quickly turned away and proceeded to get a carry out tray. He was tempted to go up and speak to her, but something in her eyes told him that now was not the time.

"Man I think she likes me," Holly said, interrupting Davis' train of thought.

Davis responded to Holly's comment, "Say what?"

"The lunchroom lady? I think she likes me."

"Yeah right Holly," Davis said sarcastically. "Well look how many French fries I got." Davis burst into laughter as he stood up and said, "C'mon man, so I can watch the news."

As they walked to the dorm, Davis noticed Tyrone jogging across campus as if he were late for an appointment. In a deep non-serious voice Davis hollered, "Tyrone- where ya' headed boy?" After Tyrone turned in the direction of the shouting, he replied, "Um' going to meet a honey, I'll get up wit'cha later nigga."

Davis smiled at him as he resumed walking with Holly. The two of them saw another attractive young lady walking their way. "Unh-unh-unh," Davis murmured as she passed. He didn't have to speak because Holly felt the same way.

"Ya' know if my two cousins came up here to visit me, the number of rape cases would go up," Holly stated. Davis quickly asked his roommate to explain. "I got these two cousins at home who are not used to courting. The truth is they're only about dick satisfaction."

"Holly every man is about that," Davis replied.

"No, no- I mean quick satisfaction," Holly insisted.

"And um' saying that's what all men are about," Davis returned. Then Holly turned and looked at Davis and said in a voice that was clear and precise.

"Davis my cousins fuck cows!"

"Excuse me," Davis replied.

"They fuck cows and they have been doing it for a while now," Holly said.

"So how come you don't do it?" Davis inquired.

"First of all, it's nasty and second, they just graduated to cows. It used to be watermelons."

"Say what?"

Holly continued. "Yeah. What they would do was get a watermelon that had gone sour on the inside. They would cut a whole in it and scrape the insides out. Then they stick their wee-wees inside of it and play around with it until they had an orgasm. They said it felt like the real thing. They even named their melons. Ya' know gave 'em girl names," Holly concluded.

By this time Davis was straining to withhold his laughter. Holly proceeded. "Well right before I came up here to Atlanta the family rented a van, and we all drove to the state fair up in Columbia."

"So what?" Davis asked.

"Well on the drive back home the two of them seemed hell bent on talking my Uncle Rayford into trading all of his cows for sheep." Davis immediately fell to one knee, grabbed his stomach and let out laughter that scared everyone within listening range. He stayed on the ground until Holly, who was smiling by this time, helped him up.

Once the two of them got back to the room, Davis turned on the news so he could get a glimpse of Kia Brent. Holly began to iron. He had begun to watch his personal grooming since the first day Davis met him. After about an hour, a sweet tooth forced Davis downstairs to the vending machines. On the way back, he ran into Tyrone who was standing in the middle of the hallway with three other guys. "D.V., what's up boy?" exclaimed Tyrone in a deep voice filled with manufactured testosterone. After figuring out that D.V. must have stood for Davis Virginia, Davis responded. Tyrone went on.

"Yo fellas this is my boy Davis. Davis, this is Fred, Khalil, and ay ay,...what's ya' name again chief?" Tyrone asked.

"Cisco man," said a tall slender young man as he reached to shake Davis' hand.

Tyrone proceeded, "Yo D.V. what you think about faggots?" Davis' face lit up and he looked around to all four of them in a surprised fashion. "Damn man! Wha' ch'all up here talkin' bout?" Davis asked in a joking manner. The group fell into laughter. After they collected themselves, Fred, who was of average height, build and wore a finely trimmed beard, stumbled forward. "No man, my boy Cisco here was about to jump on this faggot muthafucka in our room the other day because he didn't know ol' boy was gay like that. See he had let the nigga up there to borrow some toilet paper, and when Cisco reached to give it to him, the faggot wouldn't let his hand go. Then he made some wise-crack about how the toilet paper couldn't clean an ass like he could.

"Ya' bullshitting," Davis exclaimed.

"No shit," Fred continued.

"What exactly did he say Cisco?"

Cisco, who wore a lot of San Francisco 49ers paraphernalia and was from the Bay area, had gotten enraged as Fred had been telling the story. He had folded his arms across his chest and his facial expression turned sour. "Man I don't remember what that fucka said."

"Well anyway," Fred went on. "That's how we ended up in this conversation."

Tyrone jumped in. "Now myself. I don't understand how a man could want to fuck another man with all these beautiful women around here."

"Ya' see the Quoran and the Bible both say its an abomination basically," Khalil interjected. He was a very neat looking young man from his pressed shorts to his finely groomed facial hair to his dreads. Being from Augusta, Davis really didn't understand the concept of dreadlocks. Where he was from, it would be considered "nappy hair."

"I told Cisco to forget about it and stay away from the bastard," Fred said as he turned and looked at Cisco, "or dawg if you want to beat his ass we can do that too."

Then Davis spoke. "Man the only problem I have with them is the way that they recruit people, particularly the lesbians. Ya' know they always trying to rub on a sista' when she's having problems with her man or when she is weak after a break-up or some shit like that. But according to the Bible, we're no better off than they are."

"How you figure?" Fred asked. Davis continued.

"Well a sin is a sin and no one sin is greater than another. Only here on earth do we consider a murder less or greater than something like lying." Tyrone jumped in.

"That's a good point D."

Davis continued. "So when it's all said and done they have too much to worry about than to care what I think about them. So I keep homosexuality at a distance and just keep on moving."

Tyrone started to talk. "Listen to this shit that happened my freshman year. It was my first semester as a resident assistant here and this guy asked me for a physician referral. He said he needed one of them ah— what ya' call them doctors that specialize in the ass and rectum?" Tyrone looked around at all the guys in the circle awaiting some type of an answer. No one was able to give him one, even though they knew what he was talking about. Tyrone continued. "Well anyway I looked it up for him and he went. When he got back he was pissed. I asked him what happened, and he told me that his ass started hurting all of a sudden and that's why he went to the doctor. But he said that the doctor told him that he needed to stop having anal sex."

Everyone in the group looked up in astonishment at Tyrone's statement. Tyrone proceeded. "Well two weeks went by and ol' boy's ass started hurting again. This time he went to a different butt doctor. I think they call 'em ah-proctologists. Yeah that's it. But anyway, it turns out that this doctor told him the same thing. Ol' boy was really pissed then cause he knew he wasn't doin' no kinda shit like that. So after that he went upstairs to pack his stuff so he could go home to see his family doctor. But when he was packing his stuff he found something under his roommate's bed."

Everyone was really listening now and salivating with anticipation. The anxiety finally forced Cisco to ask, "What nigga? What did he find?"

Tyrone responded. "Well man it turns out that his roommate had a rag and a bottle of chloroform under his bed that he had stolen from one of the chemistry labs.

"What the hell is chloroform?" asked Khalil.

Tyrone went on. "Well I don't know what they use it for in the lab but his punk ass roommate was pouring it into a rag and putting it over ol' boy's nose when he was sleep. So once he was out cold, this bitch ass nigga would fuck him in the ass."

There was a deep moment of silence after Tyrone spoke his last word. Then all of a sudden, "Hell n'all," Cisco exclaimed. The rest of the guys started shaking their heads in disbelief.

"Man I'd still be kickin' that muthafucka's ass," Fred

yelled. The others quickly agreed with him.

Tyrone finished his story. "Man when the dorm found out about that shit, ol' boy must have had forty different niggas begging him if they could wait in the room and surprise that faggot when he came in from class. Man, half of the police department had to come and smuggle his ass out of the dorm. 'Til this day I still haven't seen that sissy." No one said anything after Tryone finished his story. Instead they all just looked around at each other with anger in their eyes. Then Cisco broke the silence.

"Ya' know dawg, I may have to take you up on that offer," he said while looking at Fred. Fred nodded his head in understanding. Davis could only assume he meant Fred's offer to jump on the allegedly gay guy whom Cisco had the problem with.

The group dispersed after that and Davis headed up to his room. As he was opening the door he heard Holly exclaim, "Wait a minute! He's walking in now. Davis! Someone's on the phone for you." Davis took the receiver from him and spoke into it.

"Hello."

"I hope I'm not disturbing you," said a sultry voice on the other end.

"No, you're not," Davis replied. He had no clue who was on the other end.

"Do you know who this is?" the voice asked.

"To be honest with you, I don't," Davis responded.

"It's Kee-Kee."

He became very silent. On the inside he was ecstatic, but he didn't want to show it no matter how happy he was to hear from her.

She continued after the silence. "I was hoping I could see you tonight." By this time, he had collected himself and was able to respond in a dignified manner.

"Yeah that's possible," he said. The two agreed that Davis would come to her dorm room in an hour before ending the call.

Davis started scrambling around the room trying to get himself together. He started ironing and pulling out his toiletries in order to take a shower. Meanwhile, Holly, who was studying, got a kick out of watching his roommate. After his shower, Davis threw on his freshly ironed jeans and some cologne and headed for the door. He rushed down the three flights of stairs and made it to the exit before he stopped at the door. "Oh shit, almost forgot the condoms," he said to himself as he turned around and darted back upstairs. He entered the room in such a frantic pace that he startled Holly. He grabbed a condom from the top shelf and headed for the door again.

"Hey Davis!" Holly nearly shouted. Davis turned and looked at him roommate.

"Be careful man, there's only one thing a woman wants at this time of the night."

"Hey Holly," Davis said with a wicked smile on his face as he took a deep breath and looked Holly square in the face before belting out the sound of "Mooooooo!" They both laughed as Davis closed the door behind him.

Kee-Kee greeted him at the front door of the dorm as he walked up. She quickly led him to her room and shut the door.

"Wow, what's the rush?" Davis asked in an attempt to start conversation.

"People around here will get into your business if you give them the chance," she replied. Davis took a seat on the bed. He looked around the room. It was very neat and orderly. He wondered if she always kept it clean, or was it clean because she was expecting company? She had candles burning on the desk and some soft music playing. He recognized it as Will Downing. She was still moving about the room and he couldn't help but notice that the atmosphere was very tense.

"I thought that visitation hours were over," he said in an

effort to break the tension.

"I'm an R.A., so the rules don't apply to me," she said quickly. She had not looked at him since he entered the room. She continued to move about the room frantically as if she were looking for something. "She's nervous," he thought to himself. "How can I calm her down?" After watching her for a few seconds more he finally fixed his lips to say something. "I missed you." Kee-Kee stopped instantly and turned around. It was as if he had squeezed all of the air out of her modest little body. She walked over to the bed, looked him in the eyes and said, "Me too." She sat down and reached for his hand while looking in his eyes. "Davis I want to apologize for not speaking to you since that night."

"Oh it's okay, I understand," he offered. He was casually avoiding eye contact when he felt her squeezing his hand. He looked up as she said, "You have some lovely brown eyes."

"Thank you," he responded as he noticed the look in her eyes. There was no mistaking the look. He had seen it just two days ago. She slowly got up and turned off the lights.

The alarm clock was cruel the next morning. It tortured his subconscious when it rang at 7:15. He opened his bloodshot eyes in preparation to get up. It seemed like he had only been asleep for a few minutes. The truth is that he had gotten in about 4:30 a.m. Today was Tuesday and he had two classes, and of course, the tutoring session. The door suddenly opened and Holly walked in. He had just gotten out of the shower and was perky, as was evident from his greeting.

"Judging by the time you got in, I guess you had a good time last night," he said.

Davis started to collect his thoughts. Holly was right. This was the first time in his life that he had awakened and was no longer a virgin. He smiled at the thought.

In the shower, scenes from the previous night came back to him. All of the heavy breathing, kissing, sucking, exploring and biting along with the moaning, panting, climaxing, and eventual massaging made him become aroused in the shower. He reached to adjust the water. He needed to soothe his anxiety. Anxiety and passion that was now just as strong as it was last night. He continued with his thoughts. He remembered his tongue exploring her mouth, then her breast and her aroused nipples. He also remembered his teeth grabbing her bottom lip and then her neck, the area outside of her belly button and finally her firm thighs.

Of all the things he did before intercourse. He still wanted to do so much purely out of instinct, but he didn't want to be too aggressive and ruin the moment. He then thought about how he couldn't help but realize the fact that although he got a lot out of it, his satisfaction didn't come close to hers. She was so into it. And she was so sexy, especially when she would arch her back as if to guide the orgasms out of her tensed body. He recalled the way her soft feet would rub the side of his thighs in a rhythm that was identical to his rhythmic thrusts. Her hands would grab his head in and intense but painless fashion. He couldn't explain it but it was as if each moan, growl, and heavy breath expressed a different side of pleasure. By the time he came back to reality, he was in an ice cold shower.

He wasn't really looking forward to this day. On Tuesdays and Thursdays classes were two hours instead of the normal hour and ten minutes. What was even worse was that after classes ended, he still had to go to tutoring. After a heavy dose of Maze and Frankie Beverly, Davis was out of the door.

His first class was Religion and the Media. He found the class to be quite interesting because of the discussions that took place. They talked about everything under the sun. It was mostly the females who would sit and talk the entire time.

One thing Davis liked about the class was the professor. Her name was Abigail Upshaw. Other faculty members called her Gail. He hadn't had a chance to appreciate her southern beauty and wit the way he normally would have because his mind had been occupied with Kee-Kee. But he knew that Ms. Upshaw was definitely someone he could appreciate. She looked to be in her early thirties and stood 5' 9" tall and weighed about 185 pounds. She had naturally curly hair that fell just below her shoulder. She wore a deep red color on her full and beautiful lips. Her eyes were a modest brown, and they protruded from her head a little more than the average person's eyes. Some might say she was a little "pop-eyed." But Davis Virginia was definitely an "eyes" man. To him the eyes could make or break the beauty of any woman. A woman who did not have a distinguishing characteristic in or around her eyes just didn't attract him. She would just look average. But perhaps the greatest attribute to Ms. Upshaw was her skin. She had a dark complexion and her skin didn't have a scar, bump, or bruise anywhere in immediate sight. It seemed as if a perfectly contoured specimen had been dipped into a tub of dark rich chocolate.

Davis sat in the back of the class and stared at her all throughout the class time. However, he couldn't concentrate on her. Kee-Kee prevented that along with the constant chit-chat in the room.

5

Davis was the first one to leave class when it ended. The truth is he could have left anytime he wanted. After all, this wasn't high school. There wasn't a bell to dismiss class. After $10,000 for tuition, one could pretty much do what he wanted to in class. He began to walk across campus to his next class. As luck would have it, he saw Tyrone coming from the opposite direction. He wasn't prepared to stop because he wanted to get to his next class, but he wanted to brag to someone about last night.

"Man what the hell you doing waking me up at 4:30 in the morning talkin' bout some open the front door?" said Tyrone with a sarcastic smile on his face.

Davis responded, "Yo' man I got with Kee-Kee last night." He didn't know if Tyrone was really mad or not. But if he was, he figured that his macho excuse might lift his mood.

"Oh for real?" Tyrone exclaimed. "That girl ain't changed a bit."

With that, Tyrone shook his head as if to say what a shame. Afterwards, he continued walking and so did Davis. He couldn't help but wonder what Tyrone meant by his last statement.

He reached his next class a little early so he was able to get the seat he wanted. There were no assigned seats in college, another aspect he loved. The class was U.S. government, and the funny thing about it was the fact that his teacher wasn't born or raised in the U.S. He was born in Kenya and his English sounded as if he had only been in the States for a couple of years. In fact, out of his five classes, he had three foreign professors; each with strong accents. Davis had already surmised that he was going to read the textbooks a lot and only use the faculty for supplementary information. This class was perhaps the coolest of all though. Not only was it just an elective, but there were a lot of familiar faces. Davis' next door neighbor, Lester Philpot, was in there. Cisco and Khalil also took the class. And perhaps most interesting of all was the fact that Lisa Hargrove took the class as well. Lisa was a sophomore that he met in the cafeteria. She invited him to a Bible study. But even after Davis declined her offer she made a point to stay in his face. The first time the class met, she made it a point to sit by Davis like some annoying little sister. However, this week due to her tardiness, she couldn't sit by him. Instead, a pair of twins walked in and sat near him. They were both short with exaggerated bodily curves.

Midway through the class, Davis grew disenchanted with his professor's accent. He found himself staring embarrassingly at the chest of one of the twins. In one instance, she caught him looking and when he was discovered, he quickly turned his head like a true adolescent and tried not to blush. He heard the two of them giggle at him. He turned back and smiled at her. While looking at the young lady, he could see Lisa sitting across the room with his peripheral vision. She had obviously seen everything and was shaking her head in disapproval. Khalil, who was sitting beside Lisa, had also seen the entire occurrence. Lisa shook her head and he began laughing himself.

When the class was over, Davis spoke to all of the guys and attempted to dash for the stairs in an effort to avoid Lisa. He wasn't successful. She had already telegraphed the move and was now on an intercept course.

"Looks like somebody had something else on their mind today besides U.S. government," Lisa said as they both hit the hallway.

Davis turned and looked at her. "Not now Lisa, I've got a tutoring session. If you really must chastise me you can call me at 1479. Right now, I have to go." With that, he turned and walked away.

"Oh a tutoring session but no Bible session huh?" she shouted with a smile on her face.

Without even turning around he threw one hand in the air and gave an emphatic, "Good-bye Lisa."

As soon as he walked through the doors of the scholarship office, the strong perfumed scent of both women hit him. He saw Ms. Holman first.

"Hey darling, how are classes going?"

"Oh they're coming just fine Ms. Holman," he replied.

Ms. Nebby walked out upon hearing his voice. After the two greeted each other he noticed that the two ladies were preparing to leave the office.

"Now Davis, my niece is already in the back room waiting on you. We're headed for lunch. Have you eaten yet?"

"No ma'am but I'll grab something at dinner," he responded.

"No baby we'll get you something while we're out cause dinner is three hours away." With that, the two ladies were out the door.

Davis walked to the back. As he entered the little room, he immediately noticed a young lady reading a book. She had a very short haircut, and her hair was nicely permed. She wore glasses, and even though she was sitting behind a table, he could tell that she was impeccably dressed. Her skin was a nice creamy caramel complexion. He didn't want to make a rash judgement since he hadn't seen her face yet, but something was telling him that this was a beautiful woman. Even her hands, which lay on the table beside each cover of the book, were beautiful and her nails were professionally manicured.

She heard him come in and stopped reading. "Hello, you must be Davis," she said as she looked up at him over the rim of her glasses. The moment he saw her face, his knees nearly buckled. He couldn't believe it. What had he done in his few nineteen years to warrant all of the good fortune that he had been receiving lately? He had not only seen this lady before, but he knew he was infatuated with her. "Are you okay?" the young lady asked sensing his shock.

"Yeah, I'm okay," he replied.

She proceeded with her introduction and a smile. "As I was saying I'm Ms. Nesbitt's niece and my name is Kia, Kia Brent," she said as she outstretched her hand in order to make his acquaintance. Davis quickly shook her hand and took a seat so she wouldn't notice his excitement. "Well Davis, I hear you're having trouble with Cal III," she said as she took her seat again.

"Are you a math teacher or something?" he asked. He knew very well that she wasn't, but he was just interested in hearing her credentials for teaching math. She giggled as she began to answer his question.

"No I'm a journalist. And let me guess, you're next question is why am I tutoring math? Well first of all, I would do anything for my aunt. Secondly, I was a math minor and tutor all of my four years in college. I attended Northwestern because of their excellent journalism program, but I also have a strong love for mathematics." She spoke with a lot of confidence. In fact, he noticed a somewhat arrogant demeanor about her.

"Now Davis I have to be honest with you, I haven't looked at Cal III in a long time," she admitted. "I only came today to get a copy of your syllabus so I could see where you guys were in the class. That way I can review before our next meeting."

Davis watched her beautiful face as she made her statement. Her eyes were lovely. She could smile as easily and as quickly as some people could blink an eye. He knew he couldn't let her see him sweating over her. "Oh yeah let me copy it for you," he replied as he made his way to the copying machine in the corner.

As he made copies of the syllabus, he watched the machine as if it were making gold. He didn't want to look at her again until he had something interesting to say. He looked back for a quick second and noticed that she had opened his textbook and had begun thumbing through it. The room had grown extremely quiet. He reached deeply for conversation. He really wanted to get to know her but he didn't know what to say. Finally, she spoke. "Davis, do you know your way around the city very well?"

"Well it depends on what you're looking for," he answered. Truthfully, he knew nothing about the city but he wasn't about to miss the opportunity to help her.

"Well I'm trying to find this store on Piedmont called Jennifer Convertibles," she said.

"Looking to buy a new car?" Davis asked.

She laughed at his question before she responded to it. "No, this store specializes in furniture and sofa beds."

He sensed this as his chance to make the mood a little lighter. "Sofa bed, what's the matter that poor baby doesn't have a real bed to sleep in?" He chuckled after he made the statement. At that point, her neck reared back and her eyes got bigger as if she were saying "Oh no he didn't."

Then she spoke. "Honey let me tell you something. I've got a $4,000 bedroom set at home with satin sheets on the bed and believe me when I tell you I sleep very well."

"Okay, I was just joking," he surrendered. Her demeanor grew less serious as she heard him speak the words. Then she spoke. "No. The problem is that I only have a one bedroom apartment and no place to put guests."

"Oh I understand," Davis replied.

She continued, "You see I'm awful with directions. I've

had a few people tell me the location already but all I can seem to remember is Piedmont road. I figured that if you knew where it was maybe you could ride with me if you didn't have another class today. I've been putting this off for so long that I'm kinda' in a bind now because I just found out that my parents want to visit me this weekend. So I have to buy this sofa today and hope they can deliver by Saturday morning."

Davis really couldn't understand her urgency. If she had been from where he grew up, she would have just made a pallet out of sheets and quilts and slept on the floor. But the one thing he did understand was her desperation. She was so lovely and by now she was standing, so he had a chance to see all of her. She stood almost 6 feet tall. It surprised him because she didn't look that tall on television. The desperation in her face and voice made him cringe. There was no way on earth he wasn't going to help her.

"No I don't have any more classes so I can go with you, just let me call my roommate first."

"Oh how sweet. Are you guys very close?" she stated in a sarcastic tone.

Davis looked at her in the same "Oh no you didn't" fashion as she had looked at him just moments ago. She smiled at him as he walked up front to the reception area to make his call.

Even though he had no clue where this place was located, he figured he could call Tyrone and get directions. Unfortunately, Tyrone wasn't home. Davis dropped his head for a minute so he could think. It was a golden opportunity that was about to slip through his fingers. Then all of a sudden he got an idea.

Three minutes later he walked back into the back room and found that Kia had packed her bag and was waiting with keys in hand. "I'm ready," Davis said as he grabbed his things. The two of them started out of the office and down the stairs. They made it to her car fairly quickly. It was a brand new, jet black 2-door Honda Accord. He thought to himself how the car just seemed to fit her. Once inside he noticed how it wreaked of that new car smell. He saw her "Press" credentials hanging from the rearview mirror. "She is really on it," he thought.

As they were pulling out of the parking lot Kia suddenly stopped. Her aunt's Lincoln had pulled beside the Accord. After Ms. Nebby learned of their destination, she passed Kia a wrapped sandwich and a drink that she had gotten Davis for lunch through the window and pulled off to find a parking spot.

Soon the little black car was racing up I-85 North. Davis couldn't help but glance at her out of the corner of his eye. The way she shifted gears drove him crazy. There were few things sexier than a woman driving a standard transmission. What made it even sexier was that she was wearing a skirt and stilettos. He watched her in these heels as her feet went from clutch to gas to break. She had also taken off her reading glasses and exchanged them for a pair of dark sunglasses. Davis screamed to himself as he thought about how intoxicating she looked. He was so caught up in her that he almost didn't hear her next question. "Davis, where do I get off?" He panicked for a second because he had to read the directions from a sheet of paper that he had placed between his legs. He rattled off his answer smoothly so he would look like he knew what he was talking about. "Yeah we get off at ah— 14th street." He had called information to get the store number and they had given him directions.

Once inside the store, Kia shopped cautiously while entertaining the small talk of the salesperson. After about twenty minutes of this, Kia decided on a beige sofa bed, which she insisted would go perfectly with the furniture already in her apartment. She stepped up to the counter where the sales clerk was preparing the bill of sale. When the clerk called out a final total amount of $1102, Davis who was now standing behind Kia winced as if he were in pain.

Kia, however, calmly pulled out her platinum Visa and handed it to the salesperson. Davis, who was very impressed by the move, began thinking to himself. "Let's see. She can afford to buy an $1100 sofa, and I can't even buy an $11.00 pillow. I guess I don't have to wonder about dating her."

The two jumped back into the Accord and were on their way. The car had the aroma of the meatball hoagie, which had been locked up in the car for thirty minutes. The smell caught him by surprise and he hoped that she wasn't mad about the scent in her car. Truthfully, he wanted to eat it but he knew he couldn't do that in her new car. The car stopped at a light and he thought he noticed her looking over at him, even though she still wore the shades. The car proceeded towards the highway entrance ramp. The smell of the sandwich almost drove him crazy. He again thought that he could see her looking at him from the corner of her eye. "What is it? What is she looking at," he thought to himself. Maybe she was pissed about the smell. Davis decided that the best thing to do would be to sit quietly until they got back to campus.

That wasn't possible though because at that very instant she formed her lips to say something. "Damn," he thought to himself. "She's about to get on me about having this stupid sandwich in her car."

Then the words left her mouth. "Davis could I please have a piece of that sandwich?" The way she stressed the word please alerted him to the fact what she was really hungry. Once he comprehended what was wrong with her and why she was driving all crazy he immediately burst into laughter. And as he laughed she peered over the rim of her shades as if she were saying, "What the hell is so funny?" He continued laughing as he reached down for the sandwich. "You mean to tell me that you're hungry?" he asked.

She replied in a stunned fashion, "Hell yeah. I'm hungry. You didn't hear my stomach growling in that damn store?"

He looked at her in a very surprised manner after she finished making her statement. He couldn't believe her language. She seemed familiar now and very accessible. It was like she was from Sunset. It was like she had let go and allowed her sisterhood to come out. Even though she was attractive in the office when she was talking proper and educated, she was like a goddess now.

He began unwrapping the hoagie and reaching for the drink which was in the cup holder. "Would you like some of the coke too?" He couldn't get his entire statement out before she snatched the cup and took a big gulp. "Are you sure we shouldn't pull over or something?" Davis asked. "No I eat like this all the time when I'm driving from one assignment to another. Now hurry up and give me a piece of the sandwich."

Davis took a half of the sandwich and handed it over to her. He enjoyed watching her eat it. Even thought she was starving, she ate it very seductively, even the way she licked her fingers against those full rosy red lips made him cringe. Once she had devoured her half of the sandwich she looked over at him. He had a smile on his face, which caused her to start laughing. "What?" she said through her laughter. "I was hungry. Damn it." This sent him into laughter. She really didn't understand that most of the humor arose from happiness that she had turned out to be really down to earth.

They soon were pulling into the parking lot of his dorm. After they confirmed the next tutoring session and said their good-byes he headed for the dormitory. As soon as he walked into the building, he literally ran into Kee-Kee. It was a throw back into reality. He had not thought about her since earlier that morning. Had she seen him getting out of the car? If so, how mad would she be? He began getting a lie together when she spoke.

"Oh, I just left a message for you at the front desk."

He was very relieved to hear the joy in her voice. "Oh yeah, what's up?" he replied.

"Nothing, I was just hoping I could see you tonight."

"Yeah, I'll be there," he said.

"All right. I'll see you then," she responded. With that she lunged forward and kissed him on the cheek and walked out of the door in an obviously good mood. The kiss threw him. She had never shown affection in public before.

When he got into his room he found Holly near the end of a conversation on the phone. He took off his shoes and fell across the bed. It had been a long afternoon. He heard Holly hang up the phone and asked him if anyone had called for him.

Holly responded, "Shoot yeah, this one girl called for you five times in the last hour."

"Oh yeah it must have been Kee-Kee. I just ran into her in the lobby," he said.

"If you're talking about the lady who called for you that night it definitely wasn't her."

At this statement, Davis became puzzled and sat up on the bed. He continued to wear a puzzled look as he thought about who had called him. All of a sudden he shouted out, "Shit!"

"What is it?" Holly asked.

"That damn Lisa. I forgot I gave her my number today," Davis went on. He had began putting his shoes on again when Holly asked him, "Where you going?"

"I'm going to get this Bible study out of the way so this girl can leave me the hell alone." With that he started down the stairs and across campus.

It wasn't long before he was knocking on a door in Merner Hall. Lisa, who was totally unexpecting of a visit from anyone, answered the door in a robe and a towel wrapped around her head. As soon as she saw Davis she gasped for breath and slammed the door in his face. After about five minutes of waiting in the hall, Davis was finally allowed into the room. She greeted him with a question. "How did you find out where I lived?" "That was easy," he insisted. "I just asked for the church lady. Lisa began to giggle in disbelief. Little did she know that he had done exactly that?

During his five minutes in the hall she had obviously sprayed some air freshener, put on some shorts and a tee shirt and attempted to dry her hair as best as she could with the towel. As he looked at the wet spots in her shirt from where she had missed areas while drying off, he noticed that she had obviously forgotten to put on a bra. Is this a bad time for you Lisa." "No," she said as she reached for the Bible from the shelf. Davis couldn't help but stare. It was the first time he had seen her with her hair down. The fact that she was wet also created some type of exotic look with her. This was the first time he noticed that she had a body as well. It was evident from the tee shirt, which was fitting a little tightly, and the shorts, which attempted to hide a decent pair of thighs and calves. She turned to look at him again. "Well considering the way you were looking at those twins this morning I think we better start talking about temptations of the flesh." As she searched for the right chapter he asked her if she had been calling him that afternoon. After she confirmed that it was her, the two of them sat down and began studying.

6

The fun and unexpected surprises of black college life continued to roll on for Davis. Among the surprises were his Bible study sessions with Lisa. Maybe it was the way he caught her off guard or maybe it was the fact that he was finally paying her some attention, but whatever it was, she seemed to be less obnoxious now and she wasn't acting like a bothersome little sister. They had actually had three study sessions and Davis found that he wanted to go to her room sometimes when he was bored and didn't feel like talking to Holly. As a matter of fact, Davis had officially declared Lisa his first platonic friend. The only problem with her was that she wanted him to make the transition from Bible Study to spending Sundays in church. He had warned her to slow down, and she did for the most part, but she would politely ask him every time she saw him.

She also never caught him looking at the twins again. It's not that he wasn't looking, but he was a little more careful. She also didn't try to sit by him in class anymore. In lieu of the times that the girls in her dorm may have seen her signing him in as a guest or the times they may have been seen walking on campus together, she figured that sitting together in class might be a bit much.

Another big surprise was Holly, who was developing some type of romance with the cafeteria lady. Davis hadn't really paid much attention to the lady because he assumed Holly had been exaggerating about her. However, one night he walked in on Holly in the middle of a phone conversation with the lady. Since that point, Davis had heard four of the conversations and each one was funnier than the previous one. He deduced that they loved to talk about two topics: food and sex. Sometimes they even talked about using food to perform sex. Davis could tell that she was somewhat promiscuous to say the least and that Holly was a virgin just trying to keep up.

Since the phone calls with Holly and the cafeteria lady continued, Davis had made it a point to pay more attention to her. So that's exactly what he did the next time he visited the cafeteria. However, he wished he hadn't. She was not the world's most attractive woman by far. She was about 5 feet 6 inches tall and weighed about 210 pounds. She also had an awful blonde color in her hair that instantly drew Davis back to the ghetto. As he continued looking at her she cracked her lips and smiled. Once she did, he was able to see it all. There it was bright, glistening and very revealing as to her past and present state of mind. She was un-mistakingly G.H.E.T.T.O. This was evident from the not one, but two gold teeth, resting in the front of her mouth. After seeing the teeth, she was okay with Davis. It wasn't that he thought it was cute or sexy. In fact, he thought it was something that black people eventually needed to get away from. However, everyone he had ever met, especially the people in Sunset who had gold teeth, were strong and full of character. At that moment, Davis gladly cracked his lips and returned the smile. She seemed to be a very jolly woman. He couldn't put his finger on the cause of her merry behavior, but it was as if she had just let go of a load of guilt. She smiled just because there was nothing better to do. He would surely grow to enjoy her.

Davis now found himself at the end of his first semester. They were now in the month of December. He had continued his tutoring sessions with Kia, which meant that he often saw Ms. Holman and Ms. Nebby. The two ladies were very sweet and continued to remind him of his mother. They continued to take care of him and all of his problems at the University. In fact, the ladies were taking such good care of him that they were actually cheating him of part of the college experience. Davis had run into a lot of people during the semester that had horror stories to tell about the paperwork and dealing with financial aid and other departments. The ladies in the scholarship office, however, would push his paperwork through. In their minds, they wanted him to concentrate on school and not have to worry about such things. It would be a couple of years later before Davis realized how much he missed out on. It was an important part of matriculation for a young man to handle his own affairs.

And what was happening with Kia? It turns out that Kia had started dating shortly after the tutoring sessions had begun. The day Davis found out he was crushed. In fact, there was one day when Davis' frustration about the dating caused the tutoring session to end early. Kia had no idea why he was so testy, but Ms. Holman knew. In fact, she posed the question to Davis who quickly denied any emotions for Kia.

How could he admit that he had a crush on this woman whose very voice serenaded him for no apparent reason? He was a young doe trapped in the crosshairs of a loaded love weapon that was being aimed by her glossy vivacious brown eyes. And every time she spoke, crossed her legs in a seductive fashion, or exposed her vulnerability by reaching for a Kleenex when talking about her disappointing date the night before, she would unknowingly pull the trigger. The young doe, which was his manhood, would fall into its own pool of blood every time, and the only thing that would be left standing was the pure and unadulterated splendor that he had for her. He knew the day would come when the doe would have to charge the hunter. His heart shuddered at the thought.

What was the story on Kee-Kee? Well, as luck would have it, she continued to show her body when she wanted to show love and he was definitely not one to complain. In fact, he enjoyed himself so much that he spent one weekend recuperating after becoming dehydrated from their hour and 52 minute long animalistic sexual escapade. The two of them even ventured off into the realm of oral sex and they were both delighted with it.

The one sad truth was that they were both mistaken about the intentions of the other. Kee-Kee, who seemed to get very involved and active during sex, did so because of the genuine compassion she had for this young man. It was a pure travesty that she had no verbal skills or courage to express herself to him. She was enticed by his chiseled frame, which stood just over six feet tall. She loved his dark and smooth complexion and the huge arms that would cradle her as if she was the last child known to mankind. Every time her pelvis straddled him, it pulled an orgasm out of his body so simply that she melted upon contact. Memories of his quick wit and no-nonsense attitude often accompanied her to bed some nights. But perhaps most of all was his smile. To try to place a dollar amount on that smile would be criminal. It was clearly priceless, and every time he would flash it, she could read a little more into his sheltered word.

Kee-Kee attributed Davis' ferocity to his male branded impatience with a woman who cared for him very much and wasn't going anywhere no matter what he thought. This poor child compared the way that Davis would rip off her clothes and make love to her to the way a child would rip open his favorite gift on Christmas morning and play with it for hours. Little did she know, that every canine-like gesture he made to undress her and "get some" was just anticipation to see the type of goddess-like specimen he had heard so much about while growing up among the loveless males back in Augusta. In other words, he simply wanted to see, taste, and feel that infamous "fat cat" that he had heard so much about, while hanging around the mongrels in his hometown.

Maybe the blame could be placed on his father, a man who didn't stick around to guide him and let him in on the truly respectful delights of manhood. This way he would know that the young lady was actually giving him her heart and soul. Instead, Davis viewed her as a freak. She was a pretty one, but a freak nonetheless. There actually was a fleeting moment when he adored her and couldn't wait to talk to her again. But that all ended the first night he touched her in her special place. Now he just couldn't wait to get her undressed. The truth was that he was prepared to play the sleuth, but she unveiled the mystery too soon and with that unveiling went his respect for her.

He never considered his feelings for her until he got into Ms. Upshaw's class. Maybe it was all of the love starved, man hungry hussies that took the class with him. This was the opinion he had formed of them partly because all of their discussions centered on talking about the problems and not much mention about how to fix them. It was like a therapy session for them. That was the only good thing he could see about this class, that and the sexy Ms. Upshaw. She was a story within herself. A story that he wished he had time to read into, but with Kee-Kee and now Kia, occupying so much of his mental efforts, that wasn't possible. However, he couldn't help noticing the way she looked at him. They weren't long deceptive stares. On the contrary, they would usually be quick glances and then a turn in the other direction on her behalf when he would look up from scribbling in his notebook and catching her in the act.

There was one day in particular when the ladies of 227, as he referred to them, were having a discussion about men. It was the first time Davis had been in the presence of a male bashing session. For the most part, he would not have even noticed. He was ignoring the class discussion and trying to catch up on other work as he usually did during this time. But today, one of the other guys in the class tapped him on the shoulder to get his attention as the debate got heated. Davis couldn't believe the way the females were talking. They had gone off on a tangent. It was as if there wasn't a guy in the room. The ladies were taking turns criticizing men and their inability to love. There were a couple of statements that literally made his mouth hang open. Of course, Ms. Upshaw, who only mediated the class discussions, saw each of his amazed facial expressions.

After a while, the discussions eased up and instead of bashing men, they examined the female role and her hopelessness in the situation. One female stated, "Ya' know, I know my God in addition to creating me, also created my soulmate. Now my aunt always told me that you couldn't spend your life looking for something that is supposed to find you. I try to keep my aunt's words in perspective and believe that some day my soul mate and I will bump into each other. But I tell ya', sometimes it gets hard to keep the faith. And in the meantime, I have to deal with these bone headed men who have less than half the qualities that I know my soul mate will have. Sometimes it gets very depressing."

At this point, Davis was shaking his head from side to side as if he were saying, "I can't believe this." Then the unexpected happened. He heard Ms. Upshaw's voice make it to the back of the room where he sat. She had obviously been noticing his disbelief.

"Mr. Virginia, I would be pleased if you would add your questions or comments to this discussion," she said.

Normally he would have kept his silence, but now it was as if another part of him took over and he cleared his voice to speak.

"Well I gotta say that I must take offense to the way that she referred to men as dogs earlier. Not simply for the obvious reason that I am a man but because it's a one sided statement. Now when you call us dogs, which of our actions are you referring to? Is it our barking or the way we chase cars from the front porch?"

The ladies in the class looked puzzled as Davis continued.

"No you're not referring to these things. The actions that you're referring to are the ways that we look at, chase, and screw other women."

Every woman in the class including Ms. Upshaw looked totally stunned. The two other guys in the class knew that Davis had better clean up the statement quickly.

He proceeded. "The thing that gets me is that women never seem to realize that a man can't carry out his whorish plan on his own. And when we go to carry out our plans, who can we always count on to be there? Women, that's who. We can't do anything alone. And that's the part that makes me wonder why it is that men are the only gender who wear the very broad title of dogs when the truth is all men don't carry on like this. Oh sure, if that lone woman is caught by the girl-friend or wife she will be asked questions or maybe even cursed out. She may even be slapped, but I have yet to see the female gender given a name that had a negative connotation because of the actions of a few like males. What's really funny to me is that it has been my experience that just as many women go looking for trouble as men.

I have seen a female despise a man for years and call him names, but the one moment that the guy had to squeeze her into his promiscuity pilgrimage, she was the first one on her back moaning with pleasure. Then, as he took his tour on the road and other women came in for their appoint-ments, he was a dog again and bastard was the name being moaned under the tears. So you can go ahead calling us dogs but if we are dogs then women are cats. Y'all are sneaky, quiet dog-hungry cats. Now, as far as the statement of dealing with boneheads until your soul mate comes along, man sometimes, I think females, and for that matter people in general, can't see the forest for the trees. When you spend your time dismissing possible mates because they don't live up to some fictional preconceived character that you have in your head, you're missing the whole picture. We could look at the statistics alone. There are four billion people on this earth? Almost two-thirds of them are women. Therefore, everyone can't have a soul mate. So it's very arrogant for you to think that God created a soul mate for you and not everyone else. Can you be so naïve as to believe that you will come across that soul mate at some point in your life when you consider that there are over 50 different states in the U.S. and over 200 different cultures and native tongues on this earth? You may have that foolish, yet optimistic notion, that God not only provided the mate for you but also went out of His way to place that soul mate in the same culture as yours. That way you wouldn't have to burden yourself with overlooking differences of dealing with any other problems that may arise with that mate if he or she belonged to another race or culture.".

At this point, Davis looked at the floor as he took a deep sigh. Then he continued.

"Forgive me for rambling on, but I guess I'm just tired of women when it comes to the topic of love. They treat it like-like love is some type of destination to which God is supposed to lead them to the end of. I regret to inform you folks, but there is no Prince Charming and there is no soul mate. In short, there is no final destination where you're going to meet this great person. Love is not a destination. Love is a journey. What we're doing when we're searching for mates is looking for good candidates to take this journey with us. We want someone we can go through the make-ups and break-ups with, someone we can cry for, cry about, and cry with. Someone who doesn't necessarily fit all of the perfect mannerisms that you thought your mate would have, but someone you can love nonetheless, even with his imperfections. They used to have a saying that an artist must starve before he can be great. Ladies you're going to have to be with that man, love that man, get angry with him and everything. Then and only then does the love become sweet? If a woman ever meets a guy and things are the sweetest and they never fall upon hard times or any other problems that can bring about his full range of emotions, well then she needs to be scared of him. In the words of my favorite singer, life is joy and pain."

7

After his two morning classes were over, Davis headed to his tutoring session. He wasn't really looking forward to it. He knew it wouldn't take long before Kia started talking about the guy she was dating. It seemed as if he was the only person she could talk to. He later found out that her cameraman would also get his daily earful but since he was in his mid fifties it wasn't the same.

Davis ended up waiting about ten minutes before Kia showed up. She burst into the office in an obvious huff. She was impeccably dressed as always but her hair was a little frazzled obviously a result of her rushing. Davis grinned as he spotted it. But he didn't grin long.

"What the hell are you smiling at?" spouted Kia to his surprise.

"Ah ...nothing, not a thing," he replied with a strained look on his face.

"You okay?" he asked.

She responded, "ya know, that's why I wanted to struggle at one of the best journalism schools in America. Because when I came out, I knew I could land a job paying at least 55 a year. Know what I do with my 55 plus a year Davis," Davis looked at her with an I-don't-understand look on his face. It was clear that there was something she needed to get off her chest so he listened intently as she continued.

"I'll tell you what I do with my money. I buy my own cars and my own house. I even buy my own gun so that I can protect my own house. I buy own clothes and I even buy expensive trash bags so I can take out my own damn trash. I don't need any sorry ass unreliable man to do it for me." With that she slammed her hand on the table in a declarative manner.

He thought to himself, "Oh no I just left this male bashing in Ms. Upshaw's class. He wasn't terribly upset about it though. He was too caught up into how sexy she looked as she threw her little tantrum. "What's the matter Kia?" She looked at him and exhaled heavily before she spoke. "Well the Association of Southern Regional Journalists is having an awards banquet next Saturday night and the jerk I'm dating just canceled on me." Davis was surprised at her calling her boyfriend a jerk but it did make him feel good. "Well independence does mean doing stuff by yourself so why don't you go by yourself", Davis said. Kia who was busy unloading her bag at the time of Davis' statement looked up quickly after she heard the words.

She gave him a cold stare and spoke, "Davis, don't fuck with me today okay." Just when he thought she couldn't get any sexier she did exactly that. After that statement, the two got to work.

Later as Davis was walking back to the dorm he ran into Tyrone who was also headed that way. They greeted each other with the usual and of course Tyrone got on his favorite topic, women, or hoes as he referred to them. Davis couldn't help but remember their last conversation and what Tyrone had said about Kee-Kee.

"Hey Ty," Davis said, "what did you mean when you said Kee-Kee hadn't changed a bit?" Tyrone didn't hesitate with his answer.

"Man I used to wax that ass on the regular when we were freshmen and it only took two nights to get it." Davis went into a trance as Tyrone finished his statement. He started a slumber walk across campus. He didn't hear another word until he heard Holly speaking to him once he had gotten upstairs.

"What's up man?" Holly said.

"Huh," was Davis' reply.

Holly went on, "Damn man, you okay."

"Yeah I'm bout to hit the sack," and with that Davis went to sleep.

When Davis woke up about 2:04 A.M. Holly was on the phone talking to the cafeteria lady. They were really getting into each other. Davis continued to lie there for a few minutes until he got his bearings. He thought about his day, from the class room argument to Kia's little outburst. He couldn't help but feel some anger from her. It was as if she disliked men or something.

"Oh shit he thought, she couldn't be gay could she?" With that he shook off the thought as he sat up in bed and looked around the room for his bedroom shoes. Holly acted as if he didn't notice Davis and continued with his conversation. Davis grabbed his shoes and started towards the door. It was time to answer the calling of his bladder. He didn't notice that the radio was playing until he was closing the door behind him. As he walked into the bathroom he saw Cisco emptying a mini-crock pot behind him. From the smell of things, Davis concluded that he had been cooking Ramen noodles. As far as Davis was concerned he would have been better off taking a salt lick. It seemed as if everyone on campus had one of those pots and a huge box of noodles or liquid sodium as he referred to them.

After seeing him in the mirror Cisco turned around and began speaking.

"Yo man, I been looking for ya'."

"What's up?" Davis replied.

Cisco continued, "man that shit about to go down."

"What shit?" Davis said as he squinted his eyes in defense of the bathroom lights.

"Stay tuned nigga, me and my roomy about to set it off up in here." With that Cisco walked out suddenly as if he were trying to leave Davis with a mystery. Little did he know that Davis would not think about it again. After flushing the urinal, he went back to bed.

The next morning the ringing of the phone awakened him. It was Kia on the other end.

"Hi Davis, did I wake you?" she asked. He was ecstatic to hear her voice outside of the tutoring session.

"No ahh, I was just getting up," he responded.

"What's up?" he asked.

Her voice came back, "well, I need a huge favor from you", she said. Her voice sounded quite desperate which of course turned him on.

"Yeah, what ya' need?" he asked. "Well remember that awards banquet I was telling you about, well I kinda need you to go with me." Once she finished, Davis grew silent. He nearly fainted from the possibility of being her date. She didn't call it that but he knew exactly what she meant.

"Hello, Davis are you still there, she asked because she was confused by the silence.

"Yeah, I'm here. Ahh sure I'll go with you," he replied desperately trying to hide his excitement.

"Oh, thank you Davis," she said.

"N'all, it's the least I can do since I have a 94 average in math because of you," he concluded.

"Wait a minute, wait a minute, you mean if you were flunking Calculus you wouldn't go with me?" As Kia finished her statement they both started laughing.

Kia then continued talking, "Okay I'll pick you up on Saturday morning around eleven."

"Wait a minute," Davis insisted, "I thought it was next Saturday".

"Yeah it is, but we've got to get you fitted for a tux," she replied.

"Wow, I didn't even think about that, ahh..Kia I'm sorry

but I don't have money for all of that," he said.

"Of course you don't; you're a college student. Don't worry, I'll take care of all that. In fact I'll treat you to lunch after we leave the tux shop just to show you my gratitude."

"Okay," Davis replied.

"I'll see you tomorrow, bye-bye." As Davis hung up he grabbed his toiletries and headed for the bathroom. Just as he reached for the doorknob the telephone rang. It was Kee-Kee and she wanted to know if she could see him that night. Davis hadn't thought about her since his conversation with Tyrone. He quickly told her a lie and was about to hang up until she asked him about the next night. He sighed and unconsciously lied again. Then he hung up in her face.

The next morning, Kia was on time to pick him up. She wore some conservative blue shorts, which stopped, just above her knee. Although he could only see the bottom portion of her legs he nearly became erect just looking at them. This was the first time he had seen her in semi- casual clothing. For their tutoring sessions she was well dressed because she went to work afterwards. But today being Saturday she was able to dress down a little bit. Quarter inch brown open-toe sandals accompanied the shorts. The candy red nail polish that she wore on those perfect toes drove him to the brink of screaming. The ankle bracelet on her left leg was like putting the cherry on top of a sundae. The beige sleeveless tank top that she wore caused her breasts to almost exhibit themselves.

By that time her words were tapping him on the shoulder. "Good morning Mr. Virginia, how are we today." He followed the words back to the seductive cave from which they had emerged. The blushing red lipstick that she wore had a perfect backdrop in her pearly white teeth. The brown in her hazel eyes was complimented by the brown highlights in her hair. And the oversized denim shirt that she wore was radiating with her sweet fragrance. The ankle bracelet on her left leg was the killer.

Davis took a deep breath and thought to himself, "this is going to be a good day.

With that the two jumped into the shiny black Honda and were on their way. The first stop was the tux shop. It wasn't a surprise to him; it was just like her to get business out of the way first.

The ride to the tux shop proved to be a long one. They hadn't said anything since they exchanged pleasantries at the dorm. Part of the reason was because Davis couldn't really concentrate on a reasonable topic. Kia's leg and the way that it handled the clutch occupied his interest. In addition to that, the candy red toe-nail polish played tricks with his imagination. This part wasn't unique to Kia. He had often wondered if women knew the power of candy red toe-nail polish. He had resolved that in his nineteen years he had never seen an unattractive pair of feet that were lightly glazed with lotion and that were capped with red nail polish. Kia's feet only pushed his theory further towards law.

Once his mind, which was about to enter the fantasy and daydream stage, allowed other stimuli from the environment to enter he noticed that the radio was blaring. She had also opened the sunroof. This was a good set-up for right now because he still hadn't come up with any real conversation and even if he had, the radio was too loud.

She had the tuner set to an oldies station, which of course gave him a break from his rap. If it had been Holly, Davis would have asked that the radio be turned to a rap station. But this being Kia, he had an opportunity to learn more about her. Frankly he had learned all he wanted to know about Holly and his cow-happy cousins.

In about thirty minutes, the tux shop visit was over. Kia ended up picking out a very traditional tux for Davis that was completed with a black cummerbund. That was his first time being in a tux and despite Kia's over exaggerations about his handsome appearance, he had to admit that he looked pretty good. Once this little excursion was over, the two of them were headed to the mall. As they were riding, Kia started a little chitchat but it didn't last long. Now it was his turn and in search of a topic to talk about he figured the radio would be a good place to start. After all, she appeared to be using it as some type of therapy that morning. So he zeroed in on the song that was playing at that moment and let loose.

"Ya' know this has got to be the dumbest song I've ever heard. I thought songs were supposed to be inspirational because they were written in a moment of inspiration like the Motown songs. Who in their right mind would want to write about how some woman cleans a house." By the time he had ended his statement, Kia had begun to laugh. Then she started laughing real hard as she continued to work the clutch. Davis was trying to decide if she was laughing with him or at him. And as her laughter subsided she began to speak.

"Davis, that is a Motown song. It was written by a Motown diva as a matter of fact. And the song isn't about a woman cleaning a house even though it's called the Clean up woman. It's about a woman having sex with a married man when his marriage goes through some hard times or some arguments." Davis felt really small as she finished her statement. She had been laughing at him. He decided not to lick his wounds but play it off instead.

"Oh okay, I get it. She's cleaning up the mess that she feels was made by the wife," he said.

"Exactly," Kia replied.

Davis continued, "well since it is Motown it must be inspirational." He could barely finish his statement when the words "not to me" shot out of her mouth. He could tell that there was a touchy subject in there just by the way she uttered the words.

"I take it you don't like the song," he stated. She replied emphatically, "it's bullshit. It's not just her in the song either. It's women as well as men. A lot of my acquaintances in college thought the same way. They thought that they were supposed to have a man and that the arguments came with that of course. And when the arguments got to the point that they forced the two to spend time away from each other that's when the female would go fuck Joe blow off the street. The sad part about it was that in most cases it was a learned behavior. Most of them had rich parents who kept up the image of the home front but who also had misters and mistresses. So this led the children to believe that infidelity was good for the soul or some shit. That's why they did it." As she stopped her statement Davis tried to quickly think of something that would keep her going he was seeing a totally different side of her and he was enjoying it. With that he made a statement, "so you just detest a clean up man or woman?"

"Hell yeah," she replied. Then she continued, "I mean let's look at this realistically. A couple has a fight. Which couples are going to do, I realize that.

But instead of making up with your mate through sex you go and give your sex to someone else. Whether it is a man or a woman and let's say it's the woman who's giving her sex away. Instead of giving her loving to the man who has been there for her for years, the man who has taken care of her ass when she was sick, the man who works that overtime so that he can take her shopping, the man who takes the abuse that comes from her crazy mood swings, she gives it to a man who could care less about her. Whether she's mad at him or not, he deserves that reward. But instead she goes and gives it to Joe Blow who hasn't done anything but be in the right place at the right time. I guarantee if she would give that loving to her man, afterwards they would probably forget what it was that they were fighting about especially if he pulls an orgasm out of her. That's the way it should be.

I don't understand how you could just fall in love with a man because you have had sex with him. In fact, I wish most females would be woman enough to admit they lust after a certain individual instead of going home and breaking the heart of the man you love just because you think the grass is greener on the other side. Of course that man seems like the best. You have already conditioned your mind to equate him with good feelings. You go to see him to help you feel better after you have had a fight with your man, or you go to see him to listen to you after that fight, or you go to be with him so he can pull an orgasm. Of course he's the shit, your mind won't let you think of him any other way. But what have you actually been through with this man besides a night of sweaty sex. You don't know him you haven't cried with him, you haven't gone through hungry times with him when you're actually digging for pennies so both of you can eat until a work study check comes through. You haven't done anything to this man except fuck, showed him your most beautiful side and truth be told, he really doesn't even deserve to see the love in your face let alone your insides." With that last word, she looked over at Davis who was amazed that she was in such a zone. She wasn't done either.

"Ya' know, I applaud any man who's trying to make a relationship work because I'm sure that man has at least one friend who's playing the field and getting more sex than he's getting. As a matter of fact if given a choice, a man would have to be crazy to enter a monogamous relationship when it seems that females would prefer a dawg to a real man. Now don't get me wrong, if you a freak and you're not scared to use the word lust, then by all means go for it. But don't play one role and live another. I can't stand people who lie to themselves and others like that." With that she started shaking her head as if she were calming herself down. Davis saw this as the perfect time to lighten the mood. He placed his hand on her forehead as if he were wiping the sweat away from her brow.

"You okay reverend?" he said a he made the brushing motion on her brow. They both laughed as they pulled into the parking deck at Lenox. Davis was feeling pretty good now since they were having meaningful conversation and plus he was very proud of the statement she had just made.

After walking through a few stores looking for a dress for Kia, the two settled in for some pizza at the mall's food court. By this time the conversation was light and the two of them were laughing a lot. They even decided to take in a movie after lunch. Everything had been fine up to the point that Davis saw the darkness of the theater. Fear overtook him. Where would he sit? Would he sit next to her or one seat away from her? If he had thought about it a minute earlier he could have led the way into the theater and it would have been her decision to make. But as luck would have it she led the way. She went down to the eighth row and started making her way to the center of the row. Then she sat down. Davis made his decision and decided to sit a seat away from her. He didn't get a chance to get comfortable before he heard her.

"Davis if you don't move over here, what's wrong, you think I'm gonna bite you or something?" He quickly thought of a quick comeback.

"Well I didn't want you to make me hot since you were so hot in the car while ago," he said.

She started laughing and said, "will you let that go please." "I'm just messing with ya," he said as he moved to the seat next to her.

Two and half-hours later the Honda was pulling up to the dorm. She thanked him again as he stepped out of the car. Davis waved good-bye to her as she drove off. Just then he heard a familiar voice.

"Well, well, well, looks like someone's weekend is starting off right."

"Hi Lisa," he said as he turned around and headed for the entrance to Brawley Hall. This time she didn't attempt to follow him. He thought that it might really be bothering her.

8

There were a lot of people out on the yard that day. Music was blasting from one of the rooms and the football players were grouped around that area. Now there was a group that Davis couldn't stand. A bunch of ignorant, smelly, so-called athletes, who managed to win only one game during their football season. He had almost gotten into a confrontation with one of them with the nickname of Slow Motion. The thing that angered him so much was that they were a bunch of sorry asses who not only got a free ride to college but also jumped everyone in the lunch line as if they were world champions or something.

As he walked into the dorm, he noticed a small crowd in the lobby. They were just standing around as if they were all waiting on the same person instead of watching television, which was usually the case. As he made his way up to his floor, he passed a lot of people standing in the hallway. Besides all that, there was a strange feeling in the air. He couldn't put his finger on it, but he was sure that all of the people standing in the halls were contributing to the atmosphere. As he reached his floor and started to the door he noticed Tyrone standing in the window.

"DV where ya' been baby? I thought you were gonna' miss it." Tyrone made this statement with a huge amount of enthusiasm.

Davis asked, "what's going on Ty? What's everybody standing around for?"

Tyrone's smile got bigger as he prepared to respond to the question. "Man the shit is about to go down."

Davis looked puzzled as he responded, "What sh..." But before he could get the word out of his mouth, he heard a high-pitched voice scream out in terror, "Oh please don't!"

With that, all heads in the hallway turned to the direction of the scream. A few of them even started running towards the direction from which it came. Davis stood still as Tyrone started walking in the direction as well. "Please don't do this!" The voice was just as high and terrified as before. Davis deduced that it was a female's voice. With that, he too started running in the direction of the scream. As he was running, he heard a deeper voice shouting. "Get up, bitch— what you think I'm some kind of punk or something?" Davis concluded that one of the guys from the dorm had lost it and was attacking his girlfriend.

He instantly felt guilty that he didn't start running sooner so he could help the young lady, but then he remembered that there were a bunch of other guys that were on their way to answer the call. Surely this angry brother would be contained shortly and all of the yelling could stop. "Please- please", the voice continued. Now Davis was confused. Surely, someone had arrived on the scene that could have ended the squabble. He continued running. Maybe the fight was concealed behind doors.

By this time, he was turning the corner. As he rounded the corner, he nearly ran into the backs of two guys who were obviously standing behind the crowd. Davis started jumping up and down trying to catch a glimpse of what was going on in the middle of the circle that had now been formed. One of his leaps was timed in such a fashion that he could catch the words coming from the deeper voice just as they were being spoken. "I ain't no bitch like

you, muthafucka!" the person shouted. Davis' mouth literally hung open when he saw that it was Fred. He could-
n't bear the thought that Fred could be beating a female
with this much intensity. As the crowd continued to shuffle around, Davis was able to get a better view. He could
see that Cisco had also gotten into the act. This infuriated
him. Whoever she was, she surely couldn't bear the wrath
of these two masculine fellows. Davis made up his mind to
knock the shit out of one of them, the first one he could
reach. But just then, he noticed the crowd opening up in
his direction because it was responding to the way Cisco
had shoved or tossed the girl towards them. At that
moment, a complete hole formed in the back of the
crowd, and a body lunged in his direction. Instinctively, he
stepped forward to attempt to break the young lady's fall,
but she hit him with so much force that Davis ended up
bouncing off the wall in back of him and her body hit the
ground with a thud.

He realized that he had the opportunity to charge Fred
or Cisco before the crowd closed again. But just before he
did, he looked down to make sure the girl was still con-
scious, since he now had blood on his shirt. When he finally looked down he was totally stunned at what he saw. "Oh
my God," he said out loud. The body was still moving. It
was even making an attempt to get on its feet. However, it
was the body of a young man and not a female like he
thought. Davis stopped dead in his tracks. His mind began
to piece things together. This must have been the homosexual that propositioned Cisco earlier. This was the one they
were talking about with Tyrone when Davis first met them.
This is what everyone meant about the shit going down.
They had set the guy up. His homosexuality also explained
the high pitched voice—maybe. Maybe that's just what a
man sounded like when he was getting his ass beat.

By this time, the guy had made it to his feet and was
attempting a get-a-way but his efforts were in vain. The

mob surrounded him again. He wasn't the largest guy Davis had seen, but he definitely wasn't a female either. So that made it okay for the guys to beat him as they did— or did it? Davis clearly was not excited like everyone else. He didn't know what to do now. So he made his way past the crowd, which had started punishing the young man as well, and went to his room. As he closed the door behind him, he could hear the victim's shrill voice still pleading for mercy, and he could tell that they were coming in the direction of his room. He sat on Holly's bed since it was closest to the door and stared up at the ceiling as he was trying to decipher what was happening. There was a violent thud against the wall that caught him by surprise even with all of the excitement going on. He was scared to think that it might be the guy's head hitting the wall like that. A second thud caused a tear to drop from his eye. How could they treat a human being in such a barbaric fashion? He was frozen with fear. Fear for the young man's life that was being so brutally beaten just a few feet away from him. He also had fear of his own actions. Why was he sitting there like a coward instead of helping him? Davis could just picture his face and head. The way the thuds sounded off, hell his skull could be fractured by now.

As Davis was finishing his thought, he heard a different noise. The sound was familiar. He had just heard it, however, this time the sound was deeper, more intense and even more deadly. And before another thought could originate from his head, his animal instinct shoved this cowardice from the driver's seat that was Davis Virginia and floored the accelerator of anger and adrenaline. Within a second, he had opened the door and looked across the hall to where he heard those vicious thuds. Blood draped this portion of the wall as a testament of the vicious activity that had just occurred. This sight caused the bull, which was now driving this well proportioned black specimen, to push down on the accelerator even further.

He followed the blood down one flight of stairs where he ran into the third floor mob. It was as if everyone wanted a piece of the action. As he used his anger to throw bodies out of the way, he finally caught sight of the victim. He was covered with blood. And Davis knew that it would take a while to reach him. There were just too many people.

"Bring that faggot down here," was the cry that came from someone further down the hall. They were all getting their punches and kicks in as he stumbled past their room.

"Please help me! Please don't beat me!" were the words that the young man slipped between his profusely bleeding lips, which were now split and swollen. He was unrecognizable at this point.

Davis watched as the victim lunged for an open door. If he could just get inside maybe he could barricade himself from the mob long enough for campus security to arrive. Now the only question was if the occupant of the room would be willing to help the guy, or was he a member of these unruly savages? Unfortunately, it didn't take long to figure out his allegiance. As the victim had gotten most of his arm inside the doorway the young man who occupied the room grabbed the door with both hands and pushed it closed with all the might he could obviously muster. Davis was taking all of this in even though he was still walking with an adrenaline filled pace trying to reach the victim whom still had his forearm in the doorway. "Noooooo!!!!!!" Davis shouted as the heavy wooden door fell against the young man's forearm. Maybe he was hoping that his shouting would drown out the next sound but he didn't yell loud enough. Craaack, was the sound that reached Davis' ears. "Oh my God!" he thought to himself as he watched the arm hang limp from an unnatural pivot point. Surprisingly, the victim didn't make a sound as he pulled his arm back to his body. His eyebrows were raised to their fullest height as he looked in amazement at his forearm. Even some of the people who were beating him stopped for a second and watched in disbelief. Sadly it did-n't matter because other young men had opened their doors as they heard the noise pass their rooms. And since they had not seen what happened to the victim's arm, they didn't notice it was broken and proceeded to kick him to the end of the hall.

Davis was enraged and engulfed in tears by now. He had never heard a person in so much pain. He had never seen so many people out of control. He had never seen a person take so much punishment and he had never heard a human being beg for his life.

By this time, the young man had made it to the second floor and Davis was still in pursuit. It was hard to reach the victim with all of the onlookers in the halls. Besides, he didn't know what he would do once he reached him. He knew he couldn't fight them all, but he also knew that his conscience and being would force him to intervene. His mind was going crazy. "Damn! Move out of the way, ya' bunch of sick bastards!" he shouted. It was desperation time. Davis wasn't about to let this young man lose his life simply because of his sexual orientation. He continued to move yelling onlookers out of his way in an attempt to reach the incident, "All of us are sinners. Only man places a higher degree of sinning on sodomy as compared with lying. In God's eyes, a sin is a sin."

Just then, a sight down the hall interrupted his thought. It was as if Davis spotted the end zone while looking for a touchdown. It lay beyond the victim and the mob, but they were all moving towards it. It was the emer-gency fire exit door at the end of the hall. This was great because if the victim could get out of the door his chances of escape would increase. For one thing, Davis knew that there were a lot of cowards in the dorm who were partic-ipating in this little Malay but he also knew that they weren't brave enough to be seen hitting the victim out-side. In addition to that, it was a fire exit. It had to be unlocked from the inside by law. The only thing now was whether the victim would see it. By this time, he was vomiting blood, and his jaw hung open at an awkward angle. Davis deduced that it must be broken not to mention the broken arm. He promised himself that he would get that little prick that slammed the door. He knew that the guy was a punk.

The victim bounced off viciously and carefully calculated punches and kicks. Somehow, he made it to lunging distance for the exit. Davis, who was a few steps from the poor guy by now, shouted out "Go for the door!" But with all the whooping and hollering and down right cheering, he knew the guy couldn't have heard him. It didn't matter because the victim somehow threw off one of the mob members who was trying to impede his progress and miraculously sucked up two hallways worth of beating and kicking. He deliberately jumped towards the door headfirst as if he had inches to the end zone. While this motion was taking place, Davis had begun to cheer because he figured if the victim could get out on the second floor, then he wouldn't have to take the beatings from the people who were waiting on the first floor. They had to be waiting for the wave to come their way. But Davis was happy to see that it wouldn't go that far. Or would it? His heart nearly stopped at the next sight he saw next. The victim had hit the door with more than enough force to knock it ajar but it didn't open. It didn't even budge. Maybe the guy was too weak by now. The victim must have thought so too because he decided to give it another shot. Unfortunately, he got the same results. The door wouldn't budge.

By this time, silence had fallen over the hallway. The mob had stopped to watch the victim's desperate escape attempt. The victim himself had all but given up. And Davis had finally figured out everything as he continued to make his way through the crowd. This was definitely the answer to the riddle that Cisco had left with him in the bathroom earlier. This was also the explanation to the quiet and somber mood that he had experienced when he first walked into the dorm. They were all in on it. They had obviously lured the guy upstairs for an ambush. And they had definitely locked the emergency exits. The victim's body had lost what little adrenaline rush it had manufactured and suddenly went limp. The guy turned around from the door and faced his attackers with blood falling from nearly every orifice on his body. He seemed to be inviting death at this point.

Davis had nearly reached him and he surely didn't want him to give up now. Just then Davis caught sight of something emerging from the crowd directly in front of him. It was Slow Motion, the football player he had the altercation with. He had an industrial-sized broom in his hands as he charged the victim. He was about to take the beating to another level. At this, Davis had become truly infuriated at the thought of a 300 pound-football player charging an injured man with the intent of further crippling him. But it wasn't going to happen today. Not with Dee Virginia's baby boy in the vicinity. Slow Motion was about to make contact when an airborne Davis struck him at an angle in the midsection causing the broom to fly aimlessly out of his hands. The big man hit the ground with the madman still wrapped around him. But it was the madman who got up first and stepped in front of the victim as if he were his guardian angel.

"This shit ain't going down fellows, not today!" Davis announced to a now quiet and stunned crowd.

"Man who is this muthafucka that I'm about to beat the shit out of?" Slow Motion shouted as he got to his feet.

The spectators were still quiet. Davis was breathing very hard by now and had focused in on his likely opponent. The only thing he could think about was his friend back at home, Big Mike. "How would he handle this?"

Davis thought to himself. He had grown to have muscular features that were similar, but he had never had the heart until now.

"Uhhhhhhhhhhhh!" Davis shouted as he bent his back at the shoulder blades as if he were flexing to get ready. C'mon you fat fucker and use that broom on me!"

This took Slow Motion off guard and out of nowhere Holly came stepping out of the crowd to join Davis. He had come in shortly after Davis and ran to the room to get his "walking tall" stick after he realized what was going on. And there he stood beside his roommate ready to take an asswhooping from the football team. The next move was theirs.

After looking at the conviction in Davis' eyes, Slow Motion decided that this "wasn't the hill that he wanted to die on" and quickly ordered his clan to "leave the little faggots alone." They retreated to the cafeteria for dinner. And with that, it was all over. Davis scanned the rest of the audience for opponents, but they quickly got the message from the over six feet enraged and muscular black man to back off. Holly ran upstairs to call campus security and the halls quickly became quiet and empty. The victim, who was now in shock, was still begging for his life as Davis kneeled down beside him to fully assess his injuries.

9

The next morning found Davis sitting on the stoop in front of Pfifer Hall staring out onto Fair Street. He was still a little disoriented from the travesty of last night. He didn't sleep much at all and he still had a little adrenaline flowing through his veins. He reflected back on the eight months that he had been at Clark and tried to make some sense of it all but he couldn't. The academic experience had been fine but the socializing aspect left him a little puzzled. Now in theory, it had been perfect for the average 19-year-old. Girls liked his physique if not him. He had a hip friend in Tyrone who kept him in the middle of things and he had a funny roommate. Perhaps the most significant of all was that he lost his virginity and had somewhat of a freaky sex life with the most beautiful girl he had ever seen in his life. With all of this in mind, why was it then that he still had some sort of incomplete feeling?

For the answer to his question, he decided that this would be a good time to call his mother. Surely she was up, it was Sunday morning and she was probably up cooking breakfast, which would soon be followed by a departure to church.

Once he got her on the phone and the two of them exchanged pleasantries he immediately went into a tearless sob.

"What's wrong baby?" Dee asked as soon as she detected his mood. Of course he insisted nothing at first. "C'mon Davis, I have to get to church, I don't have time to fish for information. What is it, has that little girl you finally lost your innocence to broke your heart?" Davis let a sigh go over the phone. He was flabbergasted. How could she have known?

"Dee how did you know I was having sex?" he asked.

"Boy please," she responded as if her intelligence had been insulted.

"I smelled it on ya' when you were home for Christmas. Any decent mother can smell and tell when her children have gotten their first piece of tail. I ain't say nothing because all my friends were hanging around for the Holidays including your Godmother. By the way, remind me to cuss yo' horny ass out later for that and in the meantime make sure you using those contraceptives boy. I'll send you some in the next care package." By this time he could hear his Godmother in the background cracking up. If he weren't in such a bad mood he would have laughed himself.

He continued with the business at hand, which was crying on his mother's shoulder. He explained the situation from last night in graphic detail. Midway through his story he began to wonder if he were telling the right person. He had just remembered his mother's stance on homosexuals or he-she's as his mother called them. But he continued anyway. By the time he finished the story she had already guessed what his concerns were. Therefore she started right in.

"Now to say something about the thoughts I know you're having. Just because you helped that boy that don't mean you have some kind of homosexual tendencies. That boy was a human being before he was a he-she. And I would like to think I raised you to care for all human beings rather they like you or hate you. Second of all, were you wrong for going into your room and trying to get away from it all, no you were not. In the beginning it didn't concern you and you probably didn't think those fools would try to kill him and they probably didn't know that they were close to killing him themselves. As a matter of fact you keep up that practice of getting away from things that don't concern you. You'll live a lot longer. 'Cause you the only baby I got. As for your last question that I'm going to answer, do you have to be friends with that boy and visit him in the hospital? All I'll say to that is if you do visit him, do it because you're really concerned and not because you feel you have to. Now baby momma has to go. You know Reverend Steed hates when his congregation comes straggling in late. But listen when you happen to see that lil' bastard who shut that boy's arm in the door why don't you slap him one time for your momma ya' hear. Now I'll talk to you later. Bye-bye." And with that Dee Virginia hung up the phone. She knew from her son's silence that he was feeling a little better.

After the phone call Davis hung up laughing. He missed his mother's head-on wit. She was always direct and very convincing. He also thought about the part of the conversation dealing with him loosing his virginity and he laughed even harder. That was his mother plain and simple. And that was just another reason why he loved her so much.

He decided that he would go outside to the original spot where he was sitting and enjoy some of the serenity that he felt earlier. As he exited the phone closet he nearly stepped into someone who was also trying to use the phone. When he looked up he noticed that it was Nate. Nate was the arm-breaker from the night before. This morning he was wearing a suit. Obviously he was on his way to church. The two were now facing each other and staring. At first Davis thought this was funny. His mother had just told him to deck this punk the next time he saw him. Then Davis re-played the vision of the door slamming on the guy's arm in his mind. This made him angry all over again. Finally Davis took a look at the suit. It was nice and expensive. It wasn't the type of suit someone would wear to just sit in a pew and nod his head in agreement with the minister. Nooo!!, this was a suit of a future deacon and it was complete with finely polished wing tips and a handkerchief.

Davis began to think about the hypocrisy of it all and by this time he was looking through Nate instead of at him. Nate knew what this stare was about and for some reason he had a nerve to smile back at the taller Davis. It was like lighting a fuse to a gun-powder keg because no sooner than he could show his teeth, Davis' hand fell across his face turning his head at a 90 degree angle from it's original position of staring at Davis. As he turned his head back his hand went up to soothe the now inflamed area. He set his stare on Davis again. Davis continued to peer through him. There was no way that Nate was ready to fight this guy. As a matter of fact he rubbed his face in a manner as if to suggest that he deserved that one. Nate then quickly broke his stare and turned and walked off.

It was about 9 a.m. now and Davis still wanted to sit outside for a few minutes longer before half of the campus got up. There were three types of people on a black college campus on a Sunday morning. One third of the people would get up, dress up, and attend Sunday service either on or off campus. Another third of the people would get up to go get Sunday morning breakfast in the cafeteria. And the last third of the people wouldn't get up at all until late in the afternoon. The Sunday worship people were obviously up and getting dressed. Davis wondered how many of these people would be coming out of Brawley Hall after last night's incident.

As he was headed out of the door he ran into Lisa. It had been a few days since he had seen her. Lisa was nearly out of breath he noticed.

"I just heard about last night," she said. Davis just looked at her as she grabbed his head with both hands as if she was checking it over for injuries.

"Are you all right?" she asked. "Sure I'm fine," he responded. She insisted that he tell her the whole story and that's what he did. After about fifteen minutes he was concluding his story as Lisa continued to shake her head in disbelief as she had done throughout his narration. Then she insisted that he pray with her right there in the doorway. He was about to decline when he noticed the conviction in her eyes and he knew that she wasn't going to take no for an answer.

Once he made it back to the stoop that he had been sitting on he looked back in the distance and noticed Lisa boarding a church van which began blowing for her as soon as they finished praying. It was nice to see her he thought. And he smiled as he thought about her genuine concern. They were truly growing closer as friends.

Little did Davis know that his run-ins with people this Sunday morning weren't over. Kee-Kee was walking across campus headed toward her car when she noticed him. Of course she detoured. She walked up on him slowly and he didn't notice her until she was nearly in his face. She began to glow as she saw his face. But the look of content on his face quickly disappeared. She spoke and he spoke as he cut his eye contact with her. She expressed her remorse and concern about the events that took place last night but he had grown silent. By the time she opened her mouth to say a few more select words he had began to interrupt her. "Kee-Kee, I just need to be alone right now okay." She stared at him in a stunned fashion for a few seconds before agreeing and leaving. "Pretty bitch," Davis said under his breath as she walked off.

Poor Kee-Kee, she really missed him and couldn't understand what the problem was with Davis. She hadn't had a real conversation with him in a long time. Tears dropped from her eyes as she continued her walk to her car. Davis couldn't explain exactly why his feelings for her had changed. He knew that it was something that he would have to come to grips with later but he just couldn't deal with it right now. No matter how much she called, no matter how much she cried, he had to be selfish and put it on his to do list.

He headed back to his room where he found Holly just sitting in his bed like some type of zombie. He was obviously thinking about last night.

"Yo man," Davis said. "I want to thank you for standing by me last night, literally." Holly fanned him off as if to say "don't even worry about it." Then he went back into his trance. Davis went about gathering his toiletries and his towel and rag and was prepared to walk out of the door when he looked at his roommate again who still hadn't budged.

"Holly you alright, you not worried about the football players are ya'?"

"Man please," Holly responded, "I'm not thinking about those wannabe's."

"So what are you thinking about?" Davis asked.

"I'm thinking about Mary, ya' know my cafeteria friend." Davis smiled after he finished his statement. Holly saw the smile. He knew that Davis thought it was some type of puppy love deal and was totally hesitant to tell him anything about it. But the smile quickly turned into laughter and this angered him. Holly started conversing with himself in his head. "Who the hell does Davis think he is anyway. Does he honestly think he has the females market cornered." The more he thought about it the angrier he got. He had to wipe that grin off of Davis' face and he knew just what would do it.

"Ya know man, we almost had sex last night." Holly said. And he was absolutely right. That smile dropped off of his face like the soap that had just dropped out of his

hand. The look on his face was turning to astonishment.
He then spoke. "Y'all were going to have sex in the lunchroom, he asked. This time it was Holly who couldn't hold
in the laughter.

"N'all man", Holly said as he tried to catch his breath,
"we were over her house."

Davis, whom was even more astonished by this answer
then asked, "How ya' get over her house."

. " She lives in the projects back there," Holly responded. Davis didn't know what to say. He didn't want to come
off like a father or anything but he thought Holly was
making a mistake going to her house especially considering the surroundings. He had sort of thought of himself as
Holly's protector since they had been rooming together.
After all, Holly had obviously been sheltered growing up
in rural South Carolina. But against his better judgment he
just closed the door behind him and started down the hall
towards the bathroom.

As he passed the water fountain in the hall he looked
down and noticed blood on the floor. Obviously house-
keeping had missed a few spots in their attempt to wipe the
campus clean of last night's little ordeal. As soon as he saw
it Davis became infuriated all over again.

"What did those jack asses think they were accom-
plishing? Did they think they could beat the homosexuality out of him." It took him back to many of those scenes
buried in his head of the Klan and their attempts to pun-
ish someone just because they were a Negro. As if that was
something they could change assuming that they would
want to. Acting behind those sheets like a bunch of punks.
That was just like all of those cowards acting behind the
safety of the crowd last night when they would get their
punch or kick in for the sake of manhood. Davis thought,
"bunch of bastards, not one would have been man enough
to fight that homosexual by himself.

As he walked into the bathroom he immediately saw

two of the cowardly faces that he saw last night as part of the Malay. Davis obliged them with eye contact for as long as they looked at him. Little did he know that they still saw the same uncontrollable beast that stood in front of the almost lifeless body last night daring anyone to try to touch the victim again. Those two soon left and different faces from last night began trickling into the bathroom. Davis had the same greeting for them as he had for the first two. He was ready to take any of them on. He concluded that this would probably go on until school ended which was just a few weeks away.

The next Monday proved to be quite different. The campus had really been affected by the weekend's incident. They were talking about it in everyone of Davis' classes. Davis himself was viewed as some type of hero. The dean had even stopped him on campus to marvel at his courage. But he also saw Slow Motion on campus. When they passed each other, the football player attempted to put on his most fearsome demeanor before he uttered the words, "I gotta break ya hero, break ya down." Davis laughed when he heard the words. The big oaf just didn't understand. Not only did Davis not respect him, he just wasn't afraid of him. He had been around people who had the heart to fight for what they believed in rather it was legal or illegal. He just didn't see that heart in Slow Motion.

Later when classes were over, he headed back to his room. While he was going up the stairs he passed Holly coming down. He had books in his hand and his bedroom shoes on his feet. He looked as if he had just been kicked out of the room and was headed for the lounge. Holly looked at him and shook his head before he said, "Good luck man." Davis' eyes squinted and the corner raised as if he were saying what! But he didn't bother to say anything to his roommate.

As he opened the door to his room, a familiar fragrance jolted his head back. It was a very pleasant smell and it definitely wasn't Holly. As he looked down to remove his key from the lock he noticed a high heel shoe on the floor. That wasn't Holly's either. He then noticed that the shoe was lying beside a black dress. "What the h..." He couldn't finish his thought before he heard, "Hi Davis!" As he looked up his eyes met those of Kee-Kee's . She was in his bed with the covers drawn over her body. And noticing the articles of clothing that were on the floor he figured that she was at least half naked up under there.

"Kee-Kee," he responded in surprise as he closed the door behind him. Before she spoke again she sat up.

"Baby I don't know what you've been going through but I'm sorry that I couldn't help you through it." As she made her statement the sheet began sliding down her chest. And there were the caramel colored breasts that he had suckled with fervor on many occasions. He had forgotten how pretty they were. In the middle of that mound of caramel was a much darker and perhaps even sexier nipple, which topped each breast with perfection. She continued as she stretched out her arms.

"Please come here, I have to hug you." Her voice was very sultry and filled with anxiety. By this time the sheet had slid down to her waist and exposed her precious navel and washboard stomach. Emotions started flying through his head. He really wanted her body right now but there was also a taste of disgust. He couldn't explain it. By this time she had rose to her knees in the middle of the mattress with her arms outstretched once again.

"I know it's been a long time baby but we can pick up right where we left off," she said. He could tell now that the heels and the dress on the floor were all that she had worn over there. As he looked below her waistline he became aware of the pouch of black hair that covered her vaginal area. He loved to refer to it as a pouf. It wasn't so much a word to him as it was a sound that his mind made every time he saw a woman lower her panties and expose it for the first time. Rather it was a xxx movie or an HBO show or even in real life, that sight always made him react in the same way. And hers was just as perfect as the rest of her body. It was finely groomed and looked like an inverted pyramid pointing to the sweetest utopia ever known to him.

"Davis please come to me," she said. This time her voice had traces of tears in it. His apprehension made her nervous. Based on their last few flings together, she thought that he would be ravaging her body by now. She couldn't even conceive of a situation in which he would just stare at her naked body. Nor could she conceive of the embarrassment of going home unsatisfied. If he didn't even touch her, it would be the ultimate rejection. After all he hadn't talked to her in a while no matter how much she tried. This was her last and most powerful weapon. How could he resist it? How could he just look at her? How could he embarrass her like this?

Meanwhile the emotions were still flying through his head. He had never experienced so many contradictory feelings at one time. He wanted to touch her. The beast in him wanted to stroke every warm spot on her body. But there was anger in him as well. Anger from an unexplained source. Anger that made him detest her in every way. Even though there was beauty confronting him right in the face, the sight of her body almost made him sick in the same instance. He finally spoke.

"Kee-Kee you have to go."

"What," she spoke back.

"I'm just not ready to deal with you right now. I have to clear my head." He was sure that he had done it now. He was prepared for her to shout obscenities at him. But instead of shouting she burst into tears.

She quickly jumped from the bed and grabbed her dress from the floor. He didn't know what to do as she struggled to zip her dress in the back. He just stood in the corner. The tears really didn't phase him one bit. He continued to watch her as she finally got the dress zipped and grabbed her shoes from the floor. She didn't even bother to put them on as she darted for the door. All she wanted to do was get back to her room where she could get away from this embarrassing exposure. As she opened the door she turned and looked at him through the tears. He could- n't bring himself to return the glance. She shook her head as the tears continued to flow and she slammed the door behind her.

10

Tuesday came and went fairly quickly. When Davis went for his tutoring session he was informed that Kia wouldn't be there. Apparently she was taking this awards ceremony very seriously and was busy preparing for it. As Davis left the scholarship office he ran into Lisa and the two of them stood and talked for a while before she ended up inviting him to her room for a study session for an upcoming test in U.S. Government. He took her up on the offer and after dinner with Holly he found himself knocking on her door.

She answered the door in a long T-shirt, which almost covered the blue shorts that she wore underneath. On her feet were house slippers. He could tell that she had gotten into comfort mode. As he entered the room he noticed books and worksheets all over her bed. She had started without him and that would undoubtedly be his opening conversation piece once he finished looking her and her room over. There was some jazz playing and an incense burning. He then turned his attention to her. She was busy looking for her stereo remote so she could turn the music down. He noticed her calves again. They were very nice but he felt kinda guilty looking at them. It was as if he were looking at one of the church elders from back home. But after Kee-Kee, it felt good to look at a nice female body and not feel any type of disgust. It was reassuring.

At one point she stopped and looked towards her top shelf trying to remember if she had put it up there. While she stood still, she took one foot out of her slipper and used the foot to rub the opposite ankle in an attempt to control an itch. Davis nearly licked his lips in her presence. Her feet were beautiful and they had red toenail polish on each toe. He thought to himself, "one day I'm going to write a book about the powers of red nail polish as a male turn on. Her foot glided softly across her shin about five times before she stuck it back into the slipper.

She turned and looked at him. That's when he noticed the red lip gloss. "Is she trying to turn me on," he thought to himself.

Then her words broke the silence; "did you bring your book?"

"Yeah, it's here in my bag," he responded.

"Well let's get started," she said as she walked towards the stereo to turn it down.

Afterwards the two of them embarked upon a quiet evening of studying which found Davis asking her to repeat her last statement most of the night because he usually didn't hear her first statements on account of he was mentally undressing her. He was happy that she couldn't read his thoughts because he would surely be embarrassed. For Heaven's sake, Lisa was supposed to be his first platonic friend in college and he thought that he had come to respect her as a friend and someone who would help him out if he needed it. It just so happens that the shorts and the red nail polish caught him totally off guard. It wasn't until the latter part of their evening that she figured out what was going on. She was embarrassed herself when she realized that his obvious thoughts didn't repulse her.

After about an hour and forty minutes the two of them agreed that they were both ready for the test. By this time Lisa was feeling a little nervous and uncomfortable. She thought that it might be a good idea to get Davis out of there before her thoughts became like his. At the door Davis turned and looked at her.

"Thanks for studying with me Lisa. I didn't get a chance to study much with everything going on." Truth would have it that he didn't need to study much at all. This year was shaping up to be a pretty easy one for him as was evident from his 4.00 G.P.A from first semester. The real reason he turned to look at her was that he wanted to prove to himself that he could look her in the face without having explicit thoughts about her. After all, she was supposed to keep him grounded. At least that's what he hoped she would do. But his plan didn't work. The second he turned to look at her, it was her brown eyes that nearly beckoned him to kiss her. For Lisa it was his broad shoulders and large chest that made her want to play with his tongue. The two said good bye with some sort of regret and Lisa quickly closed her door. She would soon pray for forgiveness about her lustful thoughts and go take a nap.

Well before Davis knew it Saturday had come. The big date with Kia had arrived and the two of them spent the day together like she had planned. Davis wanted to think that this had romantic implications but he knew that truthfully it was just more convenient for her to pick him up in the morning before she ran all of her errands.

They started off with breakfast and light conversation. Suprisingly she didn't mention her male friend right away. Davis gathered that the poor boy was history by now. After breakfast they headed for the tuxedo shop to pick up his tux. Afterwards they went to the mall. He was happy that she wasn't in a rush as they walked through the mall. As a matter of fact anyone who looked at them probably would have thought that they were a couple. This was the most relaxed he had been in about a week. It wouldn't last though.

The two decided to grab lunch at Mick's. Well Kia decided, Davis just agreed since she was paying. During lunch Kia made a statement which she intended to be a joke. The statement was centered around the fact that it was a shame that she missed out on such a great story when she dropped Davis off at the dorm last week. She was of course talking about the attack on the homosexual that Davis had part in. It took him a few minutes to recall that she had just dropped him off before all of that happened. She could tell that he found her statement dis-tasteful by the look on his face. But being Kia, she attempted to rationalize her statement. She did so in vain. By the time they left the restaurant they were both pretty steamed. He was walking slightly ahead of her. She asked him to stop for a minute while she looked at a dress in the window. He did and as he stood right behind her, he thought about how much they looked like a couple. The heated discussion, the pouting with him walking fast and her walking slow. The testing came-with her asking him to slow down for some reason other than directly saying, "Will you please walk with me?"

As he stood there he looked at her. She was gorgeous as she stood there in her heels. He knew that she wasn't really looking at the dress. She just wanted to see if he would wait on her. That meant that he wasn't too mad. If she only knew that he could never stay mad at her. No matter how self centered she got. No matter how self-sufficient she tried to become. She made him feel such a way that he knew he could spend the rest of his life with her.

After she secretly determined that he wasn't mad at her anymore, she proceeded to walk off towards the escalator. This time he was right beside her until they proceeded downward. He stood just behind her for safety reasons.

As he stood behind her, he decided that this would be a good opportunity to look her over in all of her caramel splendor. He started at his favorite spot, the feet. She had oiled them carefully due to the heeled slides that she wore. This time she didn't have on the red polish. No, this time her toenails were wrapped with a dark green polish, which he would later learn, matched her dress for the evening. Her toes were just as lovely though. She played with her shoe as she waited to reach the lower floor. She let one of her feet escape the confines of her shoe and let the foot dangle right above it. Very similar to the way Lisa had done it a few nights ago. As his vision started up the rest of her leg, he could tell that they were just as carefully oiled. He smiled as he thought about the thickness of her legs. They weren't fat, just thick. He often thought that it took a special man to love a woman with small legs. He wasn't one of those men. He continued with his inspection as he made his way to her butt. Even though she wore very conservative shorts, he could still see the modest mound that was behind her. He often thought that it took a special man to love a mound-less woman, but he wasn't one of those men. He continued by noticing her hips. They had perfect female curvature. What he tended to call "child-bearing hips." He was now headed to her arms, which were in perfect view since she wore a sleeveless shirt.

Before he could get focused, something caught his attention. A pair of lustful eyes were staring at Kia. These eyes belonged to some guy who was standing in front of her. He wore an old and outdated Members Only jacket and apparently combed his semi-afro backwards instead of forward or picking it out. To Davis, all he needed was a little more facial hair before he looked like a wolfman. Kia was busy occupying her escalator ride with an inspection of all the shoppers and stores that were down on the next floor. She hadn't even noticed this pervert mentally raping her. The truth is that guys had been looking at her all day and that didn't bother Davis. After all, she was very lovely and didn't consider himself a jealous or possessive type. Besides, she didn't belong to him. But there was something different with this guy; you could almost see the offensive thoughts flowing through his head as his eyes locked in on her breast. After all, he didn't know that they

weren't together and probably didn't care. That was totally disrespectful to him. The disrespect grew more intense
as this guy who looked to be in his mid to late thirties suddenly caught sight out of the corner of his eye. And Davis
took special care to send the prick a message with his eyes
in a last resort to avoid a confrontation.

Unfortunately this message went unheeded and apparently sparked the guy on because at that moment he decided that it was time to draw Kia's attention. His best plan
obviously consisted of sucking one of the beige teeth in the
corner of his mouth while his mouth remained opened. It
took about three of these nasty sounds before Kia turned
and looked down at the person in front of her. Once she
looked, the genius decided that he would take this opportunity to show all of the beige and some brown and rotten
teeth in his mouth. By this time Davis was infuriated and
was about to move Kia out of the way when the jerk
opened his mouth even more to speak.

"Can we go somewhere together?" he said in a voice
filled with illiteracy.

Upon hearing this, Davis was pushing Kia aside as the
escalator arrived at the bottom floor. As he shoved his
chest in front of the guy, Davis said with sarcasm, "Can I
go too?"

"Look slim, Um' talking to the female, won't you take
yo' young ass somewhere," the pervert retorted. By this
time Kia stepped in front of Davis, as the anger in his eyes
grew apparent.

"Davis, calm down. It's not worth getting upset
about," she said as her hands rested on his chest trying to
shove him back.

"Yeah Day-vis, won't ya'calm down young buck," the
pervert retorted again. At that comment, Bruce Banner
was about to leave the building and Kia knew it. Her arms
dropped from his chest and she wrapped them around his
back as she buried her head in his chest. She felt this was

her only resort since her mouth and attempts to push him back had no effect. She felt so helpless but there was no way she was going to allow this to happen. Even if she had to absorb some of the licks herself. She was pleading with him now as her words came out of his chest. "Please forget about this Davis", she said. Normally he would have enjoyed this tight hug but right now her words were falling on deaf ears. In the process of getting closer to the guy, he almost walked through Kia who was literally praying at this point. She could feel the anger as his body, especially his arms, began to tense up. No matter how much power a woman thought she had over a man, it was times like these when any female could recognize the pure beast of the male species. She felt so helpless as Davis leaned down and got directly into the face of the guy. Kia was now buried between the two.

"Man as soon as she let's go, I'm gonna fuck you up." With every word Davis spoke the bass in his voice got lower and lower. Right now Kia was hoping that the words had the same effect on the guy as they had on her. Her wish was granted. Just as Davis was reaching to remove her, she could feel the man's presence behind her disappear. A few seconds later she could hear Davis' voice say, "Kia he's gone, you can let go." As she released her grip, raised her head, and backed away she turned to make sure the wolfman had indeed left. She then looked up and thanked God that Davis' words had the same effect on the guy as they had on her, which was fear. Afterwards she looked up at him. Despite the fact that she was flattered with his so-called chivalry, she was also pissed with his behavior and took the female's way out and only let him see the anger inside of her. She just stood there and stared at him for about ten seconds before she turned and walked off. He followed a safe distance behind as he constantly asked, "What's wrong- what I do?"

He only did this to mask the laughter inside of him. He

thought it was humorous how she went from pleading with him in one instant to giving him her so-called evil eye. He adored those eyes; they couldn't scare him even though she got her point across to him.

The car ride to her apartment was very quiet. It was about 6:00 p.m. and they had to get ready for the banquet. When they were inside the apartment, he was about to comment on how nice it was when she grabbed him by the arm and pointed.

"There's a bathroom in there, could you please be ready by seven?"

With that she walked off into another room and closed the door behind her.

After about thirty minutes he emerged from the bathroom fully dressed in the tux. He would have been done sooner but the tie took up about five minutes itself. As he walked past the kitchen he found her in the refrigerator retrieving a container of apple juice. She was wearing a shower cap and a bath robe. As their eyes locked contact with each other he raised his arms in a fashion as if he were saying tah-dahhhh! Then he broke the silence;

"I'm ready."

"Awesome," she replied sarcastically as she took the glass back to the room and closed the door again. Davis decided to entertain himself with the television as he waited for her to emerge.

The rest of the night was totally uneventful. The banquet was very boring and the silence between the two continued. However she did spend a large part of the night wearing a smile and locking her arm inside of his as she introduced him to everyone as her friend. She was definitely going to get her tux and dinner's worth out of him. The whole thing was funny to him and it was becoming funny to her as she tried to sink back to pissed mode after she had made the introductions and they were alone again. She wanted to talk to him but she felt that it was important to continue to show her anger by barking instructions at him instead.

The banquet finally drew to an end and she was fortunate enough to walk away with two awards. He had hoped that would lift her mood but the ride to campus was just as quiet. When the car came to a stop in front of the dorm, he opened it to get out. At that moment she spoke in a very stern voice, or at least attempted to.

"Thank you for accompanying me tonight." He turned around to look at her as she spoke the words. It sounded pretty corny to him but he just figured that she was trying to cover all bases as only an independent Kia could do. As they locked eyes, he stared intensely at her and was about to ask her was she serious about her anger all evening but then he thought about how corny her last statement really was. This caused him to laugh instantly. Upon seeing him laugh she started to do so as well. And the two of them laughed together for a few seconds before she said with a smile and a trace of laughter, "Get out of my car, ya' crazy boy." Davis was joyful to see her smile and decided to go quickly while all was well. "Thanks for the evening," he said. "Thank you," she replied in a much more sincere tone this time. Then he walked off as she drove away.

As he walked into the dorm he ran into Tyrone. It was the regular with Ty. He just wanted to talk about the pitfalls of the university and the administration and then talk about some female he had recently screwed. The truth is he just wanted to talk to Davis to see if he was angry about the beating incident and investigate as to why he was so dressed up. He couldn't bear the thought of Davis becoming a bigger womanizer than he was. He decided to tell Davis that Vernell, the homosexual who was beaten, was now in the hospital with a cracked skull, broken arm, jaw, and six broken ribs. Davis knew that there was more but he was just happy to hear that the guy would be better if he just got some quality healing time.

As he walked into the room, he found Holly playing some soft music and studying by a lamp. They started a little conversation about Davis' evening as he got out of the tuxedo. Davis noticed that his roommate was sounding different tonight. It was as if he were hurt. Maybe he and Mary were going through something. That would definitely explain why he wasn't on the phone with her as he usually was during this time of night.

Davis decided to bypass his shower until the morning. He didn't want to wash off the seductive smell of Kia just yet. As he turned back the covers on his bed, he continued his conversation with Holly. He decided to pry and ask about Mary. Holly said that everything was fine and left it at that. Davis believed him but still couldn't put his finger on what was different about him tonight.

The telephone rang and Davis answered it. At first there was silence and then a very solemn voice called his name. It was Kee-Kee. Davis winced when he discovered it was her. But this time he really felt obligated to talk to her considering all of the embarrassment she had suffered the last time the two of them saw each other. After she called his name there was more silence on the phone. She was waiting to see if he would hang up and he was trying to think of what to say to her. His eyes wandered around the room as he thought.

"I'm sorry," she said.

"What are you apologizing for?" he asked.

"I'm sorry for embarrassing you the other day," she continued.

He responded, "you don't have t..." He stopped then. In the process of his eyes roaming around the room, he saw something that shocked him. On the floor, partially hidden under Holly's bed was something that caused him to lose his train of thought. He peered under the bed even closer to make sure he was seeing what he thought he was seeing. It was a towel. A white towel covered in blood.

"I'll have to talk to you later," he said as he hung up the phone. Poor Kee-Kee was devastated as she hung up too. It almost seemed that she was getting somewhere.

In the meantime, Davis had grabbed the towel from under the bed and jumped up to turn on the main light.

"What the hell is this Holly?" His roommate looked up in astonishment as Davis stood over him. Then Davis' eyes grew big as he looked at Holly's face. The entire right side of it was bruised and swollen. His lip was also swollen and still trickling a little blood.

"What the hell happened to you?" Davis yelled. After Holly calmed him down he explained that he had been ambushed while leaving Mary's house a little earlier that evening. Davis was listening intently until he found out that it was Slow Motion and a couple of football players who had jumped on his roommate. He immediately started to get dressed again until Holly grabbed him by the shoulders and stopped him. He calmed Davis down and tried to convince him that it wasn't as bad as it looked. He even made Davis promise that he wouldn't retaliate. He didn't want him to get kicked out on account of some bullshit. Davis agreed for the moment but was secretly plotting to address the situation during the last week of school.

11

Davis had a little trouble falling asleep that night. He felt responsible for Holly's ambush. He was also upset with his roomate at the same time. "Why in the hell does he keep going to the projects anyway," he thought to himself. But he knew that he was just angry. Holly had just as much right to go and see Mary as he had when he would creep over to see Kee-Kee. He soon drifted off to sleep.

The next morning Davis woke up ravaged. He quickly got dressed and woke Holly for breakfast. He, himself, hated being woken for something like that but he knew it was okay to wake Holly for food. The two of them hurried off to the cafeteria. This was the best meal of the day. And once Davis got his tray, he quickly picked out a table. Holly was preoccupied with Mary. He was explaining his wounds from the previous night. Davis watched the two over in the corner. He couldn't hear their words but he watched their gestures. Davis could tell from her facial expressions that she was really concerned for his roommate. After about 10 minutes, Holly joined Davis and Mary went back to work. She was visibly shaken.

The two guys always sat in the back of the cafeteria so they could see everyone who entered. This was another reason why the two had found resistance from the football team. This was their hang out. But this morning it wasn't the football players but Kee-Kee who walked in and caught their eyes. She was accompanied by one of her sorority sisters. Davis recognized her as the same girl who went with them to the party the night when he first met Kee-Kee.

Davis and his roommate proceeded to devour their meal and when finished, they started to conversate a little. Davis would soon wish that he had left immediately.

"So, did you ever call Kee-Kee back last night?" Holly asked.

"Ahh man!" was Davis' response and Holly concluded his answer from there.

"I got so caught up in your situation that I forgot to. I really didn't mind talking to her last night either. Well, I'll talk to her tonight, I know she'll call back." "Yeah I guess you're right," Holly said, because she can't take her eyes off of you right now." After hearing this, Davis was reluctant to look in her direction for fear of looking her in the face.

Although he made a valiant effort, he noticed movement in the direction of her table using his peripheral vision. When he eventually looked, he saw that the girl had Kee-Kee's arm. And Kee-Kee, who was now standing, was wrestling with the girl trying to pull free. At that moment the young lady's voice got louder and Davis heard her say, "No Keandra, don't do it." By that time Kee-Kee had broken free. She quickly started walking towards Davis and Holly with a deliberate and determined pace.

Once she reached the two of them she looked directly at Davis. He sat in fear of the obvious scene that was about to take place. With a child-like tone Holly spoke.

"Hey Kee-Kee, what's up?" Davis immediately dropped his head and shook it from side to side. Holly obviously had no idea about what was about to take place. While maintaining an intense stare at Davis, she lifted her open palm in Holly's direction to acknowledge him. She then took a second to take a slow and deliberate breath.

"Ya' know for the past few weeks I've been beating myself up and literally pulling my hair out because you've been ignoring me." She was speaking in a somewhat angry voice that grew in volume as she continued.

"For a minute I thought I had finally found a mature individual who could treat me with as much tenderness and endearment that I showed him. But like always I have to end up disappointed." By this time, heads began to turn in the direction of her voice and Davis was getting embarrassed.

"Can we talk about this somewhere else?" he asked. She didn't even understand the words he was speaking. She started to shake as she continued.

"I've been upset with people before but I've never been so upset that I couldn't talk to that person to let them know what it was that I was upset about. I never considered anyone not worth me speaking to. That's why I have such a hard time dealing with this." As she was talking Davis was calling her name trying to get her attention and attempting to avoid any further embarrassment. She never heard him. She just continued.

"So I decided that I wasn't going to treat you like you treated me. That's why I had to come over here to speak to you even though my friends don't want me to say anything to you. I had to do this for myself. So what I need to know before I leave you alone is why? By this time Davis could hear the stress and tears in her words. She then broke into tears as she asked him again.

"What Davis, what did I do that was so bad that you couldn't even bring yourself to speak to me?" She didn't care about who was listening now. She was hurt and Davis could tell. He knew he had to get her to a secluded place and fast. He jumped up and took her wrist in an effort to lead her out of the cafeteria. Kee-Kee, who now seemed in her own world with the trembling and crying, didn't object to his leading her out at all. People all around the cafeteria continued to watch as Kee-Kee asked why repeatedly as Davis pulled her limp body out of the cafeteria. As he neared the table where Kee-Kee's friend sat the girl jumped to her feet in his path in the interest of welfare for her friend. With his eyes and a nod of the head, Davis assured her that he wouldn't harm her in the slightest. The young lady sat down again.

The area beneath the stairs of the cafeteria served the purpose for the discussion. It was relatively secluded. Davis turned around and looked at Kee-Kee and released her arm at the same time. She was now trying to wipe away some of the tears that poured down her face but her attempt was in vain. She didn't imagine that it would be this hard to talk to him. As she looked in his eyes she realized just how much she cared for him. Davis could see her affection as well. It didn't matter. She knew that this conversation would probably make her feel bad but it couldn't be any worse than she had been feeling for the past few weeks therefore she was determined to clear this up.

The two of them stood in silence for a while, each of them waiting for the other to speak. Finally Kee-Kee broke the ice. With her arms folded across her chest and her right foot slightly bouncing in an impatient and waiting fashion she asked, "So are you gonna tell me the reason you've been treating me like shit!" Davis looked at her intently as she spoke. The tears had stopped but her face was wet. With her arms folded, leg bouncing, and her hair looking a bit frightful, from not being done in a few days, she looked quite funny to him. At least that's the image he chose to concentrate on since he was reluctant to have this conversation. In fact he started to giggle slowly with hopes that she would join in. She didn't. As he laughed she continued to watch him. After he saw that she was patiently waiting for him to grow up for a second, he felt very small. He realized that she was waiting on a tangible answer.

At that moment he got serious himself and searched his insides for the answer to her question.

"You know I thought I was special to you," he started out.

"But then I learned you had sex with Tyrone. I mean what is that. How can I feel special if I know you have been with womanizers like that?" Kee-Kee's face was squinting as she was searching for a handle for what he was talking about. He continued but her facial expression puzzled him and he began to babble.

"I mean isn't that what trust is all about? All of the good times we've shared this year only to realize that you've showed the same affection to somebody like Tyrone, I mean what is that," he said. By this time the perplexed look had disappeared and she had raised a hand to cover her face and started shaking her head from side to side as if to say I don't believe this. Davis tried to continue.

"I mean, I was really hurt and,"

"Just stop," she interrupted him.

"Stop before you embarrass yourself with your nonsense. You mean to tell me that you have been treating me like this because that sorry bastard said that I slept with him. Please tell me that's not what you're saying." At that moment Davis' heart sank to his stomach. He had never bothered to find out if Tyrone was telling the truth or not and it was definitely within his character to lie. He couldn't believe that he had acted this way based on a lie. His face began to squint up as if to say damn. Kee-Kee spoke again.

"You know that's just typical of a stupid ass man. All of this because of Tyrone and what he had to say. Well Davis he lied to you." As soon as he heard the words, Davis put his hands up to his face and continued to listen as she spoke.

"I didn't sleep with him, I made love to him." Davis looked up in total surprise. It was true after all he thought to himself.

"The muthafucka slept with me, but I loved him. And if you don't understand the difference Mr. Virginia then you're even more immature than I care to believe. Ya' see the problem with me is that I have a big heart Davis and as much as I hate to admit it sometimes my heart does the driving and not my head. Who the hell are you anyway. Why should I have to apologize to you for something that happened to me before I even knew you? You think I'm some kinda whore who's just looking to fuck incoming freshmen?"

"Ya' fucked Tyrone, and he was a freshman," Davis interrupted.

"So is that what I did to you Davis? I fucked you? Let me tell you something little boy, I don't know what was going through your head when you were inside of me but let me tell you what was in my head. I didn't want that feeling to end. Not just the pounding of your 200 pound body on top of mine, but the heat that I felt from trying to make you a part of my world and a part of me with every contraction, with every thrust of my hips. I wanted you inside of me, I needed you inside of me, to be a part of me. I reached ecstasy Davis. Oh sure I've had a few orgasms but I never had such a feeling. And pleasure like that doesn't come from wanting to get fucked. No, no, you can only reach such a stage by loving someone. Like I loved you. Ecstasy comes from a loss of inhibitions. And let me tell you that you don't just lose your inhibitions to get fucked. So if you're feeling like a man right now because you made me cry and treated me like a trick these last few weeks, well I guess I shouldn't be looking for anymore men." With that she quickly turned away and walked off.

Davis stood there for a few seconds digesting the words he had just heard. He started to feel bad. He then walked towards the door to exit the cafeteria. At that moment Holly was on his way out as well. He had obviously gotten tired of waiting on his roommate and was headed to the dorm without him. The two proceeded to the dorm together. Holly quickly noticed Davis' solemn behavior and knew better than to ask what happened with Kee-Kee.

When the two of them reached the door of Brawley, Slow Motion walked out in a deliberate fashion. Holly was the only one to notice him since Davis was walking with his head down. Before he lifted his head up, Davis' shoulder was rammed by Slow Motion's shoulder with so much force that he had to shuffle his feet to maintain his balance.

"Watch where ya' going ya' bitch ass nigga," bellowed Slow Motion. By this time Davis' head was up and he had locked sights with the conceited football player. He only stared at him though before he proceeded into the dorm. Davis knew his head wasn't right to deal with the big oaf. Once upstairs, he fell on his bed and went to sleep.

A very loud and unpleasant telephone ring woke him up a couple of hours later. It was the twins from his government class. They were interested in studying with him. The final exam was on the following Monday and this would have been his first official study group outside of Lisa. He wondered why they wanted to study with him but he soon remembered that the only two A's going into the final belonged to him and a very conceited female who sat at the front of the class. In his lethargic state he agreed to meet them in twenty minutes in the same place where they usually had class. After he hung up he realized that he didn't have much time and dashed for the shower.

Twenty minutes later Davis stepped onto the second floor of Haven Warren and was headed for the classroom when he noticed the twins standing in the hallway. They explained to him that the door was locked and that they would have to use the room next door. He quickly agreed and the three of them entered the room. It was a little smaller than the rest of the rooms on the hall and it had much more furniture.

Davis was the first one in and he turned on the lights as he entered. As Tyra and Terry entered behind him one of them quickly turned off the lights. This drew his attention and he turned around. As he did he noticed the both of them staring at him. They did this for a few seconds and then one of them walked across the room to draw the blinds. As she did this the other one went into one of the bags they had brought along and pulled out what appeared to be a sheet and a quilt. They both proceeded to the back of the room. He could still see them even though there was little light in the room. They were now moving furniture around and his chivalrous nature nearly made him go back and help them. However, the precision with which they moved and the fact that he was totally engrossed with trying to figure out what was going on made him stand patiently in one spot.

Once they finished moving the furniture, still in team-work fashion, they both carefully and quickly spread the quilt on the floor and then the sheet. By this time Davis decided to say something.

"Okay y'all, what the hell are you doing?" They were now headed back to the front of the room. Terry reached in the bag and grabbed a towel to hand to Tyra. Tyra took the towel by both ends and began twirling it so that it would twist up very tightly as if she were going to pop someone on the butt with it. As she finished twirling she handed the towel back to her sister and began to answer Davis' question.

"Oh, this is nothing, we just have a little surprise for you before you go home for the summer." Davis was about to tell them that he wasn't going home for the summer when he noticed Terry had dropped to one knee and carefully stuffed the twisted towel under the closed door. His imagination really started to run away with him now. What did they plan on doing. He had never smoked marijuana and wasn't about to start now. He started to think how he would tell them since they had obviously gone through a lot of trouble planning and preparing this, whatever it was. Once Terry got up, she went into the duffel bag that they had brought and started handing stuff out to Tyra. Once she finished she stood by her sister's side and the two of them started walking towards him very slowly and in synchronized stride. He had moved to the back of the room now. He noticed what they had in their hands. It was a canister of whipped cream, a plastic bag filled with ice, and a bowl filled with sliced fruit held in place by plastic wrap. It was a wonder that he could tell what they were carrying because his eyes had not adjusted to the darkness and he could barely see their physiques. It was a lovely sight as always but now that they were walking towards him in such a slow manner, it was an especially awesome sight to behold. At least he had finally figured out what was going on now. For some strange reason they wanted to have an indoor picnic. That's why they placed the towel under the opening of the door, to prevent anyone who may be in the building this Sunday afternoon from smelling the food. He would later learn that the purpose of the towel was to prevent the escape of sound and not smell.

"Ya' know, we've been doing this for a long time but what we're doing with you today is a first for us," said one of them. He had lost whatever advantage he had for telling them apart. Davis responded, "This your first time having a picnic indoors?" The girls laughed at his naïveté. They had finally reached him and placed everything they had in their hands on a nearby desk. After they giggled one of them spoke.

"Boy, this is no picnic! Well, on second thought... it pretty much is." As she finished her statement, she reached for his face and drug her fingers in curling fashion around his cheek. She spoke again as she did this.

"It's just not the picnic you had in mind."

His face looked puzzled after the last statement. He was about to ask for and explanation when he noticed the two of them fall into what he considered a trance. They were now both standing in front of him and facing each other. The two girls looked each other in the eyes and their hands started moving. They both reached towards their waists and grabbed their shirts and proceeded to pull the shirts over their heads in a choreographed fashion. He was just noticing that they were wearing the exact same outfits which was strange to him since he had never seen them wear the same thing in class before.

By the time the shirts hit the floor, they had both began unclipping their bra straps. As they did this they looked up at Davis who was now comatose with anxiety. This was the first time he looked them in the eyes since he saw them in the hallway a few minutes ago. And there was no mistaking the look he saw in both of their eyes. He had seen it before and knew exactly what it meant. By this time the braziers had hit the floor and their breasts were exposed. "Oh my God," were the words that slipped involuntarily from his mouth. The breasts were just as big as he had imagined them and they were perkier than anyone's imagination. He deduced that they both wore bras just to be lady-like because it was clear that they didn't need them. At that moment they both reached for his waistline and he threw both his hands in the air so they could remove his shirt with ease.

The girls were just as impressed with his upper torso as he with theirs. The sight of his flesh seemed to snap them out of the trance they were in because they both made a noticeable lunge for his body. The lips of one of them landing on one of his nipples and the lips of the other landing on one of the six tight muscle bulges in his stomach. As each one of them explored their respective regions of his upper body that they had selected, they slowly undid the button and zipper to his shorts. They were working as a team once again as one removed his shorts and the other removed his underwear. All the while they were still caressing his body orally. They were literally doing two things at one time. It was clear that they were very skilled and used to working together.

Once they had him undressed, they carefully pulled him to the floor and placed him on his back. Then they simultaneously stood up and reached for their pants to remove them.

They were still looking down at him when they noticed his face wince as if he were in pain. Davis had just remembered that he didn't have any condoms and knew that the heat of this moment wouldn't allow him to turn back now. Anticipating his concern, one of them reached for a small black pouch that Davis hadn't noticed sitting by the bowl of fruit. She unzipped it and emptied its contents. Davis was happily reassured as a dozen Trojan condoms hit his chest.

"Oh shit, look Tyra!" The both of them looked down at Davis and noticed his arousal. This caused both of them to noticeably speed up their attempts to remove their undergarments and join him on the floor. The next sound he heard was the spraying of whipped cream.

12

Davis woke up the next morning feeling extremely good. Unfortunately he was late for his Physics final. He ran for the shower and was soon under a hot stream of water. The water revived his thoughts from the previous evening and a soft smile fell over his face. He proceeded to wash the dried fruit and whipped cream stains from his midsection. His pace had slowed even though he was still late. He really wasn't too worried about the final – after all, he had one of the highest grades in the class of 37 people. His philosophy had always been not to necessarily stress himself out to be the best, but to always do better than most. Besides the final was from 8:00 to 10:00a.m. The time was now 8:03.

He strolled into the lecture hall about ten minutes later and picked up a test and scantron sheet from the graduate student who was proctoring the exam. He looked around and saw that the class was filled with intense students hovering over their papers as if it may blow away. Since his graduation day in high school, he was determined not to ever be that stressed. He had learned from high school that the secret to education was time management and this year he had managed his time well. He was really feeling good. His good mood caught the attention of the graduate student who was used to seeing students act like nervous wrecks around this time of the year. But why should he worry? He had just had a night that would even impress James Bond, and besides this was the last week of school. He finally found a seat and got started on the exam.

He emerged from the exam 50 minutes later and headed for his room. His next final, PE, was at 3:00 p.m. He wasn't worried at all. This would be a great time to catch up on some sleep. When he walked into the room he discovered Holly on the phone with Mary. She was obviously on her break over at the cafeteria. The two of them had been maturing as a couple and their conversations had moved beyond topics of food. They were planning something big together since this was Holly's last week. Davis had no idea what it was. He kicked off his sandals and quickly passed out on the bed.

It was 3:15 p.m. when he emerged from the gym after completing his last final - at least until Wednesday. He was quite pissed because the test was a joke and it almost felt like a waste of time. "Oh well, an easy A. I'll take it," he thought to himself as he walked down the hill to the main campus.

While walking he noticed all of the young ladies scattered about. This was a funny time to see the nice looking females on campus. During finals, most of them didn't have time to concentrate on their looks. A lot of them wore caps or plain ponytails with no make-up. He laughed as he continued walking. However, he soon found himself walking behind a very attractive dark-skinned female. She was thick and toned. She was also relatively tall. He found himself walking faster trying to catch up with her and get a better look. As he got closer he couldn't help but think that she looked a little familiar.

"Ms. Upshaw!" he exclaimed as he got close enough to get a good look. It was his teacher. He hadn't seen her in a while and he obviously didn't know that she had cut her hair. She was wearing jeans and Nike tennis shoes. This wasn't hard to believe since it was finals week. And besides, she was really wearing those jeans. She smiled when she saw it was Davis and reached to give him a hug. The two started conversating.

"How are finals going for you Mr. Virginia?" she asked.

"Oh just fine ma'am," he replied. "I can't complain."

"Son, don't call me ma'am. You can call me Gail before you call me ma'am," she said with a hungry smile. Davis was about to answer when his head was rocked from the side by a vicious open hand slap. It was a solid lick that brought a look of total surprise and anger. Once he got his head back at a level position he noticed Ms. Upshaw peering around his large shoulder in an attempt to get a better look at the assailant. Davis thought to himself that it couldn't be anyone but Slow Motion and this was about to get ugly because he had had enough of this shit. But then again it couldn't be that football player because he didn't have the heart to do that in front of a faculty member. All of this was running through his head as he was turning around to confront the person. After he had made his 180-degree turn the assailant spoke.

"Boy you know how long I been running around this hot ass campus looking for your ass?" Davis' face lit up once he saw whom it was talking to him. He was looking eye to eye with a young man with a low haircut and a Miami-style silk T-shirt covering a massive chest. Hanging from the sides of this chest were two huge arms that almost made Davis' arms look small.

"Big Mike! Wuz up?" Davis yelled as he moved in for an emphatic hug. Mike's mouth found room to speak over Davis' shoulder during the embrace.

"Wuz up boy? How ya' been,? Mike asked.

"Ahh man, I'm good. I can't complain a bit," Davis responded.

Davis introduced Mike and Ms. Upshaw to each other. He didn't want to be rude to her so he took another minute to finish up the small talk with Ms. Upshaw so that he could start entertaining his friend. She reached and gave Davis another unexpected hug as the two of them ended their conversation. It was a little different from the greeting hug she had given him a few moments ago. But in his happy state, he never noticed. As she walked off he turned to Mike so they could start reminiscing.

"Boy, that's ya' lady?" Mike asked. Davis laughed as he answered.

"Man n'all, that's one of my professors."

"Damn, I gotta get into college," Mike said in a bewildered fashion.

"Why?" Davis asked.

"Boy that professor wanna get wit' you."

"Hell no, she just cool like that," Davis returned. Mike then said in a condescending voice, "Good ol' Snap; can't see the forest for the trees."

Snap was Davis' nickname from back home. He got it as a result of snapping back with a little common sense and education whenever someone said something that was a little too outrageous to believe.

"Trust me Snap. I saw the way she was sweating you when I walked up from behind, the way she sweated you while I was standing there, and your young ass probably didn't even notice the hug she left ya' with. Trust me, you can bag that one whenever ya' ready," Mike concluded. Davis was about to write Mike's statement off as nonsense, but then he started thinking about how Mike was the kinda' guy who always put his cards on the table. He was very primitive and could easily detect primitive emotions such as lust. It was this quality, along with his physique that allowed him to get in between the legs of many attractive women.

"Enough of the bullshit, I came to take care of some business," Mike said.

"Yeah, wha'cha doin' here?" Davis asked.

"Well, I ran into ya' moms in the grocery store back in Augusta. She told me about the group of football players you were having a lil' trouble with. Now I didn't tell her what I was going to do so she doesn't know about me visiting you. But I gotta make sure you don't get kicked out of school for fighting some hard asses. We gots to keep you in college Snap!" After Mike had finished, Davis was scared to confirm the story. He knew that Mike was willing to die trying to remedy this situation. Those were the type of friends they were. It was true that their lifestyles eventually made them grow apart, but Mike loved Davis more than Davis would ever know. Mr. Virginia had to ask himself if he wanted Slow Motion to get hurt. Then he thought about his last encounter with the football players. When his thoughts were on the conversation with Kee-Kee and Slow Motion bumped into him coming out of the dorm. Since he didn't retaliate, Davis knew that there would be more harassing to come. So right then he decided to let Mike handle it.

As the two of them continued walking for main campus, Davis confirmed the story and gave his friend a few details. By this time they had reached the dorm and low and behold there were the football players. It was Slow Motion and five of his henchmen. Since Davis saw them first, he quickly pointed them out to Big Mike. Mike took a good look. "Them muvfuckas right there," Mike said in a disappointed voice. Davis confirmed as Mike looked on.

"Here, hold this," Mike said as he pulled a silver 45 caliber handgun from beneath his shirt. Davis' eyes enlarged as he quickly and carefully grabbed the gun and slipped it into his book bag. Mike had already started walking towards the unsuspecting gathering of football players when he quickly looked back and shouted to Davis, "Don't get caught with that, I'll be right back."

Mike had made it into the center of the guys when they finally noticed them. Davis looked on wondering what the hell Mike intended to do with six guys who were just as big as he was and some even bigger. At the same time he looked around nervously to make sure no campus police had seen the gun exchange. Mike, meanwhile, had put on his warriors mask and had begun staring each one of them in their eyes. It was like he was looking for something. He soon found it. After about five seconds staring individually at each one of the guys his biceps began to flex. He was now staring at Slow Motion and in a calm, calculated move his open palm swiftly flew across the face of the huge individual and it created a whacking sound that was unmistakably flesh. No sound or move was made as Slow Motion turned his head to its original position.

Mike then turned and pointed at Davis and while leaving his hand in the air he looked back at his victim and licked his lips as he wagged his head from side to side as if to say no. He then resumed the stare down procedure that he had engaged in before the slap. In giving each one of the guys their five seconds of stare-down time, he was making certain that each one of them got the message. As he turned and looked at the leader again, he spoke.

"I trust that we won't have to have this conversation again." With that he turned and left the semi-circle. He started what seemed to be an incredibly slow walk back to Davis. Davis never took his eyes off of him as he walked back. He now understood what Mike was doing during the initial stare-down. He was looking for the leader while at the same time taking the heart or what little bit there was left of it from each one of them with each five-second look. Davis could see that Mike wasn't worried about his back being turned. He could also see the six guys in the background. They had all turned and walked off in the opposite direction. Once Mike reached Davis the two of them retired up to Davis' room.

It was about 5:38 p.m. when Mike and Davis emerged from Satterwhite's soul food restaurant. Both of them were stuffed and belching. They were riding in Mike's 1978 Cadillac Deville. The next stop was the mall at

Lenox. Davis had forgotten that Mike was pretty familiar with Phatlanta. As Mike sat back in what was an unmistakable gangsta' lean with his left hand on the steering wheel he reached into the right pocket of his khakis and pulled out a wad of one hundred dollar bills.

"Here," Mike said as he handed Davis the bills.

"What is this," Davis asked.

"It's your college fund, I've been saving it for a while now." A sudden fear came over Davis. For as long as he knew Mike, the guy had never asked him to do anything illegal, why would he start now. Mike already knew what was going through the freshman's mind though. Mike started to speak.

"Ya' know you've been my best friend all of your life. In 87' we started going in different directions. Since I started selling this shit I have done and seen a lot of bad stuff. I've put men in comas with baseball bats, broken the jaws of punks trying to jack me and even caused women to starve their new-borns while they used their government checks to buy my shit. I have made over $468,000 dollars in the last four or five years and I don't have much to show for it except for this hogg we're in. I can say that there are two things that I have done right since I started this shit. The first one is that I have never done any of this stuff one day in my life, not even reefer. The other thing I did right was started saving for your college fund. And ya' know what, I don't even regret wasting all of that money because it helped me to live my life on the edge just the way I like it. You the best thing to ever happen to me dawg and when you left my world I cried like a bitch for 'bout a day. I still have no regrets. Don't make me start regretting it now, take this money man and use it to help you live your life the best way to make you happy. That's the only serious favor I've ever asked in all the time I've known you." With that Davis took the money and broke it down into two different stacks so they wouldn't stick out in his pockets.

After emerging from the mall with bags of clothing and shoes the two went back to Mike's motel room. After showering and getting dressed they headed for the club. Davis was a little nervous at first, how could he get into a club at nineteen years of age but he knew Mike would handle it some kinda way. The other thing was that it was Monday. What type of clubs would be opened on a Monday.

Davis' question was soon answered when they walked into the club that Mike had chosen. It was loud and bustling with people. It was women mostly. Very attractive and dressed in seductive yet tasteful clothing, for the most part. They were on the two gentlemen right from the start too. As the two of them took a table, a waiter delivered a bucket of champagne. It was compliments of two women at the bar.

"Well shouldn't we invite them over here?" Davis asked. He was eager to show Mike his newfound confidence with women.

"Naw Snap, they not my speed. We'll just return the favor with the drinks in about thirty minutes. It turns out that Mike had his eyes on a woman sitting across the room dressed a little skimpier than most of the women in the club.

It didn't take long before Mike joined the lady. Davis could see that the first thing she asked him to do was buy her a drink. He also noticed that the woman didn't seem very interested in Mike. Davis on the other hand was soon approached by one of the women who had sent over the champagne. She sat down at the table and pursued an aggressive role while talking to the young man. He thought this was refreshing and different so he played along for a while. However it didn't take him long to become disenchanted with the woman. All of her conversation centered around money and materialistic items. The attire he was wearing had obviously thrown her off. He did look nice and affluent in the new sport coat he was now wearing. He ordered a club soda for himself and a drink for the lady but she left before the drink arrived. She was obviously displeased with the lack of interest that he showed to her.

As soon as Mike saw the lady get up from the table he went over and acquired his original seat near his friend.

"Why did the lady leave so soon?" Mike asked.

"She is on a money hunt and I guess a brutha wasn't putting out enough vibes. What about you and that little sexy thing over there?" Davis said.

"Man that bitch ain't sexy, she fine as hell, but she ain't sexy."

"What's the difference?" Davis asked. Mike went on to explain.

"With a sexy woman, you watch her body especially her face while y'all fucking to see how exotic the dick makes her. With a fine woman you could care less how she looks, you just want to see the ugly faces and how the titties jump or how the head hits the wall while ya' stroking it. After all that you don't care what happens to her, in fact ya' hope she leaves or you just jump up and go. But that sexy woman, you just want hold for a while and wipe the sweat from her forehead. One of them you fuck in a dark car and the other you fuck on a moon lit beach."

As Mike concluded, Davis couldn't help but laugh. He understood what Mike was trying to say but he had never seen him give something so much thought or use such a vocabulary. Mike spoke during the laughter.

"Fuck you, anyway it's time for round two." Mike took a sip of the Long Island Iced Tea that Davis ordered for the lady and left the table. He noticed that Mike had to buy another drink when he rejoined the lady.

Davis sat by himself for a while and looked around the club as he did so. The women were exquisite in appearance and most of them were bobbing with the music. It was clear that the DJ had some type of fascination with Al B. Sure. Before long the second woman arrived at Davis' table. He concluded that the two of them had a bet going or something. He wasn't going to get too excited though. He had already assumed that in this case birds of a feather really did flock together.

"Ooh, you than already bought me a drink," the woman said as she took a sip from what was now Mike's Long Island Iced Tea.

"That's what I like, a man that takes care of his woman's every need." Davis draped his hand over his face to hold in the laughter. Obviously the assumption was true. He then sat back in the chair to get comfortable. He was going to let her make a fool of herself.

Around 11:30 a hand fell over Davis' shoulder as he bent over to strike the eight ball at the end of his second game of solo pool. It was Mike and he was angry. He informed Davis that they were leaving and then he literally ran out of the club. When Davis caught up with him outside he found his friend in a precarious predicament. Mike had followed the woman he had been talking to out of the club and almost cornered her at her car even though he was standing at least five feet away from her. He had most likely startled her as she was trying to open her car door. She now had her back against the door in a submissive position as she faced Mike. Davis could tell that she was scared. Davis hurried to Mike and asked what was going on. But Mike ignored him and continued with the statement he was making.

"Look, I spent $18.00 on you for drinks, now bitch if you knew you weren't gonna give me the time of day, you shouldn't have kept juicing me for the free drinks. I don't want no trouble but you're ain't leaving until I get my money back.

"I don't have any money," the woman said under a veil of tears.

"Well take your purse out and turn it upside down," Mike responded.

"Mike," Davis shouted. "What is going on".

"Snap, all she had to do was give me a fake phone number when I asked for it. But she gotta be the shit and tell me she's not interested. I'm cool with that, just tell me before you ask me to buy you three damn drinks." He turned his attention back to the woman after looking at Davis. "Now lady don't make me kick your window out. Just show me that you have no money in your wallet."

The woman now had mascara running as she looked at Davis for reasoning. Davis' expression suggested that the woman should do what Mike asked so this could end. And that's exactly what she did. As soon as her compact, lipstick, and a pack of gum hit the pavement, Mike turned and headed for his car. The huge Cadillac was soon headed down 75 south and neither of its two occupants said anything.

thirteen

Kee-Kee stood and looked in the mirror of her bathroom. The reflection was that of a puffy-faced individual who had been crying for the last 19 hours. She didn't even know why she was preparing to take a bath. She didn't want to go out, but her best friend Toi wouldn't leave her alone until she promised to accompany her and a few of her sorority sisters to a late night meal and a cocktail. Toi had witnessed the scene in the cafeteria earlier. She had also seen Kee-Kee lose it over a guy before. But Toi knew that the scene with Davis was a little different. She couldn't explain it, but Davis Virginia had a strong hold on Keandra Dixon that even he wasn't aware of. Toi knew it was important for her friend to get out and she told Kee-Kee it was the stress of the finals that made her concerned instead of the turmoil with Davis. However, Toi and Kee-Kee both knew the truth.

Kee-Kee continued to stare in the mirror for a minute before she undid the clasp of her towel that sat above her breast. As the towel hit the floor, she placed her numb body into the waiting tub of hot water. She began to think about how much make-up she would need to cover the traces of her tears. No one had seen her in the last half of a day. Even Toi had only just talked to her by phone to make plans and schedule a departure time for their evening venture. Therefore, no one had seen the pain that she was feeling and she would prefer that it stay that way.

She reached for the shaving foam and razor that sat at the edge of the tub and prepared to shave her slender legs. She spread the foam out of habit and without thought. Her mind was elsewhere. In fact it was still under the staircase in the dining hall. She thought about the things she said to Davis and the things he attempted to say to her. She was pissed because she had realized that he really didn't have anything to say as was evidenced by the babbling that he carried on. He simply wanted to prevent her from making a scene. He probably even laughed at the fact that he had the power to make a female cry over him like so many other men have done at one time. Just laugh and talk gibberish until they can get out of the confrontational situation and run back and tell their boys. Then she thought about how even then he looked adorable even though he was making an ass out of the both of them.

By this time her razor had already cleared two different paths through the foam on her right leg as her toes rested on the tip of the tub. She continued with her solemn thoughts. She thought of one of the passionate nights they had shared together in that same tub. Then she realized why Davis was always anxious and never seemed to show the emotion that she showed during sex. He was a typical male dog and she had simply given him too much credit by assuming his anxiety came from him losing his virginity. She was sure he would get past that immature stage and she was willing to wait because she knew they could be so much more. Then there was the reason he shunned her in the first place. How could he be so chauvinistic as to label her dirty and polluted the minute he found out that she had been with someone else even before the two of them met?

Tyrone was the next thought through her head. The right leg was almost completely shaven by now and she had started to look for stubble that she may have missed. She proceeded to add foam to those areas. "Yeah Tyrone, his sorry ass," she said softly to herself as her head dropped in sorrow. If it hadn't been for Tyrone none of this shit would have happened. She could all but imagine how the story unfurled too. Davis had probably been bragging about his conquest to the jerk. And not to be undone he had to brag about the time when she was vulnerable to his worthless ass. The tears really started to flow from her face now. In an instant her thoughts had gone from anger to sorrow, sorrow for herself. She thought about the four failed relationships she had had during her college career. Why didn't any of them work? Why did they all have to end the same way? Why was this happening to her?

At that moment an artery in her calf felt the sting of the cool metal blade. This snapped her out of her thoughts and she looked at her leg. Two rich red drops of blood had already hit the clear water. She looked at the wound in confusion as the blood continued to drain from her leg. Then, strangely, the feeling of confusion turned into a sense of peace as the heavy concentrated drops dispersed into a cloud-like appearance as each drop hit the now redish water. This was the most relaxing feeling she had felt in weeks. Instantly the blade started searching for more satisfaction as it swiped back and forth against another smooth portion of her calf. After 11 attempts, the razor found it's mark and she had created another wound. She watched it peacefully drain as well.

Her thoughts continued in a condescending fashion for a few more moments and then reality hit her and she asked herself, "Am I committing suicide, is that what this is?" Then a moan exited her throat. She begged once for her mommy as the blade went to work in search of more gaping wounds on her leg. And after about two minutes of crying and moaning, Keandra passed out.

On the other end of campus, Big Mike's 78 Cadillac

pulled into the Fair Street parking lot. It was about 12:40 a.m. and the two of them had just come from the 24 hour supermarket. Davis had wanted to stock up on cereal and noodles while he had a ride. It wasn't much of a good bye. Mike just told him to study hard and that he would visit him again in a few months. The Deville then drove away slowly.

Davis walked swiftly with bags in hand. He had gotten to the door and was reaching in his pocket to pull out his identification when a faint red light flashed on the wall above his head suddenly. The light flashed two more times by the time he had a chance to turn around and investigate its origin. It was coming from across campus near Holmes Hall. He dropped the bags by a pole and started walking in the direction of the lights in an effort to investigate. As he got closer to the female dorm he noticed a crowd of onlookers on the lawn in front of the building. Then he saw the ambulance. Its doors were open and so were the doors of the dorm. The paramedics were obviously inside.

Once he had gotten up on the crowd he started looking for someone familiar. Someone who had been there longer than he had and who could tell him what was going on even though he had already developed his own theory. He had heard that suicides were possible in Atlanta during this time of year. That's because it was a town with more than eight different colleges and the stress of finals could easily bring on horrible incidents. That's exactly what he figured this to be. Some poor sap had not figured out the secret to handling college as he had and now as a result some poor parents had to hear about this.

At that moment his eyes made contact with those of Toi's as she stood on the stairs in front of the dorm. He naturally looked for Kee-Kee. He wasn't familiar with Toi, he didn't even know her name but she was now headed towards him. Once she reached him she stuck out her hand in his direction and in a quiet and sad voice, she spoke.

"Hi Davis, I'm Toi. I guess it's time we were formally

introduced." Davis shook her hand and returned her introduction not knowing that she knew far more of him than he of her.

"Wow, I guessed some poor student couldn't handle the stress of finals huh," Davis said in a search for conversation. He really didn't feel like going through the small talk that came with meeting people for the first time. He looked on at the doorway waiting for the paramedics to emerge from the dorm as he awaited a response to his last statement. Toi was only looking at him.

"Davis, there's something you should know," she said. The sadness of her voice caused him to look at her. With apprehension in his face he asked, "Yeah what is it?"

"Davis that poor sap," Toi hesitated with her statement as tears began to flow down her cheek. He was now a little surprised at the amount of sadness that she was showing.

"Damn is it that bad, I thought everything might be okay since I saw an ambulance instead of a hearse," he said. After his last statement Toi raised her head from it's dropped position and looked him in the eye.

"Davis, Kee-Kee tried to kill herself tonight."

His eyes searched Toi over for evidence of laughter or anything that would make him think that she was joking but the steady stream of tears proved otherwise. Davis raised his right hand up to his large chest in an attempt to ease the sharp itching feeling that came over him. "What...what happened," he asked. Toi raised her hand to wipe the tears from her face as she began to tell Davis the story.

"Well I had invited her out for a late dinner and a night cap to take her mind off of things. You should have heard her on the phone she sounded awful. Well I got ready and then walked down to her room and knocked on her door. I knocked a few times but I didn't get an answer. I knew she was in there and that she wouldn't dare leave the room the way she was feeling. By the time I knocked again I felt water hit my toe. When I looked down the water was coming from under her door. I felt that something was wrong. As I looked more closely I could see blood in the water. At that point, I ran to get the dorm director so we could open her door and yelled for someone to call an ambulance. When we got in there she was passed out in a tub of water. It's a wonder she didn't drown." Toi had stumbled through her whole statement.

Davis had listened intently.

"Well will she be okay, will she make it?" he asked.

"We're not sure, campus security put everyone off of the floor. From what I could tell she was still alive but she had lost so much blood. All we can do now is wait for them to bring her out." A lot of things started to flow through his head but he couldn't make any sense out of any of them. The two of them waited for the paramedics to emerge from the building. The only question was would they have the entire body covered on the gurney or would they still be working trying to revive Kee-Kee.

The crowd outside fell quiet as they heard the paramedics wrestling the gurney around the narrow corner of dormitory. The first paramedic emerged into view with his back towards the crowd. The face of the second one could then be seen but Davis wasn't tall enough to see if Kee-Kee's head was covered or exposed by the sheet. They moved fast in an effort to get to the ambulance. So he pushed forward in the crowd of people to look for signs of life from the young lady with whom he'd had sex with on more than one occasion. As the gurney was carefully and quickly tipped down the stairs Davis saw the long flowing hair of Keandra Dixon and the itching he had been feeling finally stopped. She didn't look pretty though and Davis knew that the fight for life was far from over. He just hoped that she was indeed fighting.

Toi's head had fallen into his chest as she saw the same sight. He tried to comfort her as best he could a person whom he hadn't known long at all. It wasn't long though before campus security led Atlanta police to Toi and asked her to come inside to answer some questions.

"I'll call you tomorrow," she said as she walked towards the dorm while being escorted by several men in uniform. He didn't think that he would be able to sleep that night. But since Holly hadn't made it in, he turned to the school's jazz station and fell asleep an hour later from mental fatigue. He awoke the next morning to an irate Holly yelling into the phone.

He was obviously having a fight with Mary. Davis proceeded to grab his toiletries in an un-enthused fashion and headed to the showers. From the pieces of Holly's conversation that he heard he gathered that Holly hadn't spent the night with Mary but with her male cousin out running the streets. He also noticed that his roommate hadn't undressed yet and had probably just gotten in a few minutes ago.

After his shower, Davis spent a lot of the day watching television without sound and listening to heavy doses of Maze and Frankie Beverly with his headphones. Holly spent the rest of the day catching up on sleep but Davis woke him up about 2:30 in the afternoon to go and take a final. He didn't even have time to tell Holly about what had happened the night before. His roommate was definitely going through something but Davis just didn't know what it was.

A little after four o'clock in the afternoon the phone rang. It was Toi on the other end and she wanted to meet Davis somewhere to talk. After deciding on a location he hung up the phone and proceeded to get dressed. He was the first to arrive at the destination that they had decided on. He soon watched Toi approach the library staircase. She looked just as disheveled as he imagined he looked. It was clear that she had a sleepless night. She began talking as soon as she got into earshot.

"Well I picked her parents up from the airport and drove them to the hospital this morning. While I was there

I learned about her status." He listened with anxiety.

"She's in critical condition and she had to have a blood transfusion last night. It's too early for them to tell if her brain was deprived of sufficient oxygen long enough to cause permanent brain damage," she said. There was a silence after she spoke. Davis was concerned he just didn't know to what extent. He was also visibly shaken the night before, but why? Was it because of what happened or was it because he had never had a friend do something like that? After a few seconds she broke the silence.

"Davis I feel I owe it to my friend to tell you a few things about her. I hope that you will listen to me and not say anything. I'm having a hard time with this and I would like to get through this conversation without crying. First of all, she loves you very much. Regardless of how you feel about her I know that she cares for you dearly. Now I know you've heard different things about her and I'm not going to sit up here and deny anything. The situation with Tyrone, well it was true. But let me tell you, that girl was on a whole different level than that fool was but neither one of them knew it at first. I knew it because she would tell me things that she should have been telling him but she couldn't. She always had problems expressing her emotions to guys and that goes back to the idiots that she dated back in New Orleans. Her beauty pushed her into dating at a young age. She was at an age where you are too young to know anything about expressing your emotions to your mate. After sensing this, the guys would quickly begin dominating the relationship. As a result, she never learned to express herself to guys. The only way she could relate to guys was to show her body when she wanted to show love. That's what happened with Tyrone and two other guys before you. As naive as it may sound, she was simply trying to show interest when she lay down with them and believe me, those fools took it and ran with it. After the abuse and a talk with me she would usually wisen up. And

I'm telling you all of this because her capacity for love is great and I think she deserves a little better than to remembered as a slut. She's just a confused and frustrated little girl inside."

Toi walked off in a solemn fashion after she spoke her last word. She really didn't care to hear a response from him she just wanted to do a favor for her friend. He couldn't help but notice that she didn't bother to tell him the hospital and room number and he wasn't sure he wanted to know. He walked quietly back to the dorm. He was busy retrofitting all of Kee-Kee's past actions and behavior to the conversation that Toi had just had with him. He still wasn't sure how he felt about the whole thing.

Later that night in Augusta Dee Virginia picked up her phone on the fourth ring after rushing into the house. She was just getting off of work. It was her baby boy on the other end and his voice sounded just as depressed as the last call she received from him after the beating of the young man in the dormitory. Davis proceeded to tell her about the previous night's activities and she listened intently. After he finished talking he noticed that his mother had grown quiet.

"Dee," he called to make sure she was still there. His verification came in the form of a statement from her.

"Baby I'm starting to wonder if we shouldn't try to get you in school a little closer to home because this is ridiculous. In the nine months that you've been away from home you've managed to lose your virginity, risk your life in front of an angry mob, and have a young lady try to kill herself because of yo' ass." Davis said in his defense, "Dee we can't say definitely that it was because of me." Dee shouted back in a tone that suggested that he not try her patience, "Oh boy please. Save it for somebody else. This isn't about you trying to keep anything from your mother. This is bigger than that. This is about trying to get my baby back home with his mind and morals in tact. Now I truly feel sorry for that young lady and her parents. She most likely did all of that because of you. That doesn't scare me as long as I know you didn't intentionally treat that little girl wrong. And if I thought you did, I'd be on my way up there to deal with you right now. In the meantime, I need you to take your lumps from this and keep moving because you the only baby I got and I can't lose you to that girl, that city, or your own guilt. So do what you have to do to get over this and I want you to know that it's okay to feel grief, in fact it can be helpful to go ahead and get those tears out. But you gotta stay strong because if I lose you then I'm as good as lost."

His mother was direct and efficient as always and he felt better after talking to her as always. And afterwards the two moved on with their conversation. Davis told his mother about Mike's visit and after telling her about the money that he had gotten from Mike he wanted to know what she thought he should do with it since he knew that it was drug money. Dee went into a silence after Davis asked her the question. This was usually the result when she struggled with decisions about good and bad and she leaned to the bad side. Her silence caused him to laugh and his laughter caused her to laugh.

"I mean we've been asking the Lord to get you through college, who are we to question how he does it," she said. This caused him to laugh even harder. In her defense she offered to tell him a story.

"Listen to my story now," she exclaimed. "There was this man in Mississippi. Now his area was experiencing heavy rains and the town officials had begun evacuations for fear of flooding. Now being the faithful man of God that he was, when they came by in the off road vehicle to pick him up he said "no, no-don't worry, God will save me so you just go pick up my neighbors". Well the truck left and the water rose chest high. This time the officials came back in motor boat. "No, no - God will save me, have you gotten all of my neighbors yet?" Well on the third go round, the water was over the doorway and a helicopter found the man on the roof. They offered to drop a ladder for him but he just fanned it away. So sure enough he drowned and went to Heaven. Once in Heaven he thanked the Lord for bringing him to rest beyond the Pearly Gates but he asked God why didn't he save him. God looked at the man and simply said, "child I sent help for you three times and you turned it down, what else did you want me to do."

Once his mom finished her story, Davis broke the silence with laughter. They both knew that she was rationalizing the whole situation but her point was well taken. He got off the phone and started to tell his roommate about the incident from last night. Holly expressed his sorrow and then grew uncharacteristically quiet. Davis knew that something was wrong and decided that this was as good a time as any to find out what was going on with his roommate.

Holly told Davis that he and Mary had begun a sexual relationship but problems had begun occurring as well. He wouldn't go into detail about the problems but Davis could tell that they were upsetting to him.

"It's not just her," Holly said. "I've gotten myself into a little trouble lately and it's all because of her cousin." Davis asked him once to explain but Holly refused. Davis knew his roommate well enough to know that he would tell in due time. In the meantime Davis grew secretly upset with Mary. Holly didn't have any problems before her. He also wondered about her angle too. Did she just want a college man? Or maybe she thought his gullible nature came with a decent cash flow that she could milk when the time was right. He didn't know and that's what upset him.

14

Davis finished up his last final that Wednesday. He felt relieved about it too. In the midst of everything that had been happening his freshman year, the year as a whole had gone by very fast. And to top everything off, he had finished his first year in college with a 3.9 G.P.A., which was no small feat. After he completed the exam, the instructor asked him to take the results of the survey on the class to the registrar's office. This was a survey that all classes had to fill out after every final. Since it evaluated the teacher and the class, the teacher was prohibited from turning it in themselves. Even though the evaluation was supposed to cover the entire semester, teachers usually found that they received favorable reviews if they gave a realistic final.

While in the registrar's office he ran into Ms. Upshaw. She was turning in her grades from the semester. She greeted him with a smile and glowing eyes as she always did. She expressed her sorrow for Kee-Kee. Davis was dumbfounded as to how she made the connection between him and Kee-Kee. As she continued, she inquired about the status of his finals. He told her that he had just finished up and that he thought he did very well. She then proceeded to invite him to lunch as a release from the depression that he may have been experiencing lately. He quickly agreed to. He knew that the cafeteria food wasn't going to cut it today.

The restaurant Ms. Upshaw chose was a trendy little outdoor cafe. The food didn't appear to be much outside of gourmet sandwiches but the vodka and tonic that she ordered told him that she hadn't come there to eat. It was just casual conversation at first but once she took a sip of her drink he could feel the conversation shift into another gear.

"Davis, I don't say this to many students but I must tell you that it is very refreshing to meet a young man such as yourself. You have a responsible outlook on life and a small chip on your shoulder that I believe is healthy for all brothers to have. I believe Keandra knew this too, that's why she fell so hard for you." Davis' eyes grew large after her last statement. He had to inquire about how she knew about Kee-Kee and himself.

"Oh I was sort of a mentor to Keandra and Toi when they first arrived at this university three years ago. We all have been good friends since. They still come to me when they need advice about something or they just want to talk." Inside Davis was deeply embarrassed. He knew now that Ms. Upshaw probably knew much more about him than he wanted any professor to know even if she was a pretty one. He also wondered if Kee-Kee had said anything about their sexual exploits. Ms. Upshaw continued to talk and the vodka and tonic was disappearing fast.

"I know that Toi has talked to you already but I feel I need to say more, that is after I find out that you are really okay in light of what happened to Keandra." Once Davis assured her that he was fine, she continued.

"Now what I'm about to say doesn't just refer to Keandra but to a lot of different women. The first thing I want to say is that I hope you have learned something from all of this. Ya' see the average man doesn't realize the power that he has over a woman if he treats her right. Sure a woman can be independent, with a nice bank account and a Mercedes but most of the independent sistas I know and see would settle for a loving man and a Toyota. Usually when you see a woman engrossed in her career trying to look out for her future as she puts it, she probably is just disgusted with the whole dating and relationship scene and just can't get a bachelor to nibble at her bait anymore. I know, it used to be me. But I got tired of looking at loneliness and trying to call it freedom. So I decided that my life was going to change. I didn't want to grow old alone. And I didn't want my obsession for success and material things to drive any potential men away. As a result, I became a lot more patient. Sure I've had to deal with a lot of nuts in the past but I'm sure that I will be nicely compensated one day." As Ms. Upshaw was finishing her statement, the waiter brought their sandwiches and another drink for her and she lit into it. Davis was relieved by the interruption because he didn't know where this conversation was going although he was sure that as the liquor entered her system, she would get looser. At least he could devour his sandwich as he continued to listen to her. As the waiter left, she continued.

"All I'm trying to say is that I hope you respect the power you have and I hope that you don't abuse it. Lord knows that I see enough of that almost every day." With food now in his stomach, Davis now felt like playing a little devil's advocate with the relatively tipsy Ms. Upshaw.

"In what form do you see it?" he asked in an inquisitive voice.

"What form?" she repeated.

"Davis I'm 31 years old and let me tell you, in all of those years I've been dogged by some of the best. I've had men who I've cared for steal money from me; rob my apartment; run up my credit cards; tear up my car; and even supposedly, leave their wives to be with me only to see the marriage continue as he continued to use my body as a toy for years. But til' this day I'm still waiting to get mine because I realize that into each life some rain must fall. And although I can't condone what that young lady did to herself I'd be lying if I said I didn't understand."

Davis was amazed at what he had just heard come out of Ms. Upshaw's mouth. It was as if he had been let down and he now had to take her off of the pedestal on which he had placed her. He wanted to blame it on the alcohol now that she had finished two drinks but he knew that the liquor was just a verbal aphrodisiac. She continued on with her talking until her speech started to slur and she was on her third drink. During that time she admitted to him that one of her male superiors at work was now taking advantage of her sexually even though he was married. Davis decided that he had heard enough and decided that it was time for the two to them to leave now.

Davis helped her sign her credit card receipt and literally carried her out of the place. He knew that he would have to drive her home, he just hoped that she could stay awake to give him directions. Once they were on their way, he struggled trying to make out her instructions. After about 45 minutes the drunken Ms. Upshaw was giving him the code to open the gate of her apartment complex. He soon got her out of the car and helped her into her apartment. He even helped her remove her shoes and jacket before getting her to the bed. During all of this, Davis thought that this was just another great entry he could put in his imaginary freshman diary. If his mother could see him putting a 31 year old female to bed in her own apartment he would have to withdraw that very day and go home where she could keep an eye on him.

Just as he was pulling back the cover he heard a gargling sound and turned his head in time enough to see her vomit all over her night-stand. He just shook his head as he headed for the bathroom to get a wet towel to clean the piece of furniture. He remembered that he hadn't seen her take one bite of her sandwich before downing those three drinks. As he removed the lamp and the alarm clock from the nightstand he caught sight of her out of the corner of his eye. She was now snoring and resting peacefully. Even though she was drunk he admitted to himself that she was very sexy and looked very exotic. Her skirt was riding up her leg and her mint green silk panties were now exposed. The sight gave him an immediate erection. He thought to himself that he could see how so many brothers could get themselves in trouble after getting a female drunk. If he had had a weak mind he knew that he could not have behaved like a gentleman.

After he finished cleaning the nightstand he wrote her a note. In the note he let her know that he had taken the train home and asked her to call him when she woke up. He dropped the note on the pillow beside her, covered her with a quilt and exited the apartment. He walked two blocks to the MARTA station that he had seen while driving and boarded an eastbound train. It took a while for his erection to subside as he thought about how lovely and uninhibited she looked while laying there. He would take a cold shower once he got home.

By the time he reached the dorm it was 6:00 p.m. and campus looked deserted. Most of the people had taken their last final and were already on their way back home. As he passed by the cafeteria on his way to the dorm, he saw Slow Motion and a couple of guys walking in his direction.

"Ahh shit, I don't feel like this today," he said to himself. He hadn't seen these guys since the incident with Big Mike. He didn't know what to expect. As he got closer to the group he noticed Slow Motion was about to say something.

"What's up man?" the football player said in a low guttural voice. Davis returned the pleasantry and laughed as soon as he got out of earshot.

As he entered the room he found Holly at his desk studying for his Thursday morning final or at least trying to. He was clearly pre-occupied with something. Davis naturally assumed that it was with the trouble he had mentioned earlier. He still didn't appear ready to talk about it. In an effort to make small conversation Davis asked if anyone had called him.

"Yeah," Holly said, that girl Kia called about ten minutes ago." Davis stopped in his tracks. Now there was a name he hadn't heard in a few days. With all that had taken place since last Saturday he couldn't blame himself for not thinking about her much. But now she was a welcome addition to his thoughts.

"Did she say anything?" Davis asked. "Just that she would try back later," Holly responded. Davis' eyes grew with enthusiasm. The only thing he wanted to do now was take a hot shower and relax in his bed as he waited for her to call back.

In the shower he found himself thinking about Kee-Kee. He hadn't thought of her all day. He even thought about going to see her if Toi would give him the necessary information. He knew that he didn't love her but she was the first female who wasn't family who loved him. And that would always keep her dear to him.

As Davis proceeded to brush his teeth he noticed that Cisco had walked in. The two just stared at each other first and then Cisco spoke to him. Davis spoke with a nod of the head and started to wash the foam out of his mouth. Once he came up from the sink he met the eyes of Cisco again who was intentionally staring at him. The two hadn't spoke since the beating incident in the dorm. Davis could tell the guy wanted to say something.

"I wanted you to know that I appreciated what you did for us man," Cisco said. "What is it that you appreciate?" Davis asked.

"Ya' know, pulling us off of that guy. If you hadn't been there, that dude would have died that night. I know he would have because everybody I talk to says the same thing— that they couldn't stop for some reason. It's like the testosterone was too high or something. Ya' know, ol' boy came back to take his finals this week," Cisco paused as he struggled to hold back some tears.

"He looked pretty bad man," he continued after the pause.

"The arm that was broken will never be the same again. He's walking with a cane and you can tell he's in some serious pain. Tears were just running down his face. I don't know if they're from the pain or the embarrassment. You can tell that he's going to need re-constructive surgery to get the bones in his face straightened out. And all I can think about is that he came out of some woman's womb just like I did." Cisco had been looking in the mirror so he wouldn't have to look at Davis and fight away the tears. But after his last statement he turned to look at Davis and the tears had begun to flow.

"Man we had no reason to do that boy like that." He was really crying by this time. Davis decided to exit the bathroom, partly because the confession had caused anger to surface in him again and partly because he didn't want to embarrass the guy by watching him cry.

Holly had fell asleep at his desk studying by the time Davis got back to the room. He decided that this was a great time to get in some television. He grabbed the remote, turned back the sheets on his bed and turned off the lights. After about forty minutes of watching television the phone rang. He became very anxious but knew he had to let it ring at least once more before answering it.

The voice at the other end of the line made him smile like a schoolboy. It was Kia and he was very happy to hear from her. Davis thought he'd open the conversation with a bit of sarcastic humor.

"Wow just because you don't have to tutor a brutha no mo' don't mean you have to stop calling me. Ya' know I was worried about you." Kia, not sensing the sarcasm in his voice, went on the defensive.

"Davis I'm so sorry. You know it had nothing to do with you. It's just that I've been going through so much at work that I just haven't had time to do much of anything." Davis responded.

"I was just kidding, don't worry about it. But what's going on at work?" Kia took a deep breath before answering him. It was as if she didn't even want to deal with the situation even though it would only be on a verbal basis this time.

"Nothing, it's just this ol' bitch at work. You know the anchor woman, Andrea Davis, well her and I sort of got into it."

"What happened?" Davis asked trying to sound curious.

"Well she is like most other anchor women in that they have their own little show on the side. It's like she only interviews celebrities and does good news stories on citizens who are doing positive things. Well it turns out that one of my stories kind of bled into one of hers. In fact I interviewed the guy on a separate story from the one for which she's going to have him on the show for. But the problem was that my interview was going to air before her show. So when she found out right, she came into the editing bay where I was cleaning some footage with my cameraman. She starts going off on me like I was two years old and ya' know that I just wasn't having it. So when it was all said and done the editor had to come in and break it up." Sensing that she was done, Davis decided to insert his comment.

"Yeah I guess that was very upsetting," he said.

"No that's not the part that will get you," Kia responded. Davis smiled because he had obviously spoken too soon and there was more to come. He didn't mind though because it was just nice to be on the phone with her.

"No the thing is that I ended up getting suspended for a week. All because she's scared of me. She knows I'm good and that she's old and she has always feared that they were priming me for her position. And the thing that pissed me off is that the editor knows that I was just carrying out my assignment that's why he suspended me with pay. But he said he had to do it because she threatened to walk off and since she makes 750 thousand a year, I guess it was me before her. That's all right though because it gave me time to work on my resume and send it to a few different stations. I also squeezed in a date in the process." Davis' curiosity was peaked with the last statement. He had to know how the date went.

"So how was your date?" he asked boldly.

"Ahh, it sucked," she said. Davis was very pleased to hear that but he knew that he still had to sound concerned.

"What was the problem, did you run him off?" he asked with a snicker in his voice. Kia came back with determination in her voice.

"No baby, it was the independence that ran him off."

"Whatcha mean?" he asked. Kia explained.

"Well I had to give him my old live with it or leave speech".

"What exactly is that?" Davis asked.

"Well that's when I let him know where I graduated from, how much I make, I told him about my investments, and the kicker was that I told him about the house I'm having built in Decatur. After all of that he had to decide if he wanted to live with it or leave while the getting was good. To top everything off, I even paid for both of our dinners. I wish you could have seen his face when I pulled out the platinum Visa."

Davis just sat for a second after she finished her statement. He was trying to think of how to change the subject. The only thing he didn't like about Kia was when she flaunted her success. But he knew he wasn't ready to get off of the phone. So after talking about her hometown of Ohio and her college days for a little while, the two got off of the phone.

Holly was moving about the room when Davis ended his conversation with Kia. And like roommates are able to do the two easily slipped into conversation. Holly talked about Mary and her sexual habits in bed. Davis tried to hide his faces of disgust as he imagined the somewhat overweight woman doing the things Holly was describing. Davis in turn talked about Ms. Upshaw and Kia. Holly didn't take particular interest until he moved on to Kee-Kee. Holly wanted to make sure his roommate was okay so he started to ask some probing questions. It didn't take long before he got what he wanted.

"Ya' know," Davis said. "I don't even know how I feel about the whole thing. I mean we shared some pretty intimate times together but here it is that I wonder if all of this would have occurred if I hadn't been so selfish."

"Selfish!" Holly repeated, just because you took some sex from a beautiful and vibrant 21-year-old woman. Just because you did what every normal young man on this earth would have done in the same situation. Just because you don't happen to feel the same way about her that she feels about you, that makes you selfish? Please, let me tell you about being selfish. Selfish is when you'll risk the lives of dozens of people cutting across four lanes of highway traffic just to make your exit. Selfish was when that dick head at the savings and loan embezzled from the accounts of hundreds of senior citizens just because he wanted to buy a yacht. Selfish is when a person commits suicide knowing full well that they are leaving family members behind that care about them dearly. Selfish is when the government pays farmers in my community not to grow food even though there are millions of people starving on the continent of Africa. Man you have performed one of the most unselfish acts I have ever seen in my 19 years here on this earth. You threw your body in front of an angry mob to save the life of another human being even though you didn't agree with his lifestyle. So until you have done something really asinine just to help yourself, don't call yourself selfish in front of me."

Davis was watching Holly very strangely when he finished his statement. This was definitely not the same sloppy individual he had met nine months ago in this same room. Holly sensing the strange look turned and looked at Davis.

"What, why are you looking at me like that?"

Davis replied, "Nothing, I'm just listening to ya'."

"I know," Holly said.

"I've been hanging around you too long huh?" With that the two of them laughed in agreement and Holly left the room with his toiletries.

The phone rang moments later. It was Ms. Upshaw on the other end.

"Davis I am so sorry," she said. Davis smiled as he thought that this was the second time tonight a beautiful woman called him apologizing.

"I just wanted to tell you how sorry I really was about my behavior this afternoon. It's just that Keandra and Toi are close to me and I really got upset when I started talking about her again. I was really concerned about how this whole thing was affecting you and believe me when I say if there is anything at all that I can do for you just let me know."

Davis was smiling by this time. He thought it was funny that she was apologizing. He started his response with a smile.

"Ms. Upshaw, please don't worry about it there's nothing wrong with me but a little stress that can easily be cured by a few laps in a pool and an hour in a weight room." Davis was sure she would leave him alone about the incident now since she owned neither a pool nor a weight room. But he was wrong. Ms. Upshaw had an offer.

"Oh is that all you need? Well maybe I can help you out after all. We have a pool and a weight room here at my apartment complex. Now my nerves could rest a lot easier if you would come over here tomorrow and take advantage of the amenities." Well since Davis wasn't in the habit of saying no to professors he told her he would indeed come over. Besides, he was looking forward to working out.

15

Davis and his roommate got up the same time the next morning. It was Friday, the absolute last day of the semester. They headed to the cafeteria to grab some breakfast. This was already the best meal but it was even better this week since there was hardly anyone in the place. Everyone had gone home once they had finished their finals. The two roommates took full advantage of every type of breakfast food the place had to offer. Holly used the waffle iron to make two waffles while Davis waited in the chef's line to get two specialized omelets made. Once they grabbed cereal and juice the two of them sat down to a feast. Midway through their meal Mary walked out of the back with her apron folded in her hand. Holly asked her if she was working and she told him that due to the lack of students she had gotten the rest of the day off. After she answered his question she made it a point to speak to Davis who hadn't looked at her once. He was still unsure of her motives and didn't want his reservations to be seen. He did however manage to raise his head and speak in a friendly tone. Afterwards she proceeded to speak to Holly again. She asked him to run some errands with her.

Once she walked off Holly turned and spoke to Davis.

"Look man I want you to come with us." Davis was just about to raise a fork filled with eggs to his mouth.

Once Holly made his statement, he put the eggs down.

"Man she asked you, not me," Davis said.

Holly responded, "look man I can tell that you're uncomfortable with her and I think that's because you don't know her. I think if you spent a little time around her you would see just how precious my boo is." "I don't think so man," Davis said.

Holly continued. "Look, I could marry that girl one day and you could be the best man. That's means both of you would be at the altar with me on the most important day of my life. Now it's only natural that you two have at least one conversation before that day comes, okay." Davis could tell his roommate was serious and concerned. He agreed on the condition that Holly would have to tell him what type of trouble he was in. With that the two-headed downstairs to the employee parking lot. Davis thought as they waited. What was it exactly that he didn't like about this lady. Was it the fact that she had a gold tooth in her mouth? Was it that she lived in a housing project? Maybe it was because she reminded him of so many ghetto girls that he went to school with. No matter what Davis thought of, he couldn't think of a legitimate reason for disliking Mary.

"Well she is working to support herself and that was the important thing," he thought to himself.

Mary soon emerged from the cafeteria and the look on her face showed her surprise to see Davis. The trio quickly hopped into the red 79' Ford Granada and were on their way. The car was extremely loud and it's exterior was a sight to behold. It still bore its original factory paint job and it was covered with rust spots. Davis unconsciously sat a little lower in the back seat than he normally would. The two up front were immediately engaged in conversation. Once in a while Holly would throw Davis an oratorical bone in an attempt to drag him into the conversation. This continued until they reached their first destination. It was the Gas Company and it was a long wait. All three had gone inside to enjoy the air-conditioned facilities. Holly and Davis sat on a bench along the wall while Mary waited in line. By the time Mary got up to the window Davis could tell that something was wrong. Mary had a complaint and Davis could tell. He was experienced at recognizing black women about to get into altercations. Dee Virginia was a master at it. She frequently went into discussions with people whom were serving her. Davis would frequently wait to the side with his head dropped low from the embarrassment.

Oh yeah he could tell something was wrong between Mary and the lady behind the window and his head was already dropping. He could only think that if Dee could embarrass him like that then he could only imagine what this woman would do if she decide to get ghetto. Davis looked under his thumb, which was now resting above his eyebrow on his lowered head. The sight he saw made him laugh. Holly had assumed the same posture and demeanor as his roommate had.

The two of them turned to see what was going on with Mary now. She hadn't gotten upset. She had asked to see the manager and was now talking to a tall slender white male a few yards away from them. Davis was impressed. He could tell that she was handling herself in an appropriate fashion by the way the manager kept shaking his head in an agreeable fashion. After a few more seconds they heard the manager apologize on behalf of the service representative and Mary walked towards them. Soon the Granada was on its way out of the parking lot and headed towards the light company.

"What was that all about babe?" Holly asked. Her anger and mumbling prevented Mary from answering right away. The two were anxiously waiting for an answer. That's when the ghetto came out. Every head-shift and curse word that she managed to hold in the building, made it's way out in the car. Between the profanity the two were able to piece the story together. Apparently the woman told Mary she had to pay her bill in full instead of the minimum monthly payment. That's when she asked to speak to the manager. Once she had calmed down her words became understandable again.

"That's what the fuck minimum payment means, shit. Don't play me like I'm stupid. Hell, don't let the gold tooth fool ya', ya' fuck around and I'll get you fired," Mary concluded. Davis couldn't believe what he had heard and he was almost breathless with laughter. She was behaving just like his mom and aunts and after she made fun of her own tooth, he knew that she couldn't be that bad. Afterwards the three had a relaxful and talkative afternoon as they strolled through the mall sipping on slurpees. After about three o'clock they were headed back to campus. Mary was about to drop them off at the dorm. Theirs was the third car from the light when it turned green. Mary stepped on the accelerator but quickly stopped before she crossed the intersection.

"Oh my goodness," Mary said out loud. Then her left arm fell on the window and her head found it's way to the palm of that same arm. Davis, who was sitting in the back seat, could tell that Mary was watching something in the rearview mirror. He decided to turn around to take a quick look. His head was about to go back to its original position when he did a double take. He turned to scan the area behind the car again when he saw it in the middle of the street. There it was, big and rusty and resting on the street. It was the muffler from the Granada. It had fallen from beneath the car. Davis turned back around and almost assumed the same position that Mary had. He began to slump lower into the seat. He was amazed to see so many people were out and about on campus this last day. He thought that everyone had gone. It was funny that all of the people were appearing at the most convenient

time. The car made so much noise that Davis had never
heard the muffler fall off. Poor Holly didn't have a clue as
to what was going on. When he asked what was happening Mary told him to take a look behind the car. Holly
climbed up so he could see over the seat. But before his
eyes looked to the street he noticed Davis, who was sitting
directly behind him, had ducked down in the seat and was
wearing a look that seemed to say hurry up and turn
around so that she doesn't notice that I'm hiding down
here. Holly began to smile as he looked out onto the street.
After about a second Holly turned around and climbed
back down into his seat. He was prepared to sit until the
car started moving again. Mary who was looking down as
if she were searching for some dignity had now looked
over at her boyfriend. She spoke.

"You ain't gone say nothing?" Holly caught the words
as they were directed at him and looked downright confused for a moment. Then he spoke.

"Oh baby it's just the muffler, don't worry about it.
The city will pick it up." With that he turned his head forward and was preparing for the car to move forward again.
After hearing Holly's response Davis had covered his
mouth to prevent laughter from escaping. Mary now put
the car in park and turned her whole body towards Holly
as if to handle business.

"Holly," she said in a deliberate and simplified tone,
"don't you think y'all should get out of the car?" Holly
responded.

"Oh yeah, the dorm is just down the street, I guess we
could walk the rest of the way." Before Holly could finish
his naive statement, Davis had already let go of his laughter. And he was already looking at Mary who was looking
at his roommate as if he were a fool. She shouted.

"The muffler muthafucka, get the muffler!"

The words had literally pushed the clueless young man
out of the car. Davis who was stumbling under laughter had

gotten out as well. The two of them walked up to the muffler and were preparing to pick it up. Davis nearly fell on top
of the part with laughter. Then almost simultaneously they
both reached down to lift the muffler and almost in unison
they both withdrew their hands quickly. It was still hot.
Davis was not laughing anymore. He looked up as he was
trying to fan the heat away from his hand.

"Where in the hell are all these people coming from",
Davis said to Holly as he observed all of the students that
had appeared out of nowhere and were now watching the
two. Davis re-focused his attention on the problem at
hand. He thought for a second then reached to take off his
T-shirt to use as sort of an oven mitt. This quieted many
of the giggling female onlookers. Once he was in position
and ready, Davis turned his attention to his roommate and
was waiting for him to do the same. Holly looked at Davis
and then at the small crowd that had formed. Then unexpectedly Holly flopped down in the middle of the street
and began removing his sandals. Soon he had removed his
socks and was now wearing them as protective gloves.
Davis was now hurting from laughter but had composed
himself to ask, "Holly what the hell are you doing?"

Holly quickly responded. "Man, I ain't letting these
people see my big ol' stomach." That was it. Davis col-
lapsed on the pavement and laughed for a few seconds
before the horns of traffic urged the two to finish the job.

Once the two got back to their rooms, they both
rushed to take a shower. Davis wanted to get over to the
scholarship office since this was the last day and he would-
n't see the Ms. Holman and Ms. Nebby until the next
semester. Holly just wanted to take a nap.

Davis rushed to the scholarship office and found the
ladies sitting around without much to do.

"Hi Mr. Sophomore," Ms. Holman said with a smile.

"How are we doing today?" she continued.

"I'm just fine," he answered. "I just wanted to say

good bye before you ladies left today." Ms. Holman looked puzzled. "But I thought you said you were staying here for the summer," Ms. Holman remarked.

"I am but it's the summer and you guys won't be here, right?" The two ladies looked at each other and began smiling.

"No Sweetie," began Ms. Nebbie. "It doesn't apply to us. We're staff not faculty. We have to work all year round. The only one who doesn't have to be here is you."

"I know," Davis responded. "But I'm confident I can get my department to pay for my dorm room this summer so I can stay up here."

"Well do you want to go to Detroit this summer," asked Ms. Nebby. "Because I got you two internships and one is in a communications lab up in Michigan." Davis didn't know how to respond. He really wanted to stay in Atlanta but he didn't want to seem ungrateful.

"Well where's the other one?" he asked.

"The other is here in Atlanta, out in Doraville in fact. It pays $8,000 for 12 weeks. I just thought you might want the one in Detroit since it pays $9,500 for the same amount of time," Ms. Nebby said. Davis felt relief. "No I'll take the one here since I'm only two hours away from my mom," Davis said. The truth is that Dee didn't want her son home for the summer. Too much idle time and too many hoodlums to get into trouble with. She would rather he stay around the campus since it was a more positive environment. The truth is, if she knew the things he had already gotten into on campus; she may have wanted him to come home after all.

"That's fine," Ms. Nebby said. "Let me get the paper-work off my desk and you can call your contact person on Monday." With that Ms. Nebby walked towards her office. Meanwhile out of the corner of his eye he could visibly see Ms. Holman shaking her head from side to side in disapproval. Davis started giggling slightly. He had an idea where this was going.

"What's wrong Ms. Holman?" he asked with a smile.

"Boy why you don't want to go up to Detroit?" she asked with a touch of manufactured but harmless anger in her voice.

"I want to be able to go see my mom," he resounded with a grin.

"Un-huh," Ms. Holman sarcastically agreed.

"You want to be able to go see Kia, that's what it is." He felgiggled after hearing her say that. He was pleased that she was concerned. He thought to himself, "If she only knew what I've been through this year, Kia would be her last concern." Ms. Nebby walked into the room again after that and handed him the paper work. As he exited the office, Ms. Holman shouted after him, "Be careful this summer Davis." He smiled as he said "okay."

When Davis got back to the room he found Holly asleep. He proceeded to make a phone call to Ms. Upshaw to cancel the work out session for the day. After hearing about his morning's adventures she was quick to understand but informed him that he would have to reschedule for the following day and he would have to stay for dinner after working out. He agreed and the two said good bye. Once off the phone, he started to wake Holly. This wasn't always an easy job.

"C'mon man, c'mon", Davis said as he shook his shoulder almost violently.

"Damn man what is it?" Holly said as he regained consciousness.

"Ah remember you were supposed to tell me about the trouble you got yourself into," Davis reminded him.

"Yeah I'll tell ya' when I get up," Holly said as he turned on one side and turned his back away from his roommate. Davis reached to shake him again.

"C'mon man, I'm not gonna let you sleep until you tell me what's going on."

"Damned Davis," Holly said as he sat up in the bed. Davis sat back on his bed and prepared to hear the details.

Holly made a haphazard attempt to wipe the coal away from his eye. He cleared his voice before he began to speak.

"Well man it's like this. I met Mary's cousin Dante one day when I was over her house. She warned me not to fall for any of his schemes but of course my testosterone wouldn't allow me to listen to her. Well sure enough he got to talking when she was out of the room. He's talking about taking my money and bringing back five times as much." Holly watched his roommates eyes get big as he wondered where this story was going. Holly continued.

"Well I rounded up five hundred dollars and gave it to Dante. He took me to meet this guy Train and we gave him the money. The next day he was supposed give Dante what he needed." Sensing something strange, Davis stopped his roommate. Davis squinted his eyes at the spotted ceiling in an attempt to get a handle on this new situation.

"Wait a minute, wait a minute, when you say he was supposed to give the guy what he needed, what was it that he gave him?" Davis asked. Holly's eyes turned away from his roommate in shame. Then he answered him.

"Well I'm not sure what it was exactly that he was sup-posed to give him. I was never told. The only thing Dante told me was that I was supposed to get five times my money back." Davis' once confused face now grew calm as if he had figured out a solution once his roommate stopped talking.

"Okay," Davis surmised with relief, "you're just out of five hundred dollars. Now I suggest you forget about that shit and go home for the summer." He looked at Holly for approval once he made his suggestion. Once Holly's expression stayed the same, he knew that there was some-thing more.

"Well it's not that easy," Holly said as he dropped his

head into his palm.

"Train threatened to hurt Mary," Holly said. Davis' eyes grew big as a result of the last statement.

"Why in the hell would he want to hurt Mary," Davis asked. Holly took a deep breath and raised his head as he prepared to answer his roommate.

"Well," Holly began to explain, now he's saying I owe him money,"

"What!" Davis exclaimed loudly. "Yeah," Holly continued.

"It turns out that Dante bought something from him and was supposed to double his money." Now Holly was up and was walking towards the window on the other side of the room.

"And to top everything off, I borrowed the money from my two cousins at home. If I go home this summer with nothing to show for it they are going to come up here looking for Train and they would be risking their lives—either by getting shot or by whipping his ass. So I don't have the money and I can't go home this summer," Holly ended. Davis interjected.

"So you were a patsy all the while. Dante let the guy Train see your face so that you could be held responsible in his absence. Meanwhile Train isn't looking for Dante as long as he has you. And by the time Dante resurfaces he doesn't have to worry about Train because Train has already taken it out on you. Damn you're stupid Holly," Davis concluded.

"Well let me ask you," Davis continued, "what does Mary say about the whole thing?"

"I was too embarrassed to tell her," Holly said as he dropped his head once more.

Davis had gotten up and started pacing by now. He had to try to bring things into focus in order to try and help his roommate.

"So Holly what did you plan to do to correct this situation?"

"I was going to try to find Train and have a talk with him," Holly replied. Davis dropped his head and started thinking again as soon as he realized how ridiculous Holly's idea was. It was clear that his roommate had no idea of the trouble he was in.

"Well how much time do we have to deal with?" Davis asked.

"Well he said that he would do me a favor and let me concentrate on finals since I was a college boy," Holly replied. Davis felt relief. He had some time to figure this out so that no one would get hurt and his roommate could learn his lesson at the same time.

"All right," Davis said in a calmed voice, at least tell me this. Since you don't strike me as the type to be money hungry, do you mind telling me why you didn't listen to your girl and not mess with her cousin." Holly looked up in tears in preparation to answer Davis' question.

"Man this is the only woman outside of my family who seems to care about me. I like spending time with her but all we have to do is sit around her place and watch TV. I mean I want my baby to have a good time on Friday nights just like other women." As he made his statement, tears began to flow profusely. Davis went over and placed his arm around his roommate's shoulder and asked him to stop talking. Once Holly quieted down a few minutes later he left for the cold impersonal bathroom down the hall to clean up.

By the time Holly came back in, his roommate had climbed into bed. The radio was tuned to the college jazz station. He was relaxing and was on the phone with his mom. Holly thought it would be a good idea to get under his covers and grab a suspense novel he had began reading.

16

The cruel ring of the phone woke the two roommates at 11:37 p.m. Holly was the half-conscious soul that actually picked it up. Davis assumed that it was Mary and was surprised to when his roommate handed him the phone. It was a sweet and pleasant voice on the other end. Davis didn't quite have his bearings yet so he couldn't say exactly who it was.

"Oh, I'm sorry I didn't think you'd be sleep," the voice said. "I'll call you tomorrow."

"No, no," Davis said frantically as he recognized the voice as Kia's. "We had just dozed off, what's up?" Kia took a deep breath before she said anything.

"I'm bored...and hungry. I know this great diner in Buckhead where you can get any type of meal at any time of day. Will you go with me?" The familiar smile fell over his face. When would she learn that she could get what she wanted from him? Hell she could've asked him to climb Mt. Kilamanjaro and he would have given the same response.

"Sure I'll go," he said.

"Great!" she responded. "I'll be there in fifteen minutes and of course I'll pay—see ya' in a few." The dial tone blasted in his ear for a minute as he wondered what she meant about the she'll pay part. He wanted to believe that she was offering to pay since she was the one to call but for some reason he didn't think that mattered. He shook his head and hung up the phone. He then performed an odor test to decide if he needed a quick shower. Satisfied with his body aroma, he deduced that he only needed to brush his teeth. Quickly scrambling for his toiletry bag he nearly fell trying to run out of the room. Holly, whose bed had been jostled as his roommate attempted to recover his balance just shook his head from side to side.

"I guess that was Kia on the phone—huh." Davis laughed at the statement and shouted back, "Fuck you Holly," he said as he shut the door and headed for the bathroom.

Davis watched the black sports car pull to a stop in front of the curb a few minutes later. When it stopped, she turned to look at him. This was a picturesque scene he thought. Her bright smile played against the silver moonlight wonderfully. And why not he thought. It was a beautiful Atlanta night. The wind was blowing just right even though Kia had on a sweater. He was pleased to see that she was wearing shorts though. Since it was dark, he could cut his eyes over in her direction and watch those powerful muscular legs wrestle with the clutch all night.

The two pulled off and neither was too intent on conversation just yet. They were both content with enjoying the southern breeze and listening to the Sade song that the radio was now blasting. The highway was pretty much like the streets- isolated. The skyline held her attention as she drove. Her legs held his. She wished that he would go ahead and compliment her legs. She knew that he was watching them and this wasn't the first time that he had done so. It turns out that he was so distracted he never noticed her eyes cutting in his direction catching him in the act.

Soon the two were being handed menus by a white female waitress with horrible split ends as they sat at a booth in the surprisingly crowded diner. Davis noticed that the air condition was working overtime. Obviously the workers at the diner were not aware of the summer breeze outside.

"You could have told me to bring a jacket or something," Davis said in a joking fashion.

"I know, isn't it cold," she replied in agreement. She then unwrapped her silverware and inspected it. Apparently it was clean enough for her.

"Do you always inspect your silver ware," he asked her.

"Hell yeah," she replied emphatically, and you better do it too if you know what's good for you." Her statement caught him off guard. This usually happened when she used profanity. He felt like Gomez on the Addams Family after Tish had spoken in French. It was just nice hearing her let go of some of her etiquette once in a while.

Davis watched her as she wrapped herself up in her own arms. Then he noticed the waitress coming towards their table.

"Getting colder," he asked with a smile and a laugh.

"Yes, I'm about to come over there and cuddle under you," she replied in an obviously joking fashion. His eyes grew larger for a second then he returned her smile.

"What can I do for you guys tonight," the waitress interrupted. Davis looked up at her and spoke.

"Yes, is it possible to turn up the air conditioner." As he finished his statement his eyes turned back to Kia whose head was now slightly rocked back to accommodate her laughter. Sensing this was an inside joke; the waitress said nothing and proceeded to take their orders. Kia ordered first and she ordered a lot. Davis ordered a hamburger and fries. She urged him not to worry about the bill and order more but he wasn't as hungry as she obviously was and stuck with his original order.

Davis deduced that the kitchen would be a while preparing her food and decided he start right in with the conversation. He didn't mind, he definitely had a funny story to tell her about what happened with the muffler. It took him about six minutes to tell the story in detail and it surely made her laugh. However after laughing she made a statement that irked him a little bit. At the end of the story she looked around for the waitress as she said, "That's what happens when you mess with those type of people." The smile fell off of his face as soon as he heard it. Unfortunately, she was too busy looking for her food to notice. He, himself, was prepared to let it go. But then on second thought he decided to ask her about it.

"What do you mean by those type of people?" he asked.

"Oh," she exclaimed as she started shaking her head in a fashion to suggest that he shouldn't worry about it.

"It's just a bad habit that I picked up from my mother."

"From your mother?" he inquired.

"Yeah, she's always saying stuff like that," Kia explained. "Get out of here," he said in a tone that was friendly again.

"No, I'm serious," she insisted.

"Don't put it on your mother," he replied in a joking tone. But it was too late. He could tell as he looked at her that she had already shifted into serious mode.

"I remember once in the tenth grade an incident that happened. My mother was a bank executive and was making a very nice salary. Well her birthday came up and I had trouble deciding what to give her. I knew I couldn't get her anything cheap. My father suggested that I give her something that I put a lot of time into and that she would appreciate it. So after that I knew exactly what I wanted to get her. It turned out that the vocational school was having a parent-child night and I decided to take advantage. Cosmetology was my favorite class and I was pretty good in there. I decided to take my allowance and pay the $10.00 fee to use the facilities in the cosmetology room plus $48.00 more dollars to buy the best hair and nail supplies and not just use the regular supplies that they had in there. I took the supplies in early so that I could surprise her. When we got to the vocational building and were about to walk into the cosmetology room my mom stopped dead in her tracks at the door. She asked me what was it we were about to do and I told her about my surprise." Kia stopped after her last statement and turned her attention away from the traffic outside which is where she was looking while telling her story. She now turned and looked directly at Davis who could see the sadness in her eyes. Kia continued with the ending of the story.

"After telling her about my surprise my mom just looked at me and said- Oh baby that's nice but mommy can't go in there with those people."

There was an awkward silence after Kia stopped talking. Davis was searching for a response but was rescued by the waitress' arrival with their order. Kia's story ended up being the last word between the two until she dropped him off in front of the dorm. Once the food had arrived, she ate viciously. She also tried desperately to hide the belching that she was performing in front of him. Once the black accord pulled to a stop in front of the dorm, she placed her hand over her mouth and released one final belch.

"Oh my God, I can't believed I ate and belched like that in front of you," she said. The two laughed and soon she punched the gas and Davis turned to go inside.

It was about 3:30 in the afternoon when he woke up and went through his mental calendar for the day. The only thing he had to do was go over to Ms. Upshaw's. After taking a shower and getting dressed, he called to make sure she was home.

"I thought you had stood me up," she commented on the phone.

"No," he responded, "I guess I was just catching up on some sleep. I'm headed to the train station now so I'll see you in a little while," he concluded before hanging up the phone.

On the train he started to wonder what she meant when she said she thought he had stood her up. He also thought about what Big Mike said about her liking him. This of course sent him into a fantasy about her. Then he quickly dismissed it since a fantasy with a professor was a ridiculous notion to him. He thought to himself that he wouldn't know what to do even if she did come on to him and there was no way on earth he was going to come on to her. He laughed about the whole thing as he exited the train.

After buzzing him into the complex, she met him outside of her apartment. She turned him around and they headed in the opposite direction. He was happy to see that there was no one else in the workout room that she had led him to. She gave him a brief tour and announced that she had to go to the store and pick up some things for their dinner later that evening. Before leaving she made him promise not to go swimming unless someone else came into the workout room. With that, she scurried out of the door. He looked around in disappointment. Part of his fantasy definitely included seeing her in work out clothes. He laughed to himself again and thought about the fact that she was a professor. After a little while he started to appreciate the equipment in the room and remembered how long it had been since he had a good workout. The facilities in college were a joke. Soon he started preparing by stretching.

He started off on the treadmill. He liked to do this because it would get him nice and sweaty. At that point he would take his shirt off and look at himself in the mirror as he did repetitions with the weights. This would pump him up mentally. And this place had a mirror blanketing an entire wall. He continued at an overzealous pace. His body would pay him back later and he knew it. But for right now, it felt a little too good and he continued with his pace.

After about an hour Ms. Upshaw stuck her head in to see how he was doing and he took this as his cue to stop. He walked back to the apartment with her. He felt impervious. He looked the same way and the professor felt embarrassed for noticing. It was all she could do to keep her vision straight and not cut her eyes over at his body which was now glistening as the sweat slowly started to dry. As they walked into the apartment, a very pleasant and cheesy aroma greeted him.

"Goodness that smells good!" he admitted.

"Thank you, we're having lasagna tonight. So once you take a shower and change your clothes, we can dig in," she said.

"Ah man," he exclaimed as his right hand fell across his face with a loud slapping sound.

"You didn't bring any clothes did you?" she asked. In a sorrowful fashion, he shook his head no. She continued.

"I started to ask you where was your bag when I first met you outside." He was pissed with himself. He hadn't worked out in so long; he had forgotten the routine. It normally wouldn't have been a problem because he was used to returning home after his work out. But he knew he had a serious dilemma on his hands because it wouldn't be long before he started stinking. He offered a suggestion.

"It's not a big deal, I don't have to take a shower and we could just eat on the patio."

"Davis," she said in a voice that suggested that she had it all figured out. He interrupted her.

"No really, I don't have to take one," he kept insisting.

"Davis," she said in almost an identical voice as last time. He interrupted again. "And if we sit on the patio you won't have to smell me," he said.

"Davis," she said in a commanding voice, it's been too long since I entertained a man in my apartment and you're not gonna mess it up by not taking a shower. Now listen,

I saw this coming and I went ahead and grabbed a pair of sweat pants and a T-shirt out of my closet and put them in the bathroom. You'll find everything you need in there. Now please go ahead and take a shower."

As he walked towards the bathroom she dropped her head. She knew she had slipped. She shouldn't have referred to him as a man in her apartment like that. He was a student that she was supposed to be helping feel better. She had to be careful. She had to stop looking at his body; it was driving her crazy. She could only hope that he hadn't caught that. Davis, on the other hand, was getting a little confused. Was she really attracted to him? Did she really consider him a man in her apartment or was that her southern hospitality. The way she looked in on him in the weight room. The way she had set up for him to take a shower. The way she was preparing food these were all things that his mother would do for him. But on the other hand she had just made that statement. And now the apartment had soft music playing. As he stood under the flowing water from the showerhead he tried to figure out the situation. Was there anything to what Big Mike had said. Then he got mad. This was the type of stuff he could ask his father if he only had one. He let go of the thought and started to concentrate on a good cleansing.

He got out of the shower and put on the turquoise cotton jogging pants that Ms. Upshaw had placed on the clothes hamper for him. He also put on the white T-shirt that was placed on the same hamper. He was surprised when he put it on to find that the front was draped with the picture of a brown kitten.

When Davis walked out he found that she had changed clothing herself. She was now wearing a black T-shirt and some cut-off blue jean shorts. She had also put her hair up in a ponytail. When she looked at him she immediately laughed. The kitten in his mid section was a cute sight. Although she laughed at the shirt, she also took special note of how it exposed the bottom portion of his stomach on account that it was too small for him.

"It was the only shirt I had," she said while laughing. He was checking her out too. She looked mighty sporty in the outfit that she now wore. He especially loved her legs. They were dark and smooth. And the way she wore the thick pair of black sports socks gave her a very comfortable-at home appeal. He had never seen her look so relaxed. The two headed to the kitchen for dinner.

The lasagna was crammed with meat and sauce and the garlic bread was the best he had ever tasted. Over dinner she updated him on Kee-Kee's progress. She had regained the use of all of her limbs and was now trying to get back control of her speech. They had now placed her in intensive care until her white blood cell count had a chance to replenish. He was told that she would probably be released within this week or early in the following week. He could have never imagined how good that made him feel. He even felt a little more relaxed.

After dinner she grabbed Davis' dirty clothes and loaded them in the washer with detergent. He then helped her clear the table after she begged him not to.

"So how did you like the dinner?" she asked.

"It was great! "It would have been totally awesome with a nice red wine," he joked. She had quietly cursed herself as she heard him say that from the living room. She debated whether or not she should have wine with dinner earlier. She decided that it might not look right since she was the professor and he was the student. She wasn't going to make the same mistake again. After loading the dishwasher, she snatched two wineglasses from the cupboard and a bottle of red wine from above the refrigerator. She headed to the living room with the wine tucked under her arm.

"Now this is for making the highest grade in my class first semester," she said as she placed the wine on her glass coffee table. At the same time she was telling herself to keep in mind that this wasn't an ordinary man whom she had visiting her but a young man whom she had recently taught. She also knew that she had to lay off the alcohol tonight. With that in mind, she poured herself half a glass and did the same for him.

After the first glass, Davis was quick to pour himself another. Meanwhile the first few sips for Ms. Upshaw increased the volume of the second voice in her head.

"Damn this young boy is sexy," she said to herself. "And look at those abs. I haven't seen abs like that in years. I wonder how he would respond if I tried him?" she asked herself as she looked at him. Poor Davis was totally unsuspecting and was about to finish his second glass of wine. He was dealing with a pro. He would never see that look in her eye until she wanted him too. She had now raised both feet onto the couch and was sitting Indian style right beside him. He started to cut his eyes in her direction when he assumed she wasn't looking. Since she had now raised her legs, the shorts had risen up her thigh leaving even more of it exposed. He felt himself growing inside of the jogging pants.

Ms. Upshaw proceeded with small talk as she saw the alcohol slowly taking effect. She knew that he wouldn't be able to go home tonight. She would let him wear himself down with the wine and then get the guestroom ready. After Davis was near the halfway point of his third glass she decided that this would be a good time to leave him and start preparing the other room? She was just about to get up when her eyes rested on a sight. What she saw nearly took her breath away. There in Davis' lap was the imprint of a serious erection. The fact that he wasn't wearing underwear and the pants were pure cotton allowed for the imprint to really grab her attention. He was concentrating on the smooth taste of the wine as she stared at his manhood, which was cocked on his left side. She grabbed her chest in a near fit of lust as her mind quickly imagined the possibilities.

By this time Davis had noticed what was going on. He decided to act as if the alcohol were pulling him under. This was partly true. At the same time she was still wrestling with the voices in her head.

"I'll bet this muthafucka could go all night," she said to herself.

"I just can't do this. He's only nineteen. Whoa, whoa, whoa, he's over eighteen. That means he's legal. Oh shit," she continued to argue with herself.

"What am I gonna do? Look at those abs. Look at that dick. It looks like it's screaming." By now Ms. Upshaw had unconsciously lowered her hand to her vagina and was rubbing it through the shorts. Davis was now staring at the wineglass trying not to see her getting hot. This in turn made him more nervous. The only thing that prevented the tiger inside of her from pouncing on her prey was concern for her job. She was no longer worried about his resistance. She was sure that the alcohol had removed all of his inhibitions. The only question was would he open his mouth afterwards.

She decided to drop the entire thing and put him to bed and take a cold shower. However as she stood to grab him by the arm something happened. Feeling the massive arm in her hand literally made her melt. At that precise moment she said out loud this time, "Fuck a job," and quickly pulled her T-shirt off so that her aroused nipples were exposed. Next she leaped on top of him while straddling his midsection. She grabbed his head with all of her might and shoved it into her chest. She almost prayed that he would do what came naturally. It took him a few seconds as he couldn't believe what was happening but he soon swallowed one of her breast into his mouth as if it were a life line. She gave a deep guttural moan of satisfaction then instructed him to carry her to the bathroom. Once inside the bathroom she proceeded to turn on the water and quickly took off her shorts and pulled off his cotton trousers. She couldn't wait to see it without the veil of the cotton pants. Once she came face to face with it she had to grab it in her hands. Once she did this she just held it for a while. She motioned for him to climb into the shower. She climbed in behind him and grabbed one handful of his tight ass as she used the other hand to draw the shower curtain closed.

17

Davis awoke the next morning trying to identify the strange mattress underneath him. It wasn't until he heard her breathing next to him that he remembered that he was over Ms. Upshaw's. After figuring this out, his thoughts immediately went back to last night. An authentic smile fell over his face as he recalled what happened. Being with Ms. Upshaw was much different than being with the twins or Kee-Kee. It was a very memorable experience with his professor. With the others it was just scenes for his brain to recall and one day say that he did it. Sure he was able to appreciate the huge perky breasts of the twins and the flawless ass of Kee-Kee but they weren't something that he could recall with a whiff of a nice fragrance or the sweet melody of a Motown slow jam. It was just sex. However Ms. Upshaw seemed to be something different. He found himself wanting more even during the sex last night. With the others he found himself wanting to part company with them as soon as he had an orgasm. After he climaxed for the second time last night he hated to see her fall asleep.

His train of thought was interrupted as the woman lying beside him turned over in her sleep. He looked at her as she continued to sleep. Her dark skin was so smooth and inviting to the touch. Her bubbly red lips seemed just as inviting. And her perfectly permed jet-black hair flowed over the white pillow in a magical fashion. He continued to watch her for a while with a pleasant demeanor. Afterwards, he started to wonder what he should do in terms of leaving or staying. Would it be proper to get up now and start getting dressed or should he wait for her to wake up. Soon he turned his head from her direction and stared at the ceiling. He was about to go into a whole other train of thought when the silence was split by a few words.

"You awake," she asked in a very raspy voice.

"Uhhhh," he screamed as his body fell to the floor after jumping from the shock of the words.

"You okay," she asked as she peered over the side of the bed and down onto the floor. After realizing what had happened, he simply placed his hand over his face. The two started to laugh almost simultaneously.

After retrieving his clothes from the dryer Ms. Upshaw sat on the bed with her chin supported by her hand. Davis didn't notice until after he had put on his pants and shirt. He was about to put on his shoes when he asked "what," in an effort to make conversation.

"How do you feel this morning," she asked. He was about to reply okay when he thought carefully about his answer.

"Oh I feel great, how bout yourself?" he replied.

"Oh I'm fine."

"Are you sure because you look like you have something on your mind," he said. She sat quietly for a minute and looked down at the bed. Then she spoke.

"There's no easy way to say this so I'm just going to come straight out and ask—do I have to worry about my job Davis," she asked. Not getting the gist of the question, he looked puzzled at first. Then after figuring what she was getting at, he responded.

"No, you definitely don't have to worry about your job. Now can I ask you a question?" Ms. Upshaw looked on in a puzzling way. She couldn't wait to hear what he had to ask. Davis then continued in a baby-ish voice, "Can we do this again sometime?"

One of her eyes squinted and a sinister smile fell over her face, as she appeared to be thinking about it. However in reality there was absolutely nothing to think about. She loved the thought that he was looking for more and acted mature enough to handle the situation. He could definitely come back as far as she was concerned.

Davis was soon on the train headed back to campus. He took advantage of this time to go through his mental calendar. The only thing he had to do was pack. He had decided to go home for a few days to see his mother since he was about to start his internship. Dee would be there around three o'clock and since she didn't have any air conditioner in her car he knew he had better not take any chances of not being ready. He also knew that he would have to drive the two hours back to Augusta. He liked this idea. He hated to be around his mother when he was feeling like this. When he had feelings for a female. Even though he had just started feeling this way about his professor, he knew it wouldn't take long before his mother's sixth sense would pick up on it. The thing that really worried him was would Dee pick up on the age of the woman he was thinking about as well. He had to concentrate extra hard not to let anything slip. This would be a grueling task for three or four days. Besides, after holding out, he knew there would be a time when he wanted to ask her for advice about the new situation. Damn he hated this. But history had shown him that his mother gave great advice most of the time.

As Davis drove he found that is mother was in a surprisingly good mood. Maybe it had something to do with the two thousand dollars he gave her from the money he received from Big Mike. The truth is that she was just happy to see her baby. She hadn't seen him since

Christmas vacation and her enthusiasm was reflected in her conversation. She talked about the people from back home. She nearly went through the whole cast of characters that he had come to know in the neighborhood while growing up. He was happy to hear about everyone even if they weren't doing so well. She made it a point not to withhold any punches. She wanted her baby to see how fortunate he was to be in college. Little did she know that her son would have too much on his mind to even hang out with any of his old friends?

It didn't take long before his imagination started to get the best of him. Ms. Upshaw was on his mind and it caused him to miss out on the last few minutes of his mother's conversation as they reached Augusta. He asked himself where would the two of them go after last night. Could the two of them have a relationship together? Did he really want a relationship with her? And what would happen once the regular school year got started again? These were questions that he couldn't readily answer so he soon dismissed them and rejoiced in the fact that the summer was just beginning and she definitely wanted to see him again.

After dinner that night, Davis and Dee sat out in the yard. He enjoyed the nice summer air. This was a scene he hadn't seen in about a year. Dee was totally relaxed in her summer dress as she played with the bedroom shoes on her feet. She also had a folded newspaper that she fanned constantly as she sipped the diet coke that she had bought outside. Davis had assumed a lazy posture as well. He was leaning in his chair against the wall with his eyes closed as he engaged in conversation. He seemed uninterested as his mother started asking about his roommate. Davis started to answer in a very nonchalant fashion until he mentioned Mary. As he described the situation between his friend and the older woman he realized that it was extremely similar to the situation that he seemed to be entering with Ms.

Upshaw. His enthusiasm grew as he talked. He was now interested in hearing what his mother thought about the situation. He then asked her directly.

Dee took a deep breath before she answered. He could tell that she didn't think that this was a simple issue.

"Well baby, love is special whenever you can find it. Whether it's older or younger it doesn't matter. Love is something that shouldn't be taken for granted because believe it or not a lot of people go through life without ever knowing what it is. Sure they have relationships. Believe me I've seen a lot of those situations. People having sexual relationships and confusing it for the real thing. Son you remember when it seemed like all of your friends started driving before you and it seemed like you would never get your license," she recalled. Davis could only laugh about what his mother was referring to because he could remember very well.

"Yeah," he said. "I remember when I finally got my license I was driving everywhere."

"And bringing the car home with no gas," Dee added.

"I would come in asking you if you needed anything from the store," Davis continued.

Dee responded, "for about three months you did. After you got used to driving, I couldn't pay you to go to the store." Both of them laughed before his mother continued.

"Yeah and if you remember, I told you that driving was something that everyone was going to do if they wanted to. Well I'm telling you the same thing about sex. Everybody will do it one day if they want to. So I'm saying this to say that the boy shouldn't be with the older woman unless he really loves her. If he's with her for the sex, he's taking a big risk because a lot of problems can develop when you get intimate with a person and there's no love there to handle the responsibility," she concluded.

Davis concentrated on what she said for a moment. He was content with her answer. Maybe she wouldn't blow up if she found out about Ms. Upshaw even though he didn't know if it was love that he felt for her. His thought was soon interrupted by his mother's voice again.

"Of course if I was that boy's mother, I would be pretty upset," she said. Davis, who didn't like the sound of this, quickly asked why.

"Well a lot comes with experience son," she continued. I would be worried about what that older woman had in mind with you. You could be totally in love but she could have some less than clean motives. And in terms of you, I would be especially protective."

"Why would it be any different if it were me?" he asked.

"Cause you my baby," she continued bluntly, "and you the only thing I got left."

"That's not true Dee," Davis responded trying to make her feel better.

"No baby you don't understand. I'm not talking about materialistic things and I know that I have my health. What I'm talking about is what matters to me the most and that's you. Baby I could probably live homeless on the street as long as I knew you were okay. And as long as I knew you were a success, the Lord could take me at any time." Davis didn't know what to say after his mom had made that statement. He didn't have much time to think about what to say either before his mother started speaking again.

"Now I don't want to put any pressure on you to succeed or anything because you know I'm gonna love you regardless. It will just do this old woman's heart good to see you successful and enjoying life. I don't care what it is you decide to do–just be good at whatever it is. I've seen enough unhappiness and failures to last three lifetimes. I mean I've seen it from family, friends, and strangers. So you can say that I have a vested interest in seeing you make it through school. Don't get me wrong. I know this is college and you gonna have fun and make mistakes as you go through college and I want you to have fun baby, God knows you deserve it as hard as you worked through high school. My job is to make sure that you don't take yourself out of the game. I've heard of people in college who just goofed off their first three or four years but when the fourth or fifth year rolled around they were looking to graduate and they had fooled around so much that they had already taken themselves out of the game. I'm not gonna let that happen to you," she concluded.

There was a noticeable silence as Davis digested his mother's last statement. And Dee was sure to give him that time and quiet to do just that. She got up and went inside. Her son decided to sit for an hour before he retired for the evening.

The next few days were very restful for him. His used mattress felt very good under his back. It was also very nice to use a clean bathroom instead of the community bathroom he had grown accustomed to over the past year. Perhaps the best of all though was the home cooked meals that his mother prepared for him each day. He realized that he had been taking her cooking for granted for the past eighteen years. It had become the benchmark to which he compared the cafeteria food at school. He made a point to compliment his mother on every meal from that day on.

On his last night before he was supposed to go back to Atlanta, he decided to take Dee to the local dollar movie. The interesting thing was that when the two were in line to buy tickets, Davis told his mother the story about the day he and Holly went to the light bill company with Mary. He then proceeded to tell his mother how happy he was that it had been a long time since she had done something similar to that. He figured that he was safe since he was leaving in the morning.

After purchasing the ticket, his mother proceeded to the restroom. During the day she would use the restroom every two or three hours. Davis headed for the theater as soon as his mother came back into the lobby. He soon stopped after he noticed that she had stepped to the refreshment counter.

"What the hell is this?" Davis thought to himself. They never got refreshments because of the prices. When he stepped to his mother's side he noticed the attendant behind the counter. He started to look for a nametag when he noticed that the guy wasn't wearing a uniform. He was a short black man with a baldhead. Davis deduced that he was probably a member of the family who owned the theater.

"Dee, what are you doing?" Davis asked.

"Oh I'm not going to get nothing but a soda," she said. Davis decided to wait patiently. He scanned the lobby and could immediately tell that the theater wasn't well kept. His eyes then fell on the handwritten price list on the wall, which his mother had obviously not seen yet. It listed the price of a small coke as $2.50, medium $3.00, and large $3.75. The man behind the counter watched Dee as if she were bothering him as she took her time deciding what she wanted. Davis couldn't blame her. After all there was no one else in line. The only explanation he could offer for the reason why the man seemed bothered by Dee was that his conversation with a plain-clothes security officer was interrupted once she stepped to the counter. Poor Dee hadn't noticed any of this. She was truly engrossed in trying to make a decision.

"Well let me have a large diet coke," Dee said as she looked at her son.

"That way we both can drink from it," she said with a smile. Just as she was saying this, the guy behind the counter had grabbed a Styrofoam cup that didn't seem very large to Davis at all. As he used the cup to scoop some ice he said over his shoulder, "That'll be $3.75." Davis was about to drop his head because he smelled one of those moments coming on. However he was surprised when his mother quickly tried to remedy the situation.

"Oh that's okay, that's okay–I'll just take a small one," she said. She figured that she wouldn't even get upset but just move on in a smooth fashion. She looked at her son again and this time she shook her head from side to side as if to say that the prices didn't make any sense. As she was looking at Davis, Davis noticed that the guy behind the counter had taken a slow and deliberate breath as he slowly emptied the ice from the cup. Davis was happy his mother hadn't noticed his behavior. As the attendant reached for a small cup he made another statement.

"That'll be $2.50 ma'am." That statement caused Dee's head to spin from Davis' direction to the direction from which she had heard the voice. And then she released those infamous words from her lips that were equivalent to the "gloves coming off."

"I beg your pardon," she said. She waited until the attendant repeated himself just to make sure she heard him correctly.

"You mean to tell me that this little cup of soda costs $2.50?"

"Yes ma'am," he said as he continued to patronize her. Davis had to give it to his mother; she was trying her hardest not to make a scene.

"All right, just give me a cup of ice," she said as she fanned her dollar towards the stack of cups. She was sure she had outwitted the guy behind the counter this time. She even turned to look at her son and proceeded to flash a victory smile. But once again the voice from behind the counter spoiled it.

"Ma'am, it's still going to be $2.50," he said. Davis found himself in a bit of a predicament. He was not going to let anyone disrespect his mother in his presence. But at the same time he was ready to drop his head from embarrassment. He also wanted to laugh at how naive his mother had been in this particular incident. As he glanced at the security officer he could tell that he was ready to drop his head as well.

"Why in the hell would a cup of ice still be $2.50?"

The attendant proceeded to explain that the cup was part of an inventory. His mother was not trying to hear anything though. She simply looked at her son and started to complain out loud.

"Now you know this don't make any damn sense. I could get a damn three liter for $2.50," she said. She was about to continue when the security officer spoke.

"Danny, ain't nobody in here man, just say you lost a damn cup and give it to the lady." No sooner than the officer had finished speaking the attendant had grabbed a large cup and filled it with ice and gave it to Dee.

"Here you go ma'am, cause I don't feel like getting cussed out today," the attendant said. Dee looked at the man and started laughing and soon everyone else started laughing as well. Davis knew that this was a scene that could have only taken place in the south. He would laugh about it many times afterwards.

The next day Davis was back at his dorm before he knew it. His Godmother had accompanied the two on the drive back to Atlanta. The two ladies talked the entire trip, which was just fine to Davis. He used the entire time to think about Ms. Upshaw. He was extremely upset that he hadn't brought her phone number with him before he left. He couldn't wait until he could see her again. He was nervous that she might not feel the same way.

The two ladies dropped Davis off and departed quickly. They were off to enjoy the city before they were to get back on the road. Once back in the room, Holly informed his roommate that a female had been calling all day. Apparently she hadn't left a name and Davis concluded that it wasn't Kia since Holly was familiar with her voice on the phone. He knew it had to be Ms. Upshaw and he had no choice but to wait for her next call.

He was agitated as he waited for the call. He and Holly

got into an argument regarding the way that Holly had taken care of the room in Davis' absence. The two cleaned as they argued. And soon they both realized that they weren't serious about the argument and they were both soon napping to some jazz.

It was 9:00 p.m. when the phone rang. Davis answered on the first ring as his heart pounded in anticipation waiting for the voice on the other end to respond to his hello. He literally gave a sigh of relief when he heard that it was her.

"Hi Davis," she said in a calm and content voice.

"Hey Ms. Upshaw," he returned.

"Davis," she said with a giggle in her voice, "you have to call me Gail, everybody doesn't need to know to whom you're talking, okay." Davis agreed and the two continued with their conversation.

He was pleased to find out that she missed him as much as he missed her. The two were officially talking sweet to each other now. It was still hard for him to imagine this happening with his professor but he was quickly getting used to the idea and it made him very erotic. The two made plans to spend the weekend together and discussed a phony excuse to give Holly.

18

The next day Davis was awakened by the telephone. It was Gail on the other end and after greeting him with a few sensuous words she told him that she would be on campus around noon. She also instructed him to walk around the corner to the projects and wait for her at a designated spot. She definitely did not want to be spotted on campus picking up a student. After receiving instructions, he hung up the phone and headed for the shower. He didn't notice that his roommate was gone until he got half way down the hall and realized that his bed was empty. Then he remembered hearing Holly going out last night. He deduced that his roommate was visiting his girlfriend. Jumping into a lukewarm shower was an attempt to calm his nerves because he was already excited. There was no doubt that he was anxious about spending the weekend with Gail but he was also happy to be in this great city with a little money in his pocket and time to do absolutely nothing. After all this was Atlanta—the black Mecca of the south and this was the first time he didn't have to worry about taking an exam or making it to class. Maybe he could convince Gail to take him to some of the interesting places that he had observed during his train rides. Maybe even to a fancy restaurant or something else like that, which he couldn't readily find in his hometown.

Around one o'clock Davis watched as Gail pulled up in the projects. She didn't see him at first because he had gone a few yards away from the rendezvous point to talk to Mary on her porch. He didn't realize it was her place until he heard her calling his name from behind. He was also relieved when she motioned for him to come to her because standing around in that area like that made him nervous. There were a couple of guys sitting on a porch who kept staring at him. Davis was sure that he wouldn't have been able to stand in the same spot unprovoked had it been dark. Besides, after their little outing, Mary was cool now and she gave him a chance to get rid of all the nervous energy by talking. However the conversation did bother him a little bit. Mary was expressing her concern for Holly and how strange he had been acting lately. He was told that his roommate was still inside of her house sleeping.

Gail stopped at the exact spot where she told Davis to wait for her. She had noticed him sitting on the porch with the female but because she recognized the lady she was definitely not going to give the woman a chance to identify her. Davis walked briskly to the car thinking about what he had just heard about Holly and trying to gain some type of composure as well before he saw Gail.

As he opened the door to the passenger's side, the smooth sounds of jazz along with the soft fragrance of her designer perfume flowed out and arrested his thoughts. He was almost instantly calmed. The smell and sound immediately took him back to the last night that the two were together. The sight of her face was also very soothing. She had her head turned completely in his direction as he sat in the passenger seat after placing his bag behind him. She wore an enchanted smile that was highlighted by her pearly white teeth against the dark red backdrop of her plumb colored lipstick.

"We making friends in the projects already?" she asked as he repositioned himself for comfort in the seat. Davis quickly explained who Mary was as Gail put the car in gear while still focusing on his handsome and hairless face.

"Well, what are we going to do this weekend?" he asked. Gail turned forward as her foot searched for the accelerator.

"We're going to make some of my fantasies come true," she replied in a sinister voice that reflected her seriousness. After hearing that, his eyes grew big with surprise and the white sedan sped off.

After stopping at a local deli, they arrived back at her apartment. Once inside, Gail headed to her bedroom and emerged a minute later after having replaced her shoes with a thick pair of socks and removing the baseball cap that she had been wearing on account that she hadn't done her hair that morning. The two proceeded to eat their meals and didn't say much in the process. After finishing, she invited him to her bedroom where she had a VCR prepared to show a tape. Davis was surprised to see that the tape contained a few soap operas instead of the porn flick that he was expecting for some perverted reason. Once he removed his shoes, he jumped on the bed. Upon finding, her remote she jumped between his legs and rested her head on his chest. After wrapping his arms around her, Davis released a noticeable sigh of comfort and relief, which caused her to smile.

At about 6:30p.m. Davis awoke to Gail shuffling around the room. She had just taken a shower and was now in the process of doing her hair. She heard him as he was waking up and was able to greet him with a smile.

"C'mon Davis, I need you to take a shower and get dressed, I'm treating you to dinner tonight," she said. Davis stood up stretching and yawning.

"You know I have a little money, you don't have to pay for everything when we're together," he said. She chuckled after hearing his statement.

"You're so sweet," she replied as she looked at him

from the bathroom mirror.

"No honey, believe me, your presence and participation is payment enough," she added.

Davis walked into the bathroom after she made her statement. He wasn't about to argue with her.

He could use all of the money he could hold on to. He started the shower and proceeded to take off his shirt. As he got to his pants, he began to wonder if he were making a big mistake. He didn't want her to think that he was being a bit bold and perverted by using that bathroom while she was in it instead of going to the guest bedroom and taking his shower. Besides, he was hoping he could get a quickie before they left for dinner. As he was getting undressed he had his back turned to her and pretended to be concentrating on the shower. However, now that he was totally nude he decided to look back over his shoulder to see if she was showing any interest. And he wasn't disappointed. By the time his eyes locked with hers, she was wearing a mischievous grin.

"I'm going to eat you up tonight," she said as she slapped him on the buttock. And with that she walked out into the bedroom to finish getting dressed.

The two of them were soon being seated at a very posh Buckhead restaurant. Davis could see now why she instructed him to bring a suit. Gail wore a very elegant turquoise gown that teased every man whom showed the slightest interest in her large and firm calves as it wrapped around her womanly curves in a horribly seductive fashion. The pearls around her neck were the only things in the building that came close to matching the gleam in her smile. She was extremely elated and Davis could tell that this was all part of some great weekend that she had planned. He would try his best to make everything go smoothly. After soliciting drink requests, the server left them alone.

Davis looked around and realized that this was one of

those types of fancy restaurants that he had been waiting to visit while in the city. After surveying the room his eyes fell on her again. She was still wearing the brilliant smile and she was staring at him with a very intense look. She looked like a kid who had just gotten the perfect gift for her birthday. In an effort to make conversation, he asked her if she was okay.

"What do you dream about Davis?" she replied not even answering his question.

"What do I dream about?" he replied in a rhetorical fashion.

"Yes, what do you want to do in life?" she said in an attempt to clarify the question.

"Well I guess I just want to be something that would make my mother proud. I've never really given it much thought, all I know is that I feel that I could be pretty much anything I want to be at this point. I think the only challenge for me is going to be choosing a career that can hold my interest and foster a good relationship with God," he concluded. It seemed as if her smile had grown as she showed her pleasure with his response.

"You know you are extremely mature for your age," she said. This caused him to go speechless and to blush. In an effort to make the moment less awkward for himself he returned the question to her. There was a quiet giggle as she dropped her head and prepared to answer him.

"Out of everything in this world all I've ever wanted to be was a DJ," she replied.

"Really, what type of music," he asked in a shocked voice.

"Oh, only jazz," she said as she gazed at the ceiling.

"In fact, that's the only reason why I wanted to come to Clark Atlanta University. They had the only jazz station in the city at one point. Davis was able to keep her talking through much of dinner and was able to learn a lot about her.

After dinner, Gail drove to a small town that was half an hour away to get what she claimed to be the best ice cream she had ever tasted. Davis was soon convinced of the same. They kept the conversation light as they rode around. They were both anxious to get back to her apartment.

As soon as they entered the apartment, she took him by the hand and led him to the bathroom and instructed him to stand still and wait for her. She left the room and came back about two minutes later carrying a small battery operated radio. She was now wearing an all red negligée. To him, she looked simply sinful and he was enjoying every minute of it. Without looking at him she went to the tub and turned on the water. She emptied two caps of bubble bath into the tub as it continued to fill. Then returning to the cupboard under the sink she tuned the radio to the jazz station and lit a candle.

She was now ready to proceed with her plans as he could tell when she finally looked at him again. She walked up to him slowly and reached over his shoulder to turn off the bathroom lights. Then she focused on him. She instructed him to remain still and quiet and she proceeded to take off his jacket and dress shirt. She lightly kissed his biceps once they were exposed. And when she was done kissing him she removed his tank top and started to kiss his massive chest and chiseled stomach. After totally removing the tank top, she rested her forehead on his stomach and stared towards the floor. It was as if she were making sure she was ready to perform the next step. After a few seconds she continued undressing him. She was now moving with an intense pace as she wrestled with his belt and zipper. The two pieces aggravated her for a little while before she won the battle which was signified by her throwing open his pants as if she were exposing a magic trick. She then slowed the pace again as she dropped his pants and underwear and stared at his genitalia for a few seconds before kneeling on her knees and wrapping her hands around his hard and warm penis. His head rocked back and his eyes squinted in pleasure as she took Davis into her mouth. He nearly passed out.

She continued an oral massage of his penis until the sound of the running water signaled a possible overflow. As she reached to turn off the water, she used her hand to continue with the massage. After about eight strokes with her hand he exploded all over the wall he was facing. She looked up in surprise and said, "I'm glad we've got that one out of the way." He replied with an extremely relaxful smile. Afterwards, she put him into the awaiting cloud of bubbles and proceeded to bathe him slowly.

After drying him off just as slowly and placing her moist full lips on various parts of his body, she told him to lie on his stomach on the bathroom floor. With the smooth instrumental jazz playing in his ear, Davis was quick to comply. He waited patiently for her next move.

After hearing her shuffle around the bathroom for a few seconds, he heard and felt her straddle his body while in a standing position. Soon he felt a hot liquid hit his back and he raised up in excruciating pain. "Uhhhhhhh", he screamed as he felt for the trouble spot on his back.

"What the hell was that?" he asked as he turned to look at her.

"I'm sorry," she said as she looked down at him and started to laugh. I should have warned you before I did it.

"What was it?" he asked in a voice that suggested that he was truly looking for an explanation.

"Davis that was some hot wax from the candle?" she answered.

"You did that on purpose?" he asked in anxiety. She started to laugh harder now.

"Davis look. It doesn't hurt," she said as she demonstrated by allowing two drops to fall on her forearm.

"You'll get used to it as they continue to hit your

back." "What the hell is it supposed to do?" he asked surprised that she wanted to continue.

"Trust me, it only intensifies the sex," she said. He turned over on his stomach again and prepared for the pain to continue. She covered her mouth as her laughter continued while she watched him squirm in an effort to save his masculinity from the pain. After about three more minutes neither could take anymore and they both retired to the bedroom.

She proceeded to remove the dried patches of wax from his back but was only half way done when he turned over and grabbed her. He couldn't wait any longer. He quickly removed the negligée and placed her in the center of the bed. She was totally cooperative. He moved himself to the foot of the bed and grabbed her under both of her calves. He then raised both of her legs in the air as he lowered himself on his elbows. Looking up at her he could see her anxiety and decided not to keep her waiting as his tongue dove into the moist hot center of Abigail Upshaw.

The next morning he awoke to find himself in bed alone. He put on some shorts and followed the smell of breakfast to the kitchen where he found a plate of waffles, eggs, grits, and smoked beef sausage waiting on him. After speaking to Gail he proceeded to devour the meal.

"I told you my little wax trick would work. You were uncontrollable last night," she said with a pleasure filled grin as she took the seat next to him.

"You okay?" he asked wanting to make sure he hadn't done anything to hurt her in his fits of passion.

"Sweetheart, I am just fine, believe me," she said with a look of content on her face.

They had a lazy Sunday after breakfast. They lounged around watching television and napping. Gail had a couple of phone calls from girlfriends but for the most part they were uninterrupted. They cuddled each other as they napped.

In the evening he decided to get back to the dorm since tomorrow was the first day of his internship. Gail offered to drive him but he declined her offer. He preferred to take the train. That way he could relish the thoughts of this past weekend in peace. He did exactly that. He wasn't sure if it was love as he thought of what his mother had said. All he knew was that whatever he felt for her before was now doubled.

When he finally reached his room he was greeted by the ringing of the telephone. It was Mary on the other end and she was hysterical. She told him that her and Holly had just had a heated discussion and he was now on his way back to the room. She asked him if the two of them could talk about Holly together. Davis agreed but informed her that it would have to be tomorrow evening. His response seemed to calm her a little before she hung up.

Holly soon walked in with an unhappy demeanor. Davis didn't want to say anything right away. His roommate sat down and began taking off his shoes when he began to speak.

"Hey man guess who I just saw."

"Who/" Davis responded nonchalantly.

"Kee-Kee," Holly said. The words froze Davis. He was speechless for a few seconds.

"Are you sure?"

"Yeah, I just saw her walking towards the registrar's office," Holly replied. Davis didn't say another word. He just bolted from the room.

As he ran across the empty campus, he wondered just what he would say to her. Saying sorry didn't seem appropriate here. And what exactly would he be apologizing for, treating her like crap and not speaking to her or would he be apologizing for not going to see her in the hospital. He wanted to go but he wasn't quite sure how her parents would take him being there. Did they even know why she did this in the first place? Did anyone truly know why she did it? He asked himself all of these questions as he got closer to the registrar's office.

As he rounded the corner out of breath he soon came to a complete stop. He saw her at the top of the stairs of the administration building. She was just ending a conversation with a professor and turned to meet his eyes. The two stood motionless for a while. Her eyes started to tear up and a lone tear raced down Davis' face. From a distance he could see that she looked a little malnourished as she began to descend the stairs. He proceeded to walk towards her and the two met in almost the exact same spot they were in when they first noticed each other. There was another pause as the two got into reach of each other.

Davis looked at her. He couldn't believe all of the weight she had lost. He could see it in her face. It was obviously a result of being fed intravenously for nearly two weeks. He also noticed the dark rings around her eyes. It was ironic to him that when he first met her at this spot that she was wearing glasses. Now she didn't care who saw her emotionless eyes- she had much more to worry about. Her hair was now in a bun, which was obviously the best her mother could do before she left the hospital. And her skin, which used to glow with moisture, was now pale and dry. None of her feminine curves were noticeable as a result on the weight loss and the loose fitting jogging pants she wore. However, in spite of all this, she was more beautiful to him now than at any time in the past. Not in the sexual sense, no now she was a survivor who wore her scars literally in the open and this made her radiate with beauty.

After investigating her physical appearance another tear fell from her face. He also noticed the tears in her eyes. He lunged at her and embraced her frail little frame. She returned his grip as she cried on his shoulder. They embraced for half of an eternity before they let each other go.

"I take it you're leaving?" he asked in a very solemn voice.

"Yeah, I just withdrew. My parents want me to attend Grambling so they can keep an eye on me," she responded.

"I ahhh-I ahhh," he attempted to say something but she cut him off.

"What you want to stay in touch?" she said anticipating his question.

"Please understand Davis that that wouldn't be good for my healing- mentally or physically. You're already a permanent fixture in my heart. We just don't need to make that fixture any larger than it already is," she concluded.

"I just don't know what to say," he said as his head began to droop.

"You don't have to say anything. You don't have to say you're sorry or that you love me or even apologize for the way you treated me. In a way this had nothing to do with you. It was all Keandra Dixon coming to grips with her emotions. And please don't think I'm angry with you because I'm not. I lóve you just as much now as I did before this incident occurred," she said as she reached to lift his head by his chin.

"I just had to learn that it's not a bad thing when love isn't reciprocated, it's just a thing." And with that she limped off suddenly as he turned to watch her.

19

Davis returned to his room that Monday afternoon around 4:30 p.m. He had just come in from a very uninteresting day of learning obvious rules and procedures and meetings with representatives from human resources. The only good thing about the day was that he discovered that he would definitely be working in a testing lab and therefore didn't have to wear suits everyday.

He found his roommate in the bed in almost the identical spot as when he left. Holly had woken up after hearing Davis come in.

"You been in the bed all day?" Davis asked with disbelief.

"No, I went looking for a job today." Holly said as he stretched and yawned.

"Did you find one?"

"Yes mother, I start at the Quik Time Supermarket tomorrow," Holly responded in a sarcastic voice.

"Wow, I can't believe you didn't go over to Mary's when you got back," Davis continued paying no attention to the sarcasm.

"Me and babygirl had a serious argument yesterday so I'm just giving her some time to cool off," Holly explained. After listening to his last statement, Davis was reminded of his appointment with Mary and after changing clothes he started out for her house.

Mary greeted him with a smile as she let him in. Once inside, he immediately noticed the cleanliness of the room. It was decorated with very ordinary furniture but it was tidy nonetheless. Mary proceeded to extend her hospitality by asking him if he wanted anything. He declined as he took a seat on the couch. As she sat down Davis started talking immediately.

"So what is it that you and Holly fighting about?" he asked. Mary shook her head and lowered it at the same time. "There's something wrong with him, he's very irritable lately. It's like something is bothering him but he won't tell me what it is. What's worse is that I think it has something to do with my good for nothing cousin, Dante. And that's what scares me the most. See cause while Holly thinks he's being a man and taking care of everything, I know for a fact that he's never dealt with anyone like my cousin and has no idea who he's dealing with. So I wanted to ask you if he's told you anything," she concluded. Davis looked at her with both cheeks full of air and suddenly expelled the air to show his discontent with being in the middle of the situation. He could see the worry in her eyes. This surprised him because at one moment while he was analyzing the situation for Holly, his mind contemplated this situation being a sting that she, Dante, and Train may be playing on his roommate. Even though he had dismissed the notion earlier, he now realized how ridiculous the notion was in the first place. He could tell how much this lady cared for the boy. But for some reason, he really wanted to know why and that prompted his next question.

"Why do you care?" he asked bluntly. The question took Mary by surprise and she responded, "What?"

"Why do you care so much for Holly, what is it that attracts you to him," he said trying to clarify the question. She looked at him as if she were saying that was a fair question. She expelled a little air from her cheeks just as he had done earlier and her eyes tilted backward as she looked at the ceiling. He could tell that he was causing her to take the conversation to a level where she didn't care to take it.

"Five years ago, I was a woman with little self-esteem. I was well into my twenties and extremely overweight. Unlike the other girls I knew I didn't have a sorry nigga who claimed to love me and smack me around on the regular. And believe it or not, that's exactly what I was looking for just so I could fit in with everyone else. I soon found trouble and he was a sorry son of a bitch. But he did show me a little attention and that's all I needed. Well it didn't take long before his plan started to unfold. He thought since he showed me a little love that he could get me to do little jobs with him in return. This way he wouldn't have to trust any guys. He was right too. Davis let me tell you, when a woman loves a man, she won't do a thing to harm him or steer him wrong intentionally. So if you have a woman who loves you and asks you to do something, if you don't do it make sure it's because you truly don't want to and not because of some macho bullshit. Because that woman who loves you has your best interest at heart and if she's wrong and you go down because of the advice she gave you, oh she'll go down with her man and you can bet on that," Mary stated. Davis found her last statement interesting and decided to hold on to it for thought.

"Well anyway," she continued, "we started small at first. He would steal from department stores and hold up convenience stores and I was the getaway driver. But soon we graduated to banks and that's when everything hit the roof. On our second bank robbery, instead of running to the car, he ran past it and eventually got away. The guard who was chasing him recognized the getaway car from police reports. Knowing that he wouldn't catch my boyfriend, he decided to stick the gun in my face instead. I was lucky to only get three years since it was a federal offense. Well a month after being caught, I started my first day of school," she continued as Davis' face grew complex as a result of her last statement.

"The first day of school is just the first day arriving at prison," she explained. She continued, as his face grew calm again.

"Well as soon as we got into view of the inmates, the whistling and the threats of rape started. I saw later that they didn't only rape women for sex, but they did it for entertainment. They used objects and all type of shit. Well in the showers the first night I met a woman who was a friend of my oldest sister and she kinda' took care of me. When the mob started forming and was about to come after me, the lady instructed me to run over to the toilet and cover my whole body with shit. Yeah, I do mean feces," she emphasized on account of seeing the surprise in Davis' face.

"Well after seeing me covered in shit, they quickly moved on to the next girl. The next morning and every morning after that for the next six days, I smeared my crotch area and the area under my titties with shit. And this wasn't necessarily a full proof system, but they always decided to move on to the next girl instead of throwing me under a shower. Most people don't believe me when I tell this story but it is amazing the things you'll do to stay alive. It was those mornings when I would reach into that toilet that I would realize the mistakes I had made in my life. All the time I had wasted and all the respect that I didn't have for myself. It was all I could do not to lose my mind when I was rubbing that stinking shit on my body. I couldn't even begin to explain what that does to a person. I kept thinking that I was in this worthless place because of a lack of respect for myself. I vowed that I would spend those years trying to find the respect that I never knew."

Davis watched as tears began to fall profusely from her face. He now understood why she didn't want to go into this. He felt helpless and eventually got up from where he was sitting and was headed towards her to give her a hug and comfort her. She quickly stopped him with a gesture of the hand.

"No, no, believe me it does me good when I talk about it," she said as he took his seat again.

"Well as time went on I started going to the library because it was the only sane place in there. I would read even when I didn't want to just so I didn't have to be around those negative bitches. I ended up working there and eventually received my G.E.D. Afterwards I started to laugh at the fact that there was a college right down the street from my house and I never even thought about going to college. Well as I continued to educate myself, the self-esteem came and so did the dream of going to college. I wrote to receive some information from CAU and while reading it learned that employees could go to school for free. Well ever since that moment, my dream was to work at the school and some day receive my degree.

Now in case you're wondering what does all of this have to do with Holly, all I can say is the one thing that I learned to appreciate in lock-up was a good man, not a man who buys you all type of shit. I don't need a man who can fuck the shit out of you, although that would be a plus. But the man I came to dream for was a simple one with good intentions who just wants to be with you as much as you want to be with him. We don't have to go anywhere necessarily, just as long as we can both enjoy lying up under each other and struggling together. That's all I need. And after two years of working in the cafeteria, he looked me in the face one day. With him part of my dream is complete. All I have to do now is take the S.A.T so I can get into school and I'm supposed to do that next fall," she concluded.

Davis looked on from his seat in amazement at her story. After snapping out of it, he spoke.

"Mary, I can't tell you exactly what's going on with

Holly but I can tell you this-he's not in it alone and I'm going to help him get out of it. And unlike him, I do know what I'm dealing with and trust me, I'm not trying to get Dee Virginia's baby boy hurt in any kind of way," he said. He could see the relaxation in her face as he finished his statement.

Before he left, Davis decided to describe his situation with Ms. Upshaw. He was desperate for some advice from and older woman and felt he could now trust Mary not to tell anyone including Holly. He proceeded to describe what transpired every time that he was with her and Mary digested everything he said. When he finished, she was immediately ready to deliver a verdict.

"I'm not sure if she loves you Davis-to be honest," Mary started to explain.

"The woman has little confidence in herself when it comes to dealing with men. It also sounds like she has a little freak in her. So she'll screw those men with position to get what she wants even if it's only job security and she may even think she can snag one. But in terms of you, what she's found is a vibrant young boy who is not experienced enough to degrade her during sex. So she can help herself feel better by acting out her fantasies with you," Mary concluded.

"So you don't think she's stopped having sex with this dean since she's met me?" he asked in an apprehensive voice.

"No, not at all," Mary said frankly.

Davis walked home slowly as he thought about what Mary had just told him. He couldn't help but draw similarities between Gail's behavior and the way Kee-Kee used to act now that he had and opinion from an older woman that he believed.

Once he got to his room he decided to retire early and try to catch up on some of the rest that he had missed out on during the weekend. The rest of the week was pretty uneventful except for a call from Kia. She wanted to treat him to dinner that Friday night. Davis knew that there was more to the proposed evening but he couldn't get her to tell him what. He was also disappointed that he couldn't spend the entire weekend with Gail since he would be going out on Friday. He wasn't too crushed however since his head was now reeling from the opinion that Mary gave to him. He now questioned Gail's intentions. He was now confused about the entire issue. On one hand he didn't care about if she loved him or not as long as she could continue to turn out weekends like the previous one and pay for everything, he would be just fine. Then on the other hand he hated the thought of someone using him. At any rate he told her he would be tied up with his roommate this Friday and he could hear in her voice that she was disappointed. This confused him even more.

Friday came rather quickly and of course he was excited about seeing Kia. And since she had instructed him to dress in a suit he knew that she must have been dressed very nicely herself, which meant that he really couldn't wait to see her.

The black Honda pulled along side of the curb in a racy fashion. Judging by the way that she was acting and driving, he concluded that she was running late for something. She hardly looked at him since she was so busy driving down the highway switching gears in her one-inch heels. The black scarf that was wrapped around her neck almost flew out of the window because of the highway breeze. She started to explain to him exactly what was going on.

"Okay here's the story," she prepared to tell him. "We're going to the airport to pick up a couple that went to Northwestern with me. Their names are Frank and Deidra. Deidra was my roommate for two and a half years. She's also my best friend. We both majored in journalism and we both challenged each other all throughout college. Even though I work in a better region for covering the news and I have much more potential, she works in Rochester and has already been named the weekend anchorperson. Although she is very ambitious, she is also very quiet and reserved. Enter Frank," she said as she weaved in and out of traffic headed for Hartsfield Airport. Davis tried to take in as much as he could but he was terrified of the way that she was driving. Kia continued as Davis gripped the door handle for support.

"Now Frank is almost the opposite of Deidra. In fact, he's a certified asshole, but he definitely loves my best friend, which means I have to tolerate him, and I'm asking you to do the same for one night. He graduated in chemistry and now he works for Kodak in Rochester as well. He will definitely say some obnoxious things but I hope you won't let him bother you. We will be dining at Ray's on the River, which is a very expensive restaurant. You will pay for both of our meals with the money in that envelope," she said as she pointed to the white envelope that sat beneath the emergency brake handle.

"Now Frank is a black republican and the first thing he will try to do is figure out your political affiliation, pleases try to avoid the subject. They only have a four-hour lay over before they head out to Phoenix. Now Davis if you really care to be my friend, you'll tell him you're a graduate student," she said as she pulled the car into one of the parking spots at the airport. His eyes were so large from amazement by this time. Kia was now in the vanity mirror doing some last minute primping. When she finished, she opened her door and stuck her foot out but not before turning to look at him.

"Oh by the way, if anyone asks, we've been dating for the last seven months," she said quickly as she leaned over and planted a wet kiss on his cheek.

Davis had to run to catch up with Kia as she dashed for the baggage claim. She clearly wanted to make a nice impression on these people and after that kiss, Davis decided he'd do whatever he needed to do in order to help her.

Once inside Kia immediately saw the couple and rushed towards them. Davis tried to hold in his laughter once he got a glimpse of them. He thought that the female was fairly attractive. She was about 5' 10" in the heels that she wore. The funny thing was that the guy was about an inch shorter. Davis soon caught up to the group and Kia quickly introduced him. Afterwards they all piled into the Honda and left the airport.

As the car moved up the highway, the ladies whom were sitting up front were completely engulfed in conversation. Kia would peek at Davis using the rearview once in a while to see how he was doing with Frank. Davis had decided to peer aimlessly out the window until Frank decided he was ready to conversate. Although Davis hadn't heard him say one word, he could tell that the guy was stuffy. But it didn't take long for Frank to start his interrogation.

"So Davis, I hear you're a graduate student in chemistry," Frank commented.

"Yeah, I'm trying to wrap my thesis on up," Davis replied.

"Your thesis huh," Frank said in a tone of disbelief. "So what's the title of this thesis?" . Davis could now see Kia in the rearview squinting as if she expected him to be stomped by the last question. Davis started smiling. He couldn't believe this guy was playing this childish game. He eventually decided to play along.

"Ah my title is the effects of second order nonlinear optical materials on monochromatic light," Davis responded in a cool and steady voice. The car became silent after he disclosed the long title. It was as if no one believed he knew exactly what he was talking about. That's when Davis decided to put the icing on the cake.

"Yeah the applications of this research are as complex as improved laser beams or as simple as increased storage capacity on compact discs," he concluded. After a little more silence, Frank decided to speak.

"Oh, quite interesting," he responded. Kia was now smiling and Davis could tell she was proud of him even though he still found the whole thing funny.

Davis was impressed when they walked into the restaurant. It was even fancier than the one he had been to the previous weekend with Gail. In lieu of the wait, the two couples had to take drinks at the bar until a table was ready. Davis watched as the ladies continued to talk with smiles on their faces. He knew Kia was having a great time. He also sensed from her eyes that she was apologizing for leaving him to talk with that prick. But Davis thought it was all worth it just to see Kia looking so great and that winning smile. After placing their orders, the couples were seated at a tiny table in the corner. Things had gotten quiet.

"So Davis, how do you feel about attending a historically black institution?" Frank asked. Kia slightly dropped her head. She knew that it was about to get ugly.

"Excuse me," Davis said.

"Frank, don't get started now," Deidra said across the table.

"What I just want to know is if he feels that black colleges are relevant to our society when you consider that the blacks who attend the non-black colleges do better on the standardized tests that society uses to measure our competency," Frank said as he shrugged his shoulders and raised his hands in a defensive position. Even though Davis thought that it was quite humorous that this fair skinned man with hazel eyes and thin eyebrows chose to wear his Napoleon Complex in plain sight of everyone, he was now officially pissed at the question. But instead of showing his anger, he decided to get himself together so he could properly respond.

"Are you familiar with the Little Rock Nine?" Davis asked.

"No I can't say that I am," Frank responded. Davis

continued.

"Well they were a group of elementary school kids who were the first to integrate the public school system in Little Rock Arkansas. These young children had to withstand name-calling and physical attacks on their person with bottles and rocks. They were even spit on by racist whites that were totally against the idea of integration. All of this before they even got inside the classroom to take a seat. And you can all but imagine what happened there. The amazing part about this story to me isn't the fact that they integrated the system, no there were events like that happening all over. The unbelievable part to me is when all of this occurred. Now listening to my story, you might think early 1900s. But this incident happened about thirty years ago, which I find pretty fucking, amazing since my mother is almost fifty. So you have to excuse me if I don't understand when people question the relevance of schools like CAU, Howard, Hampton, Morris Brown, Fisk, Tuskeegee, or Spelman. Hell these schools have been educating African Americans for over 120 years. At a time when people my color couldn't even think about setting foot on the campus of white institutions let alone think of sitting in their classrooms. And yeah your little statistic may be true about the standardized testing, but you know what, I'd take the courage and perseverance of those nine little kids any day over some fucking test scores. Now if you're black and you choose to go to a predominantly white institution, well I applaud your choice. Hell, I even applaud your right to make that choice. But as a black person, don't you dare question the relevance of black colleges and don't you let a non-black person do it either," Davis concluded.

"Hey, hey Davis man it was just a question, calm down brutha," Frank said as he threw his hands shoulder high in a submissive position again.

"Oh believe me I'm calm, I was just answering your question, brutha," Davis responded.

The table grew very quiet after Davis' last statement. Kia was thankful when the maitre d' came to escort them to their dining area. She was sure to hold Davis so that Deidra and Frank could go ahead. Then she got right behind him and slapped him on a buttock as she spoke in his ear.

"Boy you better tell that muthafucka," she said in her deepest voice to let him know that she was proud of him.

The rest of the evening was pretty uneventful as Frank carefully chose the words that he spoke to Davis. It was mostly small talk between the two from then on. Kia and Deidra continued to have a good time and even started sharing their conversation with the guys after they had done their catching up.

20

Kia's car moved at a modest speed as it left the airport. She was much more relaxed now. She graciously thanked Davis for helping her out and didn't say much more afterwards. Davis was content with listening to the Hip-hop music coming from the radio and concentrating on the peaceful skyline. He didn't want to say anything to her because he could tell that she was in deep thought.

It wasn't long before they pulled up in front of the dorm. Davis was preparing to get out of the car but he was looking for some type of send off before he did so. A thank you or goodnight or even a casual glance, but she never turned her head.

"Did I do something to upset you tonight?" he asked.

"Oh no, you were just fine Davis and I really appreciate you doing this for me tonight," she said as she came out of her trance.

"Well what's wrong; you seem so distraught," he said.

"It's something that I really don't care to go into," she responded as she turned her head forward again. Davis wasn't satisfied with her answer, and was determined to find out what was bothering her.

"You know considering all I've been through tonight, it seems that you could at least tell me what's bothering you," he said boldly. He held his breath as he waited for her to respond. He wasn't sure if she was going to tell him or come out of a bag on him. She looked at him again, as her demeanor remained calm. He noticed her eyes had started to tear up and he watched a tear roll down her face. He felt funny as he looked at her. He wanted to do something for her but he didn't know what. Hell, he didn't even know what was wrong. As she watched him, she debated rather or not to tell him why she was feeling so bad. He decided to coax her a little.

"C'mon Kia, one minute you're laughing and reminiscing with an old friend, then once she leaves, you're immediately crying. Now you say it isn't me, so what is it," he concluded.

"Davis, right before Deidra boarded the plane she remembered that she had something to give me. When she reached into her pocket, she pulled out a wedding invitation," Kia said.

"So you think you're loosing a friend to marriage?" he asked.

"No," she responded.

"I just don't understand how she can be getting married and I don't even have a man in my life. I just don't understand how life can be so unfair," she stated.

"Unfair! She's marrying a jerk. You should feel sorry for her," he interjected. Kia looked at him as if he couldn't possibly understand the entire thing. She was really crying at this point.

"Davis, Frank may be a jerk but he definitely loves Deidra. And all I want to know is why can't I find a man who loves me. Someone I can call my own. Someone who is just content spending time with me and would like to spend the rest of their life with me. Someone who cares for me besides my father," she concluded as she lifted a hand up to her face to hide the tears which were flowing down the side of her face.

Davis' eyes began to water now. It hurt him to see this

confident, strong, yet fragile young woman cry. It was perhaps the words that hurt him most. The situation was so
ironic to him. Here she was wondering if there was anyone
out there that loved her and that very person was right there
beside her. Oh he wasn't sure of his feelings for Gail but he
knew that he loved Kia almost from the moment he saw her
do the first newscast. And after their first tutoring session,
there was no doubt in his mind. He just never bothered to
tell her since their worlds were so different. She was a career
woman and he was just a freshman. But now it seemed like
just what she needed to hear. But he couldn't tell her now.
What about Gail? And how would Kia react to it? He was so
confused and just sat in silence, as he looked her. She was
almost bent over the steering wheel now. Here was his
chance. He could get it all off his chest now.

He began to rub her back in an effort to comfort her.
He cleared his throat and was close to making up his mind
to tell her as another question flew through his mind.

"What if Gail would do something similar to what
Kee-Kee did?" He was frantic at this point and that last
thought caused him to back down again.

"Davis," she said as she looked up and continued to cry.

"I'm so sorry about acting like this in front of you," she
stuttered through the tears and heavy breathing. She bent
over again and started to get louder with her crying. That
was it. He had to tell her. If not for her, at least for him.

"Kia, I love you," he said bluntly. He could physically
feel a difference as the words left his mouth. He had never
felt anything like that before. He noticed that her crying
slowed significantly as she looked up at him.

"What did you say," she asked with apprehension. He
took a deep breath as he prepared to say it again. "I said I
love you. I've loved you almost since the day I first saw
you," he said. A silence fell over the car as she looked at
him as if she were trying to figure him out. Then all of a
sudden she broke the silence.

"Oh Davis, you're so sweet," she said as she wiped the tears away with a napkin she managed to find in the side compartment.

Davis looked at her in disbelief. He couldn't understand how she could patronize him at a time like this. He continued to look at her and he knew that she wasn't prepared to take him seriously. He jumped out of the car and fought his urge to slam her door. "Thanks again Davis," she yelled as she put the car in gear and slowly drove off.

Davis stood there for a minute and attempted to calm down. But it didn't work. In fact he got angrier as he thought how silly he must have looked. "What the hell just happened," he asked himself. That was not how it was supposed to go. He kicked the tree that he was standing near out of anger and headed upstairs trying to hold back the tears.

He was so happy to see that his roommate was gone for the night when he reached his room. He definitely did not feel like explaining the tears. As he changed into the tank top and shorts that he usually slept in, he reached to turn on the radio. He reclined on his bed and rested both hands in the back of his head. He stared at the ceiling in an attempt to put himself to sleep. After about forty minutes, he was successful.

Unfortunately, he wasn't able to sleep long. His phone rang shortly after he blacked out. It was Gail on the other end. "How was your evening," she asked in her sexiest voice. His face grimaced as he realized who it was. He was not in the mood for this right now.

"Ah, it was okay, he replied as he composed himself. "I missed you," she said.

"Damn," he mouthed silently to himself as he raised his free hand up to his face. He just did not feel like going through this but he had to remember that she wasn't the one whom had upset him. What could he talk about? How could he bring himself to talk to her now when he was feeling like such a fool? At that moment he remembered his earlier conversation with Mary. Now was a perfect time to go fishing since he had her on the phone. As he continued with his thought, she spoke again.

"I was hoping I could swing by and pick you up in a few minutes and you could spend the rest of the weekend over here," she said cautiously.

"Do you love me?" he asked abruptly as he ignored her last words.

"What?" she questioned.

"Do you love me?" he repeated clearly.

"I'm getting there," she said quickly.

"I'm getting there very fast," she emphasized. Unfortunately this wasn't the answer he was looking for even though it helped him feel better instantly. But he was hoping for some hesitation on her behalf so that he could get an attitude and get off the phone.

Davis sighed through the silence that now existed. His mind was still searching.

"Well are you going to say anything?" she asked softly. He looked up at the ceiling as she spoke.

"Well let me ask you this," he said after sighing again.

"Are you still fucking the dean?" he said with a lot of attitude and emphasis. Gail gasped as he asked the question. There was a noticeable pause that followed.

"How could you ask me something like that?" she said in a high voice.

"Just answer the question Gail," he said in an emotionless voice. She said nothing.

"Yeah, your silence is saying a lot right now," he said as he hung up the phone.

On the other end, the dial tone caught Gail by surprise. She slowly hung up the phone and got out of the chair she was sitting in. She walked across a hardwood floor until she reached a partially opened door. A metal plate was screwed into the door at eye level. It read Dean

Phillips. As she walked in there was a middle-aged man standing near a large wooden desk who was buttoning his shirt. He then reached for his tie and jacket.

"Aren't you going to go to the bathroom and wash up like you usually do," the man asked. She looked up as if his words had shaken her out of a trance.

"No," she responded.

"I don't feel like cleaning up anymore," she said as she dropped back into heavy thought.

"Oh, well suit yourself. Listen, do me a favor and lock up my office when you leave," the man said as he walked out of sight. Gail sat for a couple of minutes more before she walked over to her pantyhose and heels that were sitting near the door.

Back at the dorm, Davis walked into his room carrying his shaving bag after having taken a shower. The lone towel that was wrapped around his waist did very little to protect him from the frigid air that his air conditioner was putting out. He quickly put on his sleeping attire again. As he jumped under his covers, he looked at the clock. He was shocked that it read 2:48 a.m. He fell asleep to jazz soon after.

Davis woke up to a loud knock on the door. He attempted to regain his faculties. He felt terrible. He wondered how long he had been asleep. As he sat up he looked at the digital numbers on the clock. The bright red numbers read 3:52 a.m. He couldn't believe it. He had only been asleep a little over an hour. He heard the knock once again.

"Who the hell could this be?" Had Holly forgotten his keys?" If he had, he was about to get cursed out. He rubbed his eyes as he opened the door.

"What?" he barked to the person standing in front of him. As his eyes focused, his mouth literally hung open when he saw who it was. He rubbed his arm to make sure that he wasn't dreaming. He soon realized that his eyes weren't mistaking him. There she was looking as cute as a button. It was Kia. She had obviously gone home and cleaned herself up and she now had on sandals, shorts, and a T-shirt instead of the dress she wore earlier. The tears had been wiped away too even though he noticed the dark rings around her eyes. And he could smell the soap and the fresh summer air on her.

"Davis, do you mind coming outside to talk so we don't disturb your roommate. Besides it feels very good outside," she said.

"Oh don't worry, my roommate isn't here and I can open a window. C'mon in," he insisted.

"How did you get in the dorm anyway?" he asked as she walked in.

"There's this guy just smoking on the stoop outside. He let me in and told me your room number," she responded.

"Wow, you got lucky, huh?

"No, cause I was prepared to stand outside and call your name all night if I had to," she said.

"Whoa, what's up?" he said as he sat on Holly's bed and motioned for her to sit on his bed.

"Davis you sure have nice feet for a man," she said unexpectedly as she looked down. "Don't be looking at my feet," he said with an embarrassed grin on his face.

"So what brings you by this time of morning," he asked with a more serious tone.

"Well," she said after taking a deep breath.

"I went home and jumped in a hot bath hoping that I would feel better. Of course it didn't work and I realized that I wouldn't feel any better unless I apologized to you. And frankly Davis, I need my sleep so here I am. Hopefully after talking to you, my bed will feel much better," she concluded. Davis listened contentedly.

"I want to apologize to you," she continued.

"I hope I didn't make you feel small or anything like that. I heard what you said and I don't want you to feel embarrassed about it. Honestly, it helped me feel a little better," she said. Davis was now looking at her as if he were hanging onto her every word. She looked back at him as if to let him know that it was his turn to talk. He looked a few seconds longer then he spoke.

"I was hoping you had come by to hear me speak those words again," he said softly. She looked up at him instantly as a silence fell over the room.

"Because I meant what I said. I love you Kia and I'm totally convinced of that," he said.

After hearing this she jumped off the bed and stood in one spot as her face grimaced and one of her hands flew to her face to cover her eyes.

"Davis, please don't do this to me right now?" she said in an agonizing voice. At this point he stood in front of her and laid his hands softly on both of her shoulders.

"Look," he said, "you don't have to say a thing. You can leave right now and I would understand. This is just something that I need you to know. You are loved, I think about you religiously," he concluded. She relaxed her facial muscles and moved her hand down by her side. She began to stare at him. He looked back intensely. He wanted to kiss her but he still didn't have an official sign that she would welcome such a thing. As he continued to look at her he realized how relaxed he felt now that he had spoken the words again. His confidence was beginning to build on account of opening up to her. Neither was willing to break his or her stare. Then Davis slowly reached for her head and cradled it in both of his large palms. He moved in slowly and deliberately and his eyes dared her to push him away. As his lips touched hers, tears formed in his eyes. He took his time and tried to explore every inch of her beautiful mouth with his tongue. She offered absolutely no resistance as a tear ran down the side of her face. As the tear hit the tip of his nose he quickly jerked away.

"I don't want to kiss you if you're unsure," he said.

"Please don't stop," she said as she now grabbed the back of his head.

As they kissed, he slowly turned her around and nudged her backwards on the bed. As she lay flat on her back, she slid her sandals off of her feet. She proceeded to wrap her arms around his back and her legs around his midsection. He could now feel incredible suction from her mouth as she intensified the kiss. So intense in fact, that he had to break away. As he looked at her he could see in her eyes all the signals he needed. He began to cry as she lifted her head in an aggressive fashion to make contact with his lips.

He surveyed the heat that was coming from her especially in her midsection and it caused him to get aroused. Then he quickly broke away from her lips and kissed her cheek, and nose, and then neck. He sucked viciously around her neck. He was enticed by the sweet smell of her freshly cleaned skin. As he sucked her neck, he positioned his body so that he could slide her T-shirt up over her breast. He was totally surprised when the moonlight, which came through the window, fell directly on her beautiful nipple. He couldn't believe that she wasn't wearing a bra.

"Davis, what are we doing?"

"Kia, we're not doing anything if you don't want to. It's just that I can't seem to get close enough to you so I want to be inside of you," he said as he looked down at her. Her eyes were quiet but they were also very inviting. He got up to reach for a condom off the shelf and walked over to the other side of the room to turn off the lamp. He removed his shorts and underwear before he climbed back on the bed. He also helped her remove her shirt and then slowly removed her shorts and her moist panties. He leaned downward and laid his tongue right above the border of her pubic hair and slowly and deliberately licked up until he reached her breast. He felt her tremble as he did this. As he went down to do it again, she spoke.

"Davis I have to tell you that I've only done this once before and it was very embarrassing for me," she declared. As he made his way to her breast again, he stopped and looked up.

"Kia, you couldn't be in a safer place at this very moment," he said as he tore open the condom and put it on. His penis was rock hard and he reached to wipe his eyes dry. Then he carefully reached down and touched her warm and wet vagina so that he could guide himself in. She gasped and reached to wrap her arms around him as he pushed himself inside of her.

Later that morning he awoke to the sound of keys jingling in the lock. It took a second before he remembered that Kia was lying next to him.

"Who's that?" she said in a frantic voice as Davis jumped from the bed and rushed to the door, which was already beginning to open. He got there right before Holly was about to cross the threshold. He caught the door and pushed it back towards Holly.

"Hey what you doing man?" Holly exclaimed in a surprised voice. Davis got the door closed to the point that Holly could only see his mouth and one of his eyes.

"Holly, do me a favor and go down to the lounge and wait until I call you?" Davis instructed.

"C'mon man, stop playing," Holly said as he tried to push the door open.

"Holly, don't make me hurt you. Do like I asked okay," Davis said with a grin on his face. With that, his roommate headed to the lounge.

When Davis closed the door and turned around he saw Kia who was already standing and in the process of getting dressed. After she slid her T-shirt down over her arms she walked over and grabbed one of his baseball caps off the shelf and strategically placed it on her head.

"What you doing with my hat?" he asked in joking

manner.

"Do you expect me to go outside with my hair like this?" she responded. As she walked to the door, he grabbed his shorts and T-shirt and started to put both of them on as she waited. Then they quickly exited the room and descended the stairs. Once they were at her car, she turned to give him a hug and kiss. Afterwards she spoke.

"Will I see you again this weekend?" she asked.

"Hell yeah!" he said in a tone so his answer wouldn't be misinterpreted. She opened the door and started her car. The two said nothing else but bye as she drove off.

When Davis went back inside, he swung by the lounge to pick up Holly. He was about to speak when he noticed his roommate sitting over in the corner with a very worried look on his face.

"Man please tell me you're not mad about what just happened?" Davis said with a smile on his face. Holly looked at him for a second before he said anything.

"Train met me coming back to the dorm this morning," Holly said in a voice that reflected his fear. Davis' face now grew worried as he digested what his roommate said.

"What did he say to you?" he asked.

"He said that he needed his money by the end of the day while he lifted up his shirt so that I could see the gun in his waistline," Holly responded in a numb voice.

"What did you do," Davis continued to investigate.

"Well I just hung up with my cousins in South Carolina," he said as he pointed to the pay phone on the wall. "I don't think they realize how serious it is because they said it would be a few days before they could get here so they told me to stay in my room until then," Holly continued.

"Well I be damned," Davis shouted as he turned to his side and looked up at the ceiling as if he were looking for an answer.

"Y'all muthafuckas ain't gone spoil this awesome

weekend I'm having," he said as he turned to look at his roommate again.

"C'mon, lets go upstairs so we can clean up and go take care of this situation," he said as he motioned to Holly.

"What are we going to do?" Holly asked as he walked out of the lounge behind his roommate.

"I don't know yet, but I'm going to try to end this today," Davis said without even turning around to look at him.

"The question is can you stop your cousins from coming?" Davis continued as he started to mount the stairs.

"Nope, my mother couldn't even keep them from coming now since they know I'm in trouble," Holly responded.

"Damn," Davis said loudly.

21

After getting washed up, the two roommates scampered out of the dorm towards the housing project that sat across the street from the campus. They were headed in the direction in which Holly had had his encounter with Train. The two of them walked in a Laurel and Hardy-like fashion, Davis with a determined and fast paced stride and his chunky roommate literally galloping trying to keep up while attempting to gain eye contact over either of Davis' shoulders while being careful not to trip over anything.

"What cha gonna do man," Holly asked in a voice that struggled to gain oxygen.

"Didn't I tell ya' I didn't know what the hell I was gonna do?" Davis replied without even bothering to look back. It was as if Holly was a pesky little sibling who didn't understand and was only getting in the way.

"Davis, this guy is rough, besides I don't understand why ya' don't wait for my cousins to get here anyway?" Holly shouted in a voice that was really gasping for breath by now. He had literally broken into a trot trying to keep up with his roommate. But just then Davis came to a complete stop causing Holly to crash into his huge back. Something Holly had just said really caught his attention. After peeling himself off the back of Mr. Virginia, Holly was soon staring into the same angry eyes that he had just lost his breath trying to catch a glimpse of just a few moments ago.

"No, that's where ya' wrong Holly, this guy isn't tough, he's a hustler. That's probably something you don't know anything about. But let me tell ya', if he's anything like the hustlers from Augusta then he's very serious about his money and will go through anybody within reason to get it. And believe me roomy when I tell ya' —you are within reason. Now if your cousins are anything like you, they wouldn't know what a small caliber weapon was if it hit them in the face. They probably plan on coming up here and smacking this guy around or something. But let me ask you, have you ever seen a person's head swell because a bullet is lodged in their brain. Well I have," Davis responded before Holly could even answer.

"Let me tell ya' something country boy, it ain't a pretty sight. It takes years before you could stop dreaming about something like that. Now the way I see it," Davis continued as he backed out of Holly's face, "There are two things that could happen here. Number one—your cousins could get the drop on Train and beat the shit out of him. Then they go to jail or face retaliation from his crew. Or Number two, Train could get the drop on them and do what any hustler would to protect his money. I don't know about you but it seems to be a loose—loose situation to me." By this time Davis had started walking again in his frantic pace. Holly just stood there for a while trying to digest the words that were just spoken to him. Then he looked towards his muscular roommate whom was walking ahead of him. He realized at that moment that he had a true friend in Davis Virginia. He soon broke into a sprint trying to catch up to him.

The two of them were about two blocks from where Holly had last seen the hustler. Unfortunately they had to walk past Mary's apartment to get there. As luck would have it, she noticed the two walking towards her place from the window. She quickly stepped outside to greet them as they approached. Davis still had a significant lead on Holly and he was the first to step into her presence.

"Hey Davis, what's up?" she said with a winning smile. She could literally feel the wind across her face as he walked quickly past her without looking in the direction from which he had heard her voice. A few seconds later Holly came jogging by as her face began to look puzzled.

"Don't worry about it sweetie, just go inside and I'll be right back," he said as he, himself, whizzed by.

A few moments later they both came to a halt. They were now standing in front of three guys who were sitting on a porch. Davis' instinct led his eyes to gaze upon the one sitting in the middle. It was a tall wiry guy wearing a black Adidas sweat suit with red stripes and a matching red Kangol hat.

"You Train," Davis barked. The three were so stunned that their bodies jerked. They couldn't believe that this stranger had gotten so close to them without being detected. At that moment the one in the center jumped to his feet and reached in his waistline to withdraw a silver handgun. He kept it pointed at the ground since he noticed that Davis wasn't armed. However the sight of the firearm quickly caused Holly's enraged roommate to come to his senses.

"Yeah, um Train, who the fuck wanna know?" the guy said as he looked Davis right in the eyes. Davis began to speak nervously now as his eyes dropped to Train's side where the gun rested.

"Yo, take it easy man, um just here to settle up with you for my roommate."

"Yo' roommate? Muthafucka I don't even know you, let alone yo' roommate," Train replied. At that moment the sound of running footsteps and panting breath caused everyone to look over Davis' shoulder. It was Holly whom had finally caught up.

"Ooooh, you mean doughboy," Train said as a smile

grew on his face that placed the two gold teeth in his mouth on display. After giving a loud sucking noise from his teeth, the wiry figure spoke again.

"So how ya' planning on settling up fella?" Davis stood there for a while just staring at the gun which he had now determined to be a .38. He raised his hands in a submissive position as he began to speak.

"Now take it easy buddy, um gonna reach in my pocket and pull out the money he owes you okay," Davis said. He didn't dare move until Train nodded his head as if to give the okay. With that, Davis slowly pulled out a wad of bills and reached to hand them to Train. As he looked up at the wiry young man who was still holding the gun, Davis quickly recognized the look in his eyes. The villain was assessing the situation and Davis knew he was about to be shaken down for more. After leveling his head from a slanted and cocked-back position, Train stretched out his hand to grab the money. At that moment a third hand came out from what seemed to be nowhere and snatched the money out of the grasp of both of them.

"Ahh damn," Holly shouted as he recognized who had ran between Davis and Train. By the time all five guys had a chance to focus on the figure that appeared virtually out of thin air, all of their eyes rested on a chubby black woman with blond streaks in her hair with no shoes on her feet. It was Mary. She had obviously became alarmed at the behavior of the two as they passed her house. She had begun running after the two of them and lost her shoes in the process. After the silence from the shock had worn off, it was Mary who was the first one to speak as she stuffed the money in her brazier.

"Davis you ain't giving him shit," she said angrily as she focused on Train. By this time Train had tossed the gun to one of the two guys who were now both standing. Train however had began to smile as he raised his arms in position to receive a hug.

"Baby girl, it's me, what's up, Train said as he inched closer to the angry Mary. By this time she had started walking towards Holly.

"Hey baby what cha doing?" he asked nervously as he read the pissed facial expression that she wore. As she stood in front of her boyfriend, Train, who was now standing just over her left shoulder dropped his hands and rested them on his waist out of confusion. He couldn't believe that she had just walked passed him without giving him a hug. Davis had rested a hand over his face and started rubbing it as if he were trying to remove something. He couldn't believe what was going on. Mary raised her right hand towards Holly's face. As she did this she also outstretched her index finger as if she were pointing at something.

"Is this the muthafucka you been having all of the trouble out of?" she said obviously referring to Train. Holly's silence and stunned face answered her question. He had never seen her this mad before. By this time the index finger was poking him right in the center of his forehead as she began talking again.

"The next time I ask you what's going on you better tell me ya' hear," she said in staggered syllables that were matched by pokes from her finger that caused his head to bounce back and recoil with every other syllable she spoke.

"And yo' ass," she said as she turned around and looked at Train. However Train wasn't about to be embarrassed in front of his fellas.

"Mannn, you betta give me my fuckin money," he said as he cut her off. Mary, not hearing a thing, walked right up to him and got into his chest. "Do you know how much time I did in lock-down because yo' punk ass chose to run past the car and not say shit to me?" she said. Everyone looked intently at her after she released her blast from the past.

"You ever wonder why the police never came looking for yo' ass," she continued.

"Because I never told them shit—and for that I got nine more months," she concluded. By this time Train began to smile again. "Now what I suggest you do is forget about these two and me and be on your way, cause you know what— that case was never closed and I can still play the stool pigeon," she said.

"So what makes you think I won't kill yo' ass right now?" he asked curiously still wearing the smile.

"C'mon Train, as long as we were together, give me a little credit, you steal—you don't kill," she finished. There was a small silence after she made her statement. After that Train fell into laughter as he grabbed her by the back of her head and pulled her in for a kiss across the forehead. After letting her go, he bellowed in laughter.

"Baby girl I knew you was special, that's the reason why I picked you." With that he zipped up his jacket and walked off followed by the other two guys.

Holly, Mary, and Davis left the scene together. They didn't say anything as they walked back. Holly decided to go to Mary's place with her, which suited Davis fine because he didn't feel like being bothered anyway. Even though he had just been face to face with a gun, his thoughts were already on his plans for the day. He couldn't wait to see Kia again. It was almost like last night was a dream. In spite of all that had happened during his freshman year, he couldn't believe the intimacy the two had shared just a few hours ago. Of all the beautiful women he had seen and been involved with, she was definitely the one whom gave him the warmest feelings. After seeing her on the television that first day, he would have never guessed that he would have seen her in real life let alone have her in his dorm room. As he thought about her, he didn't even notice that he had began to walk faster. She's just different, he thought to himself. Unlike other times when he had accomplished a major score like when he first had sex with Kee-Kee, he didn't want to tell anyone about this. Usually when a man has casual sex with someone, it's not complete unless he tells someone. That was half of the conquest. Not this time however. He couldn't care less if no one knew about it. That wasn't the point at all. He only wanted to recreate last night and prove to himself that it was real. He also wanted to know where would they go from there. Would she want to spend time with him or would she write the whole thing off as a mistake. That would be worse than if nothing ever happened at all. His mind could only remember what that first time was like and eventually agonize and collapse trying to hold on to every detail since it would never happen again. He shuttered at the thought.

By this time he had made it to the empty dorm and had walked in. As he passed by the lounge he heard someone call his name. It was Tyrone. The two proceeded to talk right there in the hall.

"Ty what cha doin here?" Davis asked in a desperate attempt to make conversation. The two hadn't really talked in weeks.

"Ya know I live in the city, man um always here," he responded. Davis couldn't help but notice that Tyrone had called his name and ran behind him as if he wanted something.

"What 'chu doin' here in the summer?" Tyrone asked in a voice that was much more inquisitive than Davis'.

"Well I lucked up and got an internship here this summer." Tyrone just looked as if he didn't believe him before he spoke again.

"Oh, okay I get cha." Davis was about to wonder about his behavior then he realized how irrelevant it was. Tyrone had always been a strange character to him. Davis decided to offer up a few more words so that it wouldn't seem as if he was trying to rush off.

"Well I guess Atlanta is a lot different since your boys Fred and Cisco went home for the summer, hunh?"

"Man fuck them, specially ol' punk ass Cisco," Tyrone responded, catching Davis off guard. Davis was now the inquisitive one and he let go a little smirk to show it before he spoke again. "Damn what's all the hostility for Ty?"

"Oh I didn't have a chance to tell you what happened did I?" Tyrone asked after searching his memory.

"N'all, what happened," Davis asked with sheer anticipation. Tyrone began.

"Well you remember that little beating thang with the faggot right," he asked rhetorically.

"Well those two was down in my room having some beers one night about three days after that shit went down. And we was talking right and I forgot how that part of the conversation came up but anyway after they got a few beers in them, Fred said something that got me. What he said was that he had gone down the hall to wait a few minutes until Cisco had the sissy in the room talking that faggot shit. After that ya boy Fred was supposed to bust in the room and the ass whooping was supposed to begin. Well as it turns out, Fred said he got to talking to some dude down the hall and got back to the room about five minutes later than they had planned. So when he finally bust in the room, the faggot was on his knees with his hand on Cisco's zipper." Davis' head jerked back and his eyes grew as a result of the startling news. Tyrone continued.

"So when Cisco saw Fred, he reached down and punched the faggot in his nose and thatís when all the shit started."

"Damnnnnn," Davis exclaimed. "So what did Cisco say after that?" he asked.

"Well Cisco said everything was done the way him and Fred had planned it. Of course Fred denied it and the two of them started fighting right there in my crib. I put both they asses out because it was some ol' gay shit all way round."

"Well I'll be damned," Davis said as his eyes searched

for an explanation. Tyrone definitely didn't give him time to find one. He had something on his mind that he had to clear up.

"Well I sho' ain't expect for you to still be here."

"Why not?" Davis responded.

"Well I saw your sister or cousin, whoever it was come in the dorm about three o'clock last night to pick you up. In fact um the one who told her how to get to your room. I just happened to be sitting outside smoking a joint," he said in an effort to sound cool and not like he was sweating Davis.

"My sister?" Davis mouthed to himself as he tried to figure out what Tyrone was talking about. Then it hit him. Davis was right, Tyrone did want something. He wanted to be nosy. Davis deduced that he must have been the one to let Kia in the dorm last night. He also deduced that his fair-weather friend must have been feeling a little jealous. After all, Kia was extremely attractive and sophisticated and if she wasn't coming to see him then who? By this time it was all Davis could do to hold back a smile. He really wanted to flaunt the fact that the beautiful woman was there to see him last night. He was sensing that competition from Tyrone that he sensed the first semester. It was as if Ty was so anxious to make Davis his friend just so he could keep an eye on him. Like spying on the competition. Now Tyrone was really looking at Davis expecting him to confirm that the woman from last night was indeed a relative.

"No Ty, she wasn't my sister. She's just a friend who came over to talk," Davis finished.

"Talk?"

"Yeah, talk," Davis confirmed. And with that Davis ended the conversation and headed upstairs.

He couldn't wait to call Kia. He jumped right on the phone. Unfortunately Kia was very cold and impersonal, at least Davis thought so. It turns out that she was on the phone long distance and Davis just so happened to interrupt her call. However before she clicked back over she did

express interest in seeing him that day. She made a haphazard attempt to give him directions on how to get there
on the transit system but she spoke too fast for him and
eventually returned to her long distance conversation
before checking to make sure he understood. For a second
Davis thought that she was very rude but it didn't take
long for that feeling to subside. All he knew was that she
said come over and he would make it his goal in life to get
to her today.

Davis was lucky enough to bum a ride from Mary and
Holly about two hours later. They were headed to the mall
and Mary didn't mind going out of her way. She was ecstatic about driving her car now since it had a new muffler.
During the drive Mary said very little about the incident
that had transpired earlier that morning. Obviously she
and her boyfriend had discussed all they needed to discuss
a few hours earlier.

After he was dropped off, Davis decided to wait
around the corner from the apartment number that Kia
had given him just so he could catch his breath. His heart
was beating extremely fast and he knew that he must have
a look of worry in his face. He tried to think of different
things to calm down before he knocked on the door. He
stood out there for about three more minutes before he fell
into laughter. He was imagining Tyrone's facial expression
when he would watch the local news and see Kia reporting and eventually put two and two together. With that he
strolled right up to the apartment.

Kia answered the door in a huge T-shirt with her alum-
nae logo stamped across the front of it. The shirt fell over her
hips and part of her thighs, which were draped with black
stretch leggings. This slightly aroused him because he could
only imagine the sight that was covered by the shirt. Her
hair was thrown back in a ponytail. But what was most
interesting to him was the fact that she was bare footed. Her
feet were well lotioned and the tips of her feet were accent-

ed with his favorite—candy red nail polish.

Since she was on the phone, she motioned for him to come on in. Once inside he quickly took a seat on the couch. He recognized this piece of furniture. This was the sofa bed that he had helped her pick out at Jennifer Convertibles. As he sat back to relax he watched her as she paced back and forth while still talking on the phone. At one point, she paced over towards him and stood over his shoulder as he sat on the edge of the couch. She then proceeded to rub his head in an affectionate manner. She did this as if to say that she was sorry for ignoring him at the present time. After that, the same feeling that he had just fought back a few moments ago resurfaced. Now he was glad that she was still on the phone. He needed a little time to relax.

Fifteen minutes had passed by and now he could see her anxiety to get off the phone. He was happy at that sight and wished the person on the other end would let her go. He had been too nervous to listen in on the conversation but from the little that he did hear, he could tell that this was a distressed friend on the other end. Kia ended her pacing by taking a seat— Indian style right beside him on the couch. In fact her beautiful toes were touching his thigh. He became so nervous that he started chuckling. She looked at him with a raised eyebrow as if to ask what was so funny.

Fortunately he could hear the conversation winding down. Kia quickly said good bye and pushed the button on the cordless phone.

"Ohhhhh," she exclaimed as she lifted her head to the ceiling appearing to be stretching.

"I am so sorry Davis, but that was one of my girlfriends from college. I have been on the phone with her for the last three hours. She's really upset because she's debating on whether or not to leave her man." "I hope it was Deidre then," he said. Kia immediately started laughing which caused him to laugh. It helped him relax which was important since he now had her undivided attention. But then he noticed that she was no longer laughing with him. She had now rested an elbow on her knee and the corresponding fist was now supporting her chin. She was watching him as if he were some type of original masterpiece. He cleared his throat as he looked at the floor for a second in search of a response. By the time he looked at her again she was in the process of removing her hand from her chin, licking her lips ferociously, and leaning in his direction. She gave him a passionate open-mouthed kiss which melted away all of his tension. The two of them just sat there playing in each other's mouths for about half an hour. Little did Davis know that this would be the beginning of a very lazy and intimate weekend.

Ten days passed and Davis found himself on an emotional roller coaster. He had such good times with Kia that the time he spent away from her was pure agony. It turned out that he could only see her on weekends since the bulk of her reporting was done on the eleven o'clock news. The weekdays were pure torture. However he did find a little comfort in his internship.

While working a Bell Labs, he found an interest in physics that he hadn't managed to find during his freshman year. All of the permanent employees whom worked in the lab with him were constantly praising his skills. He was also doing a lot of practical applications, which beat schoolwork anytime. This particular day seemed to be like any other. He would get off at three and take an hour train ride back to campus. The ride would go by quickly since he would spend his time wondering what Kia was doing at any precise moment. While walking home he would stop at the grocery store where his roommate worked and purchase something to eat. Once in the dorm, a hot relaxing shower was usually followed by lonely hours of watching television in anticipation of seeing Kia's report. Then he would fall asleep.

21

The next day Davis was quick to exit the building at 3:05 p.m. He always liked beating everyone else out, knowing that if he didn't, he would run into co-workers who would always offer him a ride. Since most of those people were white and older he knew that the conversation would be awkward. Besides, what did he have to rush home to? Unless it was Friday, he didn't have a chance at seeing Kia.

As he walked through the parking lot at a brisk pace heading for the train station, he passed by a woman sitting in a parked car. He noticed her briefly but was careful not to stare. As he continued walking, he couldn't help but think that something was familiar about her. If not her, at least the car. As he kept walking, he heard a female's voice call him from behind. After turning around he noticed that it was the woman whom he had just passed in the parked car. She had gotten out now and he started to approach her slowly still trying to figure out who she was. It didn't take him long. He stopped walking as soon as he realized who the stranger was. By now she had started walking towards him.

"I'm sorry to meet you at your job, but I just had to talk to you," the woman said. His mouth was almost hanging open; he had never seen her look so disheveled.

"How are you?" he spoke the only words that came to

mind.

"Well, I've been better," she responded. The two were now standing face to face in the parking lot. He could see the dark rings around her eyes from either a lack of sleep or a lot of crying.

"You know I thought I'd be okay once I saw you again but I can already feel myself wailing up. So please forgive the tears," she said as her shoulders hunched over and she drew a handkerchief up to her face. He had never seen anyone more in need of a shoulder to cry on. He wanted to oblige but how would she take it considering the last words he had spoken to her. He just stood there in the interim, attempting to let her recover from her crying. But she didn't, in fact a deep guttural sound followed her next deep breath and he knew it was time for him to rush in.

With a quick step he was standing right in front of the woman and she was positioning her head into his chest in an effort to accept his support.

"Gail, I'm so sorry about this," he said as she started to take those quick breaths that usually signaled the end of a crying episode. As he looked over her shoulder, he noticed one of his coworkers exiting the building and staring intently at the two of them embraced. He convinced her to get in the car and the two drove away.

Ms. Upshaw had finally stopped crying altogether by the time they had reached the sandwich shop that they had agreed to attend. It really helped her to put her head on his chest again. As for Davis, he was trying to sum up the situation. He knew that their last conversation wasn't on friendly terms but he couldn't remember exactly what he had said. Hell he hadn't even thought about Gail since everything had happened with Kia. But seeing her again after about ten days really bought back some warm emotions. Besides, he had absolutely nothing to do until work the next morning.

As they waited for their sandwiches, they carried on a

little light conversation. Davis was listening intently as she spoke slow and steadily while staring down at her iced tea on the table. This was all so she wouldn't burst into tears again. He could tell that she was in a lot of pain and he was slowly realizing that it was because of him. As the discussion progressed, he learned that she hadn't been to work since they last talked on the phone. She wasn't even dressed, as sharply as she normally did and as he listened to her stumble over her words, he felt increasingly guilty. He couldn't believe that he was the cause of all this. He kept waiting for her to say that she had a relative somewhere that was gravely ill. That would account for some of the crying but she never did. Unfortunately he couldn't tell that she was starting to come to life again right there in front of his eyes. In spite of her cotton jogging suit, in spite of her un-permed hair, the bloodshot eyes and the ever present handkerchief, Abigail Upshaw was starting to warm up again.

"Ya' know Davis, I haven't been in love in a long time," she started.

"And I didn't say that to say that I'm in love with you right now. The truth is that I don't know one way or another. The one thing that I do know is that I care for you deeply. Now when you asked me, in a very blunt manner I might add, if I was still fucking the dean my heart literally fell to my stomach. The irony is that I was calling you from his office at that moment," she said as he fought to suppress the surprise in his face.

"After I had finished that revolting act, all I could think about was coming to get you and lay up under you after taking a warm shower. I knew I would have felt so much better. But instead, you said something that made me feel much, much worse. And at first, I was too pissed at you for hurting my feelings like that. Later I realized that you delivered just what I needed and that was verbal slap in the face. So even though I don't know what possessed you to say what you said, I know that I have to thank you for it. As of that moment, I vowed to never let a man take advantage of me again, even if it does mean remaining single for the rest of my life," she concluded.

Davis knew that he was now sitting under a spotlight. He knew he had to say something and he was trying to gather his thoughts.

"Please say something," she pleaded, "that was hard enough." He stared intensely at her as he sat up and cleared his throat. "Well, I would start by saying that I am sincerely sorry. I lashed out at you because I was facing a difficult issue at the time of your call. I would have never talked to you like that under normal circumstances," he said.

"The one thing I did mean to do was talk to you about your promiscuity with that jerk and how he takes advantage of you. Gail you are a very lovely woman both inside and out. Hell you're beautiful just because you're a black persistent female. You don't have to settle for shit," he. exclaimed as the passion started to build in his voice which caused the tears to build in her eyes.

"Now I didn't say anything before because I thought—who the hell was I to be a nineteen year old kid talking to a thirty year old woman. But you know what, I care about you a great deal and it wouldn't be me if I didn't express myself on that issue," he concluded. By this time her tears were really flowing by now and the heavy panting had begun. But it was different now. The tears were those of joy and relief and she just couldn't stop them at that moment. At that instant, Davis got out of his seat and walked around to her side of the table. After dropping to both knees right beside her, he guided her head onto his biceps. He didn't care how many people were around them; he just wanted to comfort her. This caused a floodgate of tears. He had no idea how much she had missed him up to this point. She didn't even know herself until she saw him again. The tears now were those of total joy and relief. She only wanted him to touch her again.

After about ten minutes, Gail was able to pull herself together again and decided to go to the rest room. Davis had the waiter wrap the sandwiches up and the two decided to leave. He thought it would be best if he drove just in case she had another crying attack.

Soon the two of them were pulling up on Lawshe Street, the street that separated the dorm and the projects. He parked the car and turned off the engine. For some reason, he didn't feel like now was the time to leave. He looked over at her and tried to make out her facial expression in the dark. The darkness camouflaged her face well and an occasional sniff from her nose was the only proof that he had that she was over there.

"Are you feeling any better?" he asked in an attempt to spark some conversation.

"You have no idea how much better I feel," she responded.

"Even though I made a fool of myself, today was something that I really needed," she continued. He responded, "Now c'mon baby, you didn't make a fool of yourself." His statement caught both of them by surprise. He could tell as he looked over at her. His eyes were adjusting to the light and he could see her much better now.

"Damn it," he said to himself. He didn't mean to call her baby, it totally slipped.

Gail's entire thought process began to change. In that brief instant in which he had used the term baby, her goals changed from trying to regain acceptance, to trying to gain affection. He let it be known, rather consciously or subconsciously, that he still had feelings for her.

"Now his ass is in trouble," she thought to herself. She knew just what buttons to push from that point and she started mentally preparing her strategy.

The first step was taking inventory. She knew that there were only three things she needed: her finger nails, her feet, and her lips. She knew how to work each one to his satisfaction. She had done it before.

"Davis," she said as she reached over and grabbed his biceps as if to gain his attention, "I'm totally sorry about bothering you today." After she released his arm, she carefully and deliberately drug her quarter inch nails down to his elbow. This immediately gained his attention. After removing her hand, she returned back to her original sitting position in the car. He tried to speak in a way that would hide his curiosity.

"Gail, I told you that's okay, besides I'm the one who should be apologizing."

"It was just hard for me," she continued. "Ya' know, I had gotten used to doing certain things with you. Things like playing footsie." He nearly jumped as he felt her smooth feet push his pant leg up. He didn't even hear her moving her leg over to his side of the car. Her smooth foot pushed up towards his calf muscle. He shuttered inside as he thought of times in the past when she played games with her feet. But what was she doing now.

Surely this wasn't a calculated move, he thought to himself.

If this was, that meant that everything that she had done today was a planned attack. Naaaah, she's not that good of an actress he continued thinking.

"She must be just caught up in her own emotions. Once she goes a little too far, I'll just have to jump out of the car," he concluded.

For the most part, he was right. Gail had certainly not been acting earlier that day. But now she was definitely not caught up in her emotions— she was caught up in him. His smooth back that she loved to grab when the two of them used to make love. His many grunts, his rhythmic pumping motion which would always bring her to orgasm. That's what she was caught up into. Besides if he would reject her right now, she could always say that she got caught up in the heat of the moment because she knew that's exactly how he was thinking. In addition to all of that, she simply loved to play this game with him. He was the first male that she had learned to do this with. Before, she would always put herself out there as an object and let a man have his way simply because she thought it would better her future. But that wasn't the case with this young buck. He had nothing to offer her in terms of a career. In fact, in her thirty plus years, this was the first male with whom she took the aggressor's role. It was totally exciting to her. She would later learn that this aggression would stay with her for the rest of her life and her sex life would be a hundred times better off because of it.

As she continued to caress his leg with gentle rubbing motions of her feet, she noticed that he wasn't putting up any resistance whatsoever. However the car was quiet which in turn made the mood somewhat tense. She remedied this situation by quickly turning the ignition of the car a quarter turn and hitting the power button on her car stereo. The delightful sounds of Ellis Marsalis were soon filling the car.

Gail then proceeded to lift his massive hand from his lap and drew it to her soft lips and kissed it intently. She had now used three of her major weapons and he knew that he was in trouble. After three additional moist pecks from her lips, he decided that he would have to exit the car in a hurry if need be. Dee Virginia's poor baby boy was a step behind again. Just as he was grabbing the door handle, Gail was already in the middle of her next step. Without any warning, she had quickly and precisely guided his hand down to the vaginal area outside of her sweat pants. He froze instantly. His hand sat there forever, as it seemed to Gail. This was the moment. Did he want her as much as she wanted him right now or would he just exit the car out of frustration? Then, finally she felt his hand begin to move. But it moved incredibly slowly. Would the hand dive in for more or would it retreat altogether?

Davis was prepared to pull the hand away but he just couldn't. He was torn between leaving and staying. He eventually pulled his right hand away much to her disappointment. But then she noticed him moving. He was about to get out of the car when something hit him. He grew still again in an effort to figure out what it was. He didn't have to wonder for long though. It was a very pleasant aroma that he had definitely smelled before. Gail had become very excited and the scent of her vaginal moisture began escaping the boundaries of the cotton sweat pants. The smell left him paralyzed for a moment as he started to think of the possibilities. Gail on the other hand was prepared to call it quits and had withdrawn her foot massage in the process. But just then, Davis repositioned himself in the car seat so that he could get closer to her. With his left hand, he reached across his body and forcefully dove into her panties. The move caught her totally off guard but she quickly participated by spreading her thighs as widely as she could. She gasped for breath frequently as his large fingers waddled around in the thick juices that she was producing. Her head swung wildly from side to side on the headrest as his rubbing motion between her legs picked up speed. She was seconds from an orgasm right there on the spot when he unexpectedly withdrew his hand.

"I can't do this," he yelled.

"Baby what's wrong?"

"I feel like I'm taking advantage of you," he responded. She was pissed at this statement. She wanted to explain to him that if anyone was being taken advantage of, it was him but she knew that would have been detrimental to her goal of getting him to fuck the shit out of her right there. Trying to reason with him wouldn't have been very good either. All it would do was consume valuable time. She was hot. She was ready. And she knew that she cared for this young man. The time that would be spent trying to reason with him could better be used trying to reach a climax.

She thought frantically about what she could do to pick things up again real quickly. Then it hit her. She instantly calmed herself down. After reaching into the glove compartment to grab a condom, she quickly reclined her seat as far as it would go. Davis looked on intently. With one quick motion, she arched her back and slid her pants and underwear down to her ankles. Then she leaned back until her head was almost in the back seat. With another calculated move she swabbed her right index finger on the inner wall of her labia. She then took the finger, which was now dripping with her bodily secretions and touched the tip of his nose. She lightly drug her finger from the tip of his nose to his upper lip down over both lips and eventually to his chin. Then she calmly pulled her hand away until it was resting by her side. Poor Davis was completely stuck. He had to smell it, taste it, or both. He didn't have a chance. His erection was so intense that he had no choice but to snatch the condom from her lap and quickly put it on. Once he was undressed and ready he pounced on top of her.

Once in position, he just looked at her. She did the same. They both knew what was coming next and they were both drunk with anticipation. After making a haphazard attempt to pull himself, he slid his hand down between both of their bodies so that he could guide himself in. As he did this, Gail slowly repositioned herself so that she could wrap her legs around his back and receive every thing that he had to offer. Once she felt his penis resting at the lips of her sex organ, she noticed that he looked up at her one last time for approval. By this time, her eyes were more inviting than they had ever been before and he knew he had the permission that he wanted. Then with one slow and deliberate thrust of his massive frame, he felt himself on the edges of her warm and slippery walls.

"Aahhhh uhhhhh," she screamed as her head moved forward to the point that she could lodge her teeth into his chest out of ecstasy.

It was exactly twenty-three minutes later when the two emerged from the vehicle. They both got out on the passenger side. Davis was preparing to go upstairs and Gail was simply headed to the other side of the car so that she could get in the driver's seat and drive herself home. But as soon as they got out, they were approached by two figures from the dark. Davis' adrenaline was about to kick in when he noticed that the two people were Mary and Holly.

Holly was leading Mary by the hand. "Man guess what," Holly said as Davis noticed the sniffling coming from Mary. He knew that she was crying and he quickly asked what was wrong. "Man them bastards fired Mary," he exclaimed. The words froze Gail who had made her way around to the other side of the car and was about to get in.

"You're bullshitting," Davis said loudly.

"What for?" he asked. Holly shook his head from side to side before answering, "For dating a student at The University." The words drew a silence from Davis. Holly made a suggestion.

"Let's all get in the car and I can tell you all about it."

"No," Davis and Gail shouted loudly and simultaneously. They couldn't imagine anyone getting in that car after what they had just finished doing.

"Davis, I have to go. I'll call you tomorrow after work," Gail said as she jumped in the car and drove off. The scene was shocking to her since she surmised that she was dating a student as well. In addition to that, she hadn't been to work in nine days. She was nervous as she drove home.

Holly and Davis walked Mary home. She was visibly upset. Davis knew exactly what The University meant to her future plans. He became angry as he thought about it. They all set in Mary's living room as she cried herself to sleep. They both began to brainstorm as to what they could do to help her. They even went as far as to pull out the handbook that Mary had received in her employee orientation. However, they didn't see anything that they could use to help her.

After Holly put his girlfriend to bed, he locked up her apartment and he and Davis headed for the dorm. They didn't say a word as they walked. They knew that there was nothing that they could do for her. Holly felt bad. He knew he was the reason that she had lost her job.

Once in their room, they both quietly got ready for bed.

"Damn you stink," Holly exclaimed unexpectedly to his roommate.

"Shut up," Davis responded. He wasn't offended because he knew exactly why he smelled.

"And what have you been eating, doughnuts," Holly asked.

"No, why you say that?" Davis asked with a puzzled look on his face.

"Looks like some glaze or something on your lips," Holly responded. Davis licked his lips to investigate. As soon as he did, he could instantly taste Gail. With that, he jumped up and grabbed his toiletries and ran to take a shower.

23

It was a Friday evening in Atlanta. It was a lazy summer afternoon as the setting sun created a tranquil mood. The wind caused all the leaves on the trees to dance. The smell was definitely one of summer time. The sky was a golden color and it was completely devoid of clouds. Even the people whom were sitting on their porches were quiet and restful and for the most part just motioning their wrists back and forth with whatever object that could mimic a fan in the slightest. It was much too nice to be inside under an air conditioning unit. These were the people Davis noticed as he walked from the train station to the dorm after getting off of work. Even as he crossed the Spelman parking lot, he noticed that it was empty for the most part except for a few summer school students who were also taking advantage of the weather by sitting either in or on their open -doored cars tuned to the local radio stations. No one appeared to be in a rush. No one appeared stressed, except for him. In spite of this gorgeous day that he would normally enjoy, his thoughts were focused on the two women in his life. He wondered what to do this weekend. It seemed only natural to go and see Gail after the escapade in the car that Wednesday night in addition to the two hours on the phone the following night. But on the other hand, this was the weekend, which meant Kia wouldn't have to work. He really wanted to see her but what could he tell Gail?

It was about five minutes after six when he climbed the stairway to his floor. As soon as he got to his hallway he heard his phone ringing which caused him to break into a frantic sprint. After almost falling over the bed, he spoke the normal greeting into the phone.

"Hey, how ya' been doing," a soft, sultry, and relaxed voice came over the phone line. He instantly recognized it as Kia's. His eyes squinted as his cheeks grew so big that the receiver was literally raised off of his face. He was so happy to hear her voice. It was so quenching after he had thirsted for her all week. But he had to compose himself.

"I've been okay," he responded.

"What are ya' doing?" he returned.

"Oh, I'm just sitting here listening to Anita Baker, enjoying a nice white wine and wondering why you don't have your ass over here yet," Kia answered. Davis nearly screamed inside. He could imagine the scene. She was probably in a reclined position on her couch with all the blinds closed and the wineglass in her hand. He could hear that she was already tipsy. There was only one question now.

"What are you wearing?" he asked in a deliberate tone.

"A T-shirt," she answered in a sophisticated and methodical tone. She knew that T-shirts that hung just below the waist in a teasing fashion just drove him wild.

"Now will you hurry and make your way over here mister!" she continued.

"I'm on my way," he responded as they ended the conversation. He wished that he could fly over there. Anything would be faster than the train. Besides, he knew that he would have a wonderful erection until he got to her. But at the same time, they both knew that she was in no condition to come and get him.

After freshening up in the bathroom, Davis walked back down the hall and to his room. As he was about to enter, he caught sight of Holly coming up the stairs.

"What'cha doin' off work so early?" he asked Holly.

"Man, Mary called me at the store. She was crying up a storm. So I need to go over there and make this weekend a good one for her." Davis didn't have much to say. He wished he hadn't even asked. He felt so helpless. It was even worse now that he knew Mary and knew her plans for returning to school. But there was nothing he could do to help her and he hated that.

As Davis placed his toiletries back on the shelf, Holly called Mary to let her know that he was on his way over. As soon as he hung up the phone, it rang again. As Holly waited for the traditional second ring, Davis' cheeks grew with anticipation. He could picture Kia on the other end waiting to ask why he hadn't left yet. Unfortunately the clamorous second ring brought an unforeseeable scary thought with it.

"Oh shit!" he thought to himself. He hadn't heard from Gail today. As his eyes grew big and his lips shrunk into a small circle he looked at Holly.

"Look, if that's Gail, tell her that I went home for the weekend. Ya' hear me." Holly's eyes scanned the room as if they were looking for a reason as to why his roommate had such a demonic look on his face and was now talking in such a sober tone.

"Okay," Holly stated as his eyes gave up their search. Then he proceeded to pick up the phone after the third ring. Sure enough it was Gail and Holly repeated the words that were just spoken to him and soon hung up the phone. By this time Davis was out in the hallway while still looking in as if to be sure the message was delivered correctly.

"I appreciate it dawg," Davis stated in a voice that was now empty of the apprehension that it contained just seconds ago. This confused Holly even more and he shook it off as Davis closed the door behind him.

Soon he was knocking on Kia's door. He knocked a

couple of times before she finally answered. She stood there almost posing for him. He took his time looking at her too. Her hair now contained a slight bit of a dark red color, which he would learn as she bragged later cost about $75 dollars. He loved the way that the highlights bought out the brown in her eyes. As his sight slid down her voluptuous body, her bra-less breasts were peeking through the T-shirt akin to toddlers looking out of a cracked door trying to steal any chance they could to run out and play. When his vision continued to descend, his mind began to wonder what was more fascinating, her powerful chocolate thighs or the mystery under the shirt. As he grew curious as to whether or not she wore any panties, she reached down and tugged at the bottom of the shirt a few times as if she were about to raise a window shade. This caused his eyes to grow large with curiosity. At that point she removed her hand from her shirt and reached to grab his penis through his pants. She wanted to know exactly how her appearance had excited him. As soon as her hand felt the bulge between his legs, she knew that the mirror in her bathroom wasn't lying when it told her that she looked very sexy. With her other hand, she reached to grab his cheeks and giggled as she did so.

"You're so precious", she said as she grabbed his arm and led him inside.

To Davis' surprise, the two didn't have sex right away. Instead, Kia put away the zinfandel and threw on what she considered to be her favorite movie - Mahogany.

"Boy I just love that damn Billy D. Williams. Why can't more men be like his character?" she asked. Davis must have assumed it to be a rhetorical question because he didn't bother to answer. Instead, he attempted to get more comfortable in his position, which was lying between her legs with the back of his head in her chest. The two were resting comfortably on the couch.

Davis couldn't pay much attention to the movie. He

was glowing on the inside because he was so happy to be with her. His glow didn't last too long though because Kia soon got up to use the bathroom. She took a little while and when she got back to the couch Davis was still sitting up waiting to resume his position of resting on top of her.

"Boy these things are uncomfortable," she said as she stood in front of him.

"What things?" he asked without breaking his stare at the television. He was now into the movie.

"These things," she said with a little anger in her voice at the fact that she couldn't get his attention. As she made her statement, she quickly reached under her shirt and pulled down the burgundy panties that she was wearing. Davis caught a glimpse of what she was doing and by the time he turned his head to get a better view, the underwear was draping her feet. She then slowly stepped away from the constraints of the garment in a totally seductive fashion. She put her candy red toenail polish on display as she bent her second foot in an alluring fashion attempting to free it as she had done the first one. When both feet came to rest on the beige carpet, he took a moment to marvel at them. They looked delicious as the chocolate of her shiny, well lotioned skin and the candy red brilliance of her toenails seemed to be highlighted as they rested in contrast against the light beige shade of the carpet. After getting an eyeful for his sight and imagination, he finally looked up at her. They stared at each other for a few seconds before simultaneously bursting into laughter at the artificial sexual tension that had been created by the zinfandel. As she laughed, she took her position again of lying up under his athletic frame.

He tried to concentrate on the movie again. It was extremely difficult though because the smell of her now filled the air. The aroma of her cleaned vagina filled his nose and was about to pull out the animal in him. He would learn later in life that there was a fine line between the aromas of a carefully cleaned female sexual organ and one that wasn't so clean. He would also learn that as long as the female organ was immaculate, the emission of the pheromones caused his blood to boil.

He continued to lie there as she shifted slightly every now and then trying to find a comfort zone. He thought he was imagining things when every time she moved the smell got more intense. By now the back of his head was down by her pelvis. At one point the scent was so intoxicating to him that he actually closed his eyes to concentrate on it while at the same time taking a huge breath in an attempt to pull in as much of the scent molecules as he could. Once he realized what he had done, Davis could only hope that she hadn't noticed. But she had noticed and began smiling as a result of it. He tried to concentrate on Diana Ross in the movie but there was no use. A minute later, he subconsciously took another deep whiff. This time his body began to tremble as he exhaled. This caused him to abruptly sit up and turn and look at her. She looked at him in astonishment and with concern.

"What's wrong," she asked. He didn't answer. He just stared at her. She stared back with curiosity until she realized what was wrong with him. She smiled as she realized that she had pushed every button that he had. Her smile quickly turned into slight laughter as she proceeded to open up and to feed him. He watched like a savage beast as she repositioned her legs in an inviting fashion. He dove into her. As the pallets of his tongue glided effortlessly across her warm and moist insides, he could hear the laughter melt into soft pleasure filled moans. These moans grew louder and more intense as his licking grew more pleasurable. Her sounds would have caused envy in any woman who would have heard them. Without lifting his head out of her, he gripped both of her smooth thighs with his massive hands positioned her body at an angle so that he could rest his knees on the floor while lunging his tongue into her. At this she threw her hands in the air as if to beg for more and mercy at the same time. Finally she stabilized one foot on the floor and flung the other over the back of the couch so as to make his job easier.

It was 2:49 a.m. when Davis woke up. He found himself on the floor with a sheet spread over his naked body and a pillow from the couch placed carefully under his head. He was puzzled though. Why was he on the floor alone? Searching his memory, he recalled the potent hour plus of lovemaking he had done with Kia but where was she now? At that moment he heard what sounded like sniffling. He followed the sound to what must have been the bathroom in the master bedroom. He found Kia sitting on the edge of the tub with both hands over her face. She was startled once she looked up and saw him. Once she did look up, he could see that her face was flooded with tears.

"Baby, what's wrong," he asked with deep sincerity. She attempted to answer but nearly choked. Davis reached for some tissue, then set beside her and put his arm around her in an effort to comfort her. After holding her tight for a few minutes, she finally calmed down to the point that she was able to talk.

"Now Kia, tell me what's wrong.

"Who are you?" she asked with a puzzled look on her face.

"What'chu mean?" he responded.

"How did you get here?" she continued with her questions as if she hadn't even heard his response.

"What'cha mean, here in your apartment?" Davis asked. He was more confused now. He was worried that she may not have been okay.

"No, I mean how did you get to this point in my life? I vowed never to let a man get this close. I don't even remember how you got here," she said. She was still looking at Davis and her face was filled with confusion and tears. She was just as confused as he was.

"I mean I woke up a few minutes ago right beside you. I replayed the love that we made in my head and shook, almost violently, until I nearly came again. That's just not supposed to happen. And I know that it's not just a physical thing. The only thing I can't recall is when did you sneak in— how the hell did I come to care for you so much?" she finished. Davis just stood there. He was in deep thought. It would be a few years before his young mind could comprehend the power of the statement that she had just made. As for now, it was all he could do to stop from smiling. To him it was an awesome compliment that she had just given him. Hell, he wanted to pat himself on the back. Although he didn't have a real grip on her dilemma, he could appreciate the seriousness in her tone and in her tears.

"Baby, I'm not sure how I got this close to you but I do know that I am the luckiest man alive right now," he stated. As she continued with the weeping and the sobbing, she spoke again.

"Ah c'mon Davis, this night wasn't much more than sex to you- admit it." His head jerked as he focused in on her. He couldn't believe what he had just heard.

"What the hell did you say?" he asked in a violent tone that caused her to look up at him.

"You think this shit is just sex to me?" he asked with much sincerity. He then got on his knees in front of her and held both of her hands in front of him.

"Baby let me tell ya' something," he said as he peered into her eyes.

"I hate hard situations, in fact I try my best to stay away from them if I can. Believe me when I tell you that making love to you is one of the hardest things I have ever done. You know why, because even though I may be enjoying the hell out of it, the deepest regions of my being are wondering if this will be the last time that I will get to be that intimate with you. Will this be the last time that I get to lay you down and feel your soul? It scares me just not knowing the answer to that question. Do you have any idea what it's like to feel two distinct and opposite emotions at the same time such as fear and love?"

"Yes," she said excitedly.

"Don't you understand Davis, those are exactly the two emotions that I'm dealing with," she professed. After she spoke a silence fell over the room. Davis turned and faced the wall. He rubbed his head as if he were searching for an answer.

"You know what I don't understand," Davis said as he broke the silence.

"As self reliant and independent as you are, you of all people should be running around looking for love. Try this one; try that one, and whichever one doesn't work, well fuck him. You know why, because you're Kia fuckin' Brent. You drive yourself, anywhere you want to go. You pay your own way. Shit, you even take out your own trash—just so you don't have to ask a sorry ass nigga to do it for you. So if I don't care about taking this plunge, why should you care? If it don't work out, you of all people have the strength to be without a man. You also have the independence to wait patiently until the next serious prospect comes along, " he concluded.

Kia was confused. He had a valid point. It just wasn't that simple though.

"Davis I need to be alone right now. If you don't mind, would you just sleep on the sofa and I'll take you home in the morning," she pleaded. He looked at her as if he were searching for the seriousness in her last statement. Once he found the earnestness, he just sighed and went to climb on the sofa.

By 7:00 a.m. the next morning, the two had climbed into her car and were on their way to campus. The ride was a quiet one. He really wanted to ask her questions but he didn't want to seem like a wuss. Although he was totally confused about what was going on and what she was going through, he had to keep some shred of masculinity and not ask her anything right now. He needed her to think that he didn't care.

As the little black car pulled up in front of the dorm, Davis grew even more nervous. It didn't seem as if she was going to walk him to the dorm like she occasionally did. This frightened him.

"Does this mean it's over?" he asked himself. When the car came to a complete halt, the two just sat there for a second. Neither looked at the other. Kia was hoping that he wouldn't make this any harder and just get out of the car and wait for her call a couple of days later. She wasn't that fortunate though. After about twenty seconds of silence, Davis decided to suspend his masculinity and pleaded with her to explain herself again.

"Davis please have a little compassion for me and give me a few days to deal with this," she begged. Her last remark caused him to feel a little selfish and he graciously did as she requested.

Davis ran into an excited Holly whom was leaving for Mary's as he arrived back at home. Once Davis made it to the door, Holly grabbed him by the shoulder and looked at him.

"Davis, I will never be able to thank you for all you have done for me lately," Holly said with an exuberant smile. Davis, who really wasn't in the mood for games at this point, calmly replied—

"What are you talking about Holly?"

"Well your girl Gail just called and she told me to tell Mary that she could report back to work tomorrow, say she had worked everything out. Plus the University has enrolled Mary in their preliminary S.A.T course and they are going to waive her fee for the examination in the fall," he concluded. Although he was confused, Davis had to admit that this was good news to him.

"Did Gail say how she got all of this done?" Davis asked.

"No," Holly responded. "But she does want you to call her as soon as you get in." Davis hurried to the phone so he could do just that.

Gail was noticeably chipper when she answered the phone. She got even more excited after she found out that it was Davis on the other end.

"Ya' mind telling me what it is that my roommate is rambling about?" he wasted no time in asking her.

"Nothing, I just got that sweet child her job back, that's all."

"How did you do that?" he inquired.

"Oh, I just had a talk with my friend the dean," she responded. Davis' end of the phone went totally silent. After about fifteen seconds of soundlessness, Ms. Upshaw spoke again.

"Davis don't worry, I didn't do anything with him except for talk." There was a noticeable sigh from him after she said that. After he collected his thoughts again, Davis spoke.

"I can't imagine that selfish bastard doing anything too nice for you, so how did you get him to do that?"

"Well I guess you can say that I'm blackmailing him right now as we speak." Davis began to smile after hearing her last words. He finally had confidence that Gail's metamorphosis was complete. After hearing that, he decided to move the conversation elsewhere. Lord knows he needed to get his mind off of Kia.

"So ahhh—what are you so happy about?" he asked.

"Well I guess you can say I'm celebrating my independence," she responded.

"What'cha mean by that?".

"Well, I got fired today," she said bluntly.

"What, from the University?" he exclaimed loudly.

"Yep,"

Davis let the receiver fall down to his neck as he looked to the ceiling and mouthed the words, "Could you help me with these crazy women today?" After dealing with Kia earlier, he just couldn't understand how Gail could be happy about losing her job.

"So Gail, help me understand this," he started.

"You mean to tell me that you used your pull to get the job back of a woman whom you barely know but you didn't try to get your own job back?"

"Yep," she again exclaimed enthusiastically.

"Explain," Davis demanded. He was tired of trying to figure things out at.this point and time.

"Well Davis, not to make you feel guilty or anything but I was fired because I spent nine days basically crying over you or at least what you told me. And in a funny kind of way, I can truly say that I found myself in those tears. That's why I'm not pressed about getting my job back. I want to try my dream of being a disc jockey," she concluded.

"But Gail, you're over thirty years old and you don't have a lick of experience in radio," he said in a panic just trying to get a grip on the situation.

"That's okay sweetie, because now I have something that I haven't had in a long time— and that's a belief in myself and at the risk of using a cliché, I have no one but you to thank," she said.

The two ended their conversation shortly there after. Davis took a shower and tried to watch some television. He quickly fell off into a deep sleep.

24

It was late that Sunday evening when the irritatingly loud ring of the phone was heard throughout the room. Davis awoke with a horrific headache after the third ring to answer it.

"Wow, you sound tired," was the voice of a female after he said hello. The voice was extremely pleasant and familiar but it wasn't Kia's or Ms. Upshaw's.

"No, I'm not tired at all," he responded.

"Stop lying, those people over at your must be wearing that behind out," the female said. Davis still couldn't place the voice and it was bothering him.

"Do you know who this is Davis?" the female decided to ask after a noticeable silence from him. He began to panic after the question. He was now on the spot. He searched his mental faculties to attempt to draw some similarity between the voice he was now hearing and the patterns of both Gail's and Kia's. Could it be either of them and the fatigue was just not allowing him to recognize it. After all, with the exception of his mother, those were the only two women he had spoken to this summer. He definitely didn't want to call one of their names and it ended up being the other. He had never thought about it before this moment, but he suddenly realized that the two of them didn't know each other. It also occurred to him that

that was the way he wanted to keep it.

"This doesn't make me some type of playboy does it? Nahh, after all, I truly care for both of those women. I care for them for different reasons, but I definitely care for both of them," he concluded.

"Hello, Davis, are you still there?" The voice bought him out of his private thoughts.

"Yeah, Yeah, I'm still here," he responded. By this time he had begun to sweat. He felt like he was playing Russian roulette with the name that he was about to call and he still had no idea of who this was. He knew however that he had to call someone's name or he would be convicting himself.

"Davis I don't know where it's coming from but I can hear the nervousness in your voice. This is Lisa Hargrove and I was just calling to say hello. I'll call you at a more convenient time okay." He could feel his heart rate decrease as he sighed out loudly. He was so relieved.

"No- no, Lisa it's all right, I was just getting up from a nap. I'm just a little disoriented that's all.

"Oh okay," she said. "Can you talk?"

"Yeah, what's going on in Baltimore?"

This time Lisa herself took a long sigh before she began to speak.

"I guess it's okay," she finally said.

"Whoa, are you sure? You sound a little distraught."

"Yeah I'm fine. It's just that I'm starting to wonder about the very meaning of life," she responded.

"Oh really, what's bringing on this question?" he asked.

"I can't really say. You know how you just stop to wonder about things and get all disappointed?"

"Yeah, I can identify with that," he said.

"Oh can you," she said as her voice raised an octave.

"What do you do when you get in that mood," she asked in a desperate tone. Davis could tell that she was looking for some advice, but he also knew that he wasn't in any frame of mind to give it to her. The last time he had a serious conversation with Lisa, he was still only friends with both Kia and Gail. His life had become entirely too complicated to deal with her precious yet adolescent questions right now. But then he remembered how close he and Lisa had become in such a short time. He felt obligated to help her out in some kind of way. Then it hit him. He knew how to get off the phone with her and give her some great advice at the same time.

"Well let me ask you something," he asked in a voice that attempted to hide his enthusiasm in the great idea he had come up with.

"Have you gone to talk to your pastor about it," he smiled as he finished his question. He knew how religious she was and he remembered how she couldn't wait to get back to Baltimore this summer so that she could attend her home church.

"Oh boy, ...no Davis, I hadn't talked to him," she answered. Frankly her tone and her answer shocked him. In an attempt to regroup, he went on.

"Ya' know Lisa, I know the man may be busy running the church but I'm sure he would want to know if one of his parishioners were having a problem like this."

"Oh Davis please, spare me okay," By now, he was a little confused.

"Did I say something wrong?" he asked. After a little silence, she spoke again.

"Sweetie, I'm sorry. I shouldn't have snapped like that. It's just that ...' that —well my pastor is the exact cause of my problems," she finished.

"How's that?" he asked.

"Uhhhhhhhh, I really didn't want to talk about this but I guess that it would be unfair for me to call you for conversation and then I be the one not to talk, so here goes." She took a few seconds to compose herself. "Well

— my pastor made a pass at me this summer," she blurted out. Davis was speechless. He could only wonder about the amount of trust that she must have put in not only him but his church as well. "And before you ask—yes I am sure it was a pass. He put his hands on my breast and my vaginal area," she continued.

After her confession, he really got into the conversation. The two of them stayed on the phone for two more hours before ending their talk. Davis wasn't able to help but he did comfort her. Once they hung up, he found that his headache had subsided. He decided to take a shower and iron his clothes for work the next day.

During the following week he spent a lot of time with Gail. By now he had a key to her apartment and would simply go there after work. He liked this set up—going over Gail's during the week and over to Kia's during the weekend. Well at least that's how it used to be. He hadn't heard from Kia since she had bought him home that Saturday morning. Now he had to take full stock in Ms. Upshaw and try not to think about Kia until she called him.

It was a Wednesday and Davis was sitting in his sleeping shorts and a tank top after having already taken his shower. When Gail walked in, he greeted her with a huge smile and genuine delight to see her. She was so adorable. In her power skirt and blouse, she would have grabbed the attention of any man. This obviously didn't apply to the males at the radio stations where she had been interviewing for the last few days. She had interviewed at seven different radio stations and not so much as a "we'll call you." Although her spirits were still high, Davis could only imagine her sense of dejection. She never showed any signs of it though. She would greet him with the same intense smile and kiss with which he greeted her. However this didn't stop him from feeling sorrow for her. She was a black female in her thirties, technically living alone, and trying to find a job in a field that was totally foreign to her.

To make matters even worse, her savings were disappearing fast.

"How's my baby doing tonight?" he asked after an intense lip-lock by the two of them.

"She's starving, that's how she's doing. I was hoping you would have pulled something out of the freezer,"

"And do what with it, look at it—cause you know I can't cook a lick," he returned.

"Oh yeah, I forgot, a momma's boy," she said with a sarcastic grin. He returned the grin in the same sarcastic fashion before speaking again.

"Well I did order a pizza and it should be here shortly," he said.

"Oh bless you," she said with tremendous relief as she kicked off her pumps and climbed on the sofa beside him.

"What the hell are you watching," she asked with a little disgust as she scanned the room for the remote. He had the cable on the Home-shopping network.

"I wasn't really watching it. I was just thinking about my mom."

"Oh yeah, what about her?" she asked.

"Well just thinking about the fact that I haven't talked to her in about a week," Davis answered.

"Is that such a crime," Gail asked as she began to play footsie with him.

"With my mom, yeah it's a crime alright," he said. Feeling the need to explain, he continued.

"Well I guess you have to take into account our history together. I mean for years we were the only thing that each other had. Hell it's still that way and I swore that when I got to college that I would call her at least twice a week. Not only have I not talked to her in a while but the last time I talked to her, I sort of snapped at her,"

"Why?" Gail interrupted.

"I don't know, I guess I was under some kinda' of stress," he said as his mind started to wonder. He knew that stress was exactly the reason why he snapped. He also knew that the stress came from the fact that he had been dealing with two older women at the same time and keeping them secrets from each other had begun to weigh on him. But there was no way that he was about to tell Gail that. It's not that she would get angry. He sincerely believed that she would understand and may even offer advice, but now was not the time to tell her. On the other side of town, the telephone greeted Holly as he stepped into his dorm room after having taking a shower. With the wet towel almost falling off of him, he ran to Davis' side of the room to get it. Holly was surprised to find out that it was Ms. Virginia on the other end. After greeting her properly and carefully, Holly proceeded to tell her that her son wasn't there at the present time. "In light of the schedule that he's been keeping lately, I'm not surprised," she said.

"But listen, I called to talk to you anyway," she continued. Her last statement caused his head to rock from being stunned.

"Holly, pay attention," she proceeded, "I need you to get some information for me."

By the time Friday rolled around, Davis found himself over at Gail's once again instead of in his dorm room waiting on Kia to call. She came in a few minutes after him just as she had done all week but something was definitely different. When she came in, her face was full of tears.

Davis jumped to his feet to comfort her. As he guided her to the bedroom, he asked her what was wrong. The stress of being unemployed had finally taken it's toll on her. Davis undressed her as she sat in a slumped position on the edge of the bed.

"I'm starting to wonder if I've made a mistake. I mean, I had a good job. I don't think I can do this radio stuff and obviously these people who are interviewing me don't think I can do it."

"That's enough baby. You know you can do that shit,"

he jumped in to say. He didn't have his pep speech all together but he was watching her confidence melt right in front of his eyes.

"But Davis, I've tried every radio station in the city. No one sounds like they will even give me a call back. And now I'm scared. I mean at this rate, my savings will be gone in six months," she concluded. Her last statement was a little too powerful for him to come back on. Instead of risking saying something inappropriate, he decided to just make her as comfortable as he could for the rest of the weekend. For the rest of the evening she laid in his arms drifting in and out of sleep.

By the time Sunday rolled around, Davis had decided that he would move in with her for the two weeks that were left before school started. While she slept late, he took her car to go to the dorm room and grab some clothes and toiletries. He had only planned to be there for about ten minutes. He wanted to be sure that he grabbed every-thing that he needed. Of course things didn't go as planned. While he was grabbing the last of his things, there was a loud and vicious knock at the door. It was one of those types of knocks that pissed you off and made you anxious to answer it just so you could curse out the person on the other side of the door.

He flung the door open and was prepared to greet whomever with the most evil eyes he could muster up. Unfortunately when he finally got the door open, things didn't go that way. For one thing, he didn't see another person's face when the door was ajar. The only thing he saw was chest, and lots of it. He methodically raised his head so that he could alter his vision. He ended up look-ing in the face of a very dark skinned individual whom had poorly groomed facial hair. Although he took note of the hygiene, he was more focused on the sheer size of the indi-vidual. The guy stood about 6' 9" tall and weighed about 320 easy.

Davis' mind started searching for answers as to who this guy may be. The first thing he wondered was if there were anyone looking for him to cause him bodily harm. Could this be a jealous ex of one of the women he had been seeing? Had Slow Motion sent over some of his friends to take him out, or was this just someone who was trying to take advantage of the near isolation of the building and rob the first person that he could? Davis' heart began to beat extremely fast as he realized that it was too late. He would have to fight his way out of this one and looking at the size of this fella' he was just praying that he would make it out of this one without any broken bones.

Just then the guy took an uninvited step in. Davis' head turned and quickly scanned the room in an effort to find anything that he could possibly use as a weapon. As his eyes roamed, his attention was caught as the giant began to speak.

"Yo cuz, is Holly here?" he mumbled. Davis slowly turned his eyes back towards the huge individual as he thought about the words that were just spoken. Then it hit him like a ton of bricks. Just then he was able to notice that there was a second individual standing behind the first guy. The second individual was just as huge as the first one. These were obviously Holly's cousins from South Carolina.

Davis ended up setting the two behemoths down and carefully explaining the situation that unfolded with Train and the money. He didn't want anything to be left unaccounted for and the way he explained it, everything was understood by both of them. Afterwards they were totally grateful to Davis for looking out for their little cousin. They were desperate to return the favor. However all Davis wanted to do at first was get them out of there so that he could get back to his sleeping beauty. He ended up showing them to Mary's house where he knew Holly could be found. But just before he left them, he got an idea that made him smile noticeably to himself.

"Hey guys maybe there is something you can do for me after all," he said with a mischievous grin.

The following day proved to be a long one at the internship. Davis ended up destroying a valuable tool. His mind was on the two women in his life. He worried a great deal about Gail. He couldn't help but blame himself for her quitting her job in the first place. It wasn't that bad until she came home that Friday in tears. He felt so helpless. And then there was Kia. He didn't know how to feel about her. He tried to understand what she was going through but he always came to the same conclusion that he was the one getting the raw end in all of this. But he still missed her all the same. He had stopped watching her broadcasts so that he wouldn't feel so bad. This was a perfect situation to talk to his mom about but under the circumstances, he knew that there was no way that Dee would understand.

After being chewed out about his performance for that day, he jumped on the train and was headed to Gail's. He was the one who needed to be pampered tonight. He just hoped she had had a better day than he had.

Once on the train, he kept his head low and never peeked above the rim of his baseball cap. Friday afternoons on the train were usually crowded. He seemed to draw talkers like a magnet and in the south, there was no shortage of people whom would walk up to you and spark a conversation. One Friday, this old woman managed to tell him about the three different operations she had had on her ingrown toenail all within his thirty-minute ride. Dee had always told him that his trait of seeming easy to talk to was definitely one he had inherited from her.

"Garnett Street Station," was the first sound he heard after coming out of his fifteen-minute nap. He had basically trained his sub-conscious to listen out for that stop as it was announced over the train's PA system because the one immediately after it was his. As he came back to consciousness, he noticed that there was a woman sitting next to him.

"Ahh shit," he thought to himself. He really didn't feel like talking and luckily he was about four minutes from his stop. So all he had to do was keep his eyes buried under the rim of his hat and he could get off without any conversation whatsoever.

As he sat quietly, he couldn't help but notice that all of the seats that he could see were totally empty. Why in the hell was this lady sitting beside him with all of the seats that were available? As he completed the thought, his nose caught whiff of the woman's perfume. It was simply intoxicating to the point that it almost seemed familiar. He let the thought go as he decided to set still just to ensure that the woman would say absolutely nothing to him. Just at that moment the woman repositioned her feet in a manner that he could see the shoes that she wore. He was starting to think his sleepy mind was playing tricks on him now because even the shoes seemed vaguely familiar. He stared at them for a few seconds as he tried to recall where he had seen the shoes before.

As he continued to stare at the shoes, the woman's left hand quickly entered his peripheral vision. The hand was headed towards him. His face squinted up in wonder.

"Does this woman think I'm still sleep? Is she trying to cop a free feel or something." The hand continued to move in his direction and it finally landed on his arm. "What the helllll?" he thought to himself. And just as he was about to look up from under his hat and ask her just exactly what she was doing, he heard her speak.

"What, do you think I'm going to bite you or something?" Then as he turned his head in her direction, he finally saw her face. It caused him to jerk his head back in disbelief. He would have literally expected to see the president of the United States before he saw her.

"I know it's been a long time since we talked but I had

to get some things together and I'm happy to say that I have sorted everything out," the woman said as she spoke for the second time. After regaining his composure, Davis spoke. "Kia.... what are you doing here?"

"I wanted to catch you as soon as you got off of work. I had to tell you that I was done with second guessing myself and how much I missed you," Davis still had a look of disbelief on his face and he barely heard what she said. He did a body check as the gorgeous emotions rushed into his body. He was searching for the emotions that only came from seeing her.

"Well why didn't you call me?" he asked as he still struggled to get himself together.

"No, no, no—the phone just wouldn't suffice this time Davis," she said as she grabbed his head as if she were testing a melon for ripeness. Once his head was secured in her hands, she slowly and deliberately moved in for what turned out to be a simply ravishing lip-lock. Davis slowly broke the kiss as he heard his stop announced. That's when it hit him, he was holding and kissing Kia while headed to Abigail's apartment. He almost fainted from the anxiety.

"Oh shit!" he slipped and said aloud.

"What is it?" she inquired. "Oh ahhh–nothing, just a little crook in my neck from sleeping on the train," he said in a calm and collected fashion as he remembered that the stop for campus was still coming up and he could get off there with no problem. Later on down the line, he would realize how smooth he was at that exact moment by not mentioning Gail by mistake.

25

The hallway on the third floor of Sage Hall had grown quiet and dark. The staff and faculty were always leaving at 4:55 in the afternoon in an attempt to beat rush hour traffic. Today was no exception. The only light on the hall was coming from the office of Dean Phillips. Abigail Upshaw's resignation had caused a large void in his department and he had to pick up the slack. It's not that he minded staying late. On the contrary, he had grown quite accustomed to it. The part he hadn't grown accustomed to was working late without Gail being there. He missed sexually harassing her. "That dumb, weak, bitch," he thought to himself. "Why did she have to go and fuck everything up." He began to hate Gail for that. She was so easy and accessible, much different from his wife of 18 years at home. Now he was forced to go home to his wife and listen to her talk about the old bitties in the church and refuse him any sex. He would probably never realize how sweet of a wife he had and would probably never show her the affection she deserved. He also would probably never figure out that the reason why he didn't get as much sex as he used to was because he stopped showing her any affection.

After packing his briefcase and grabbing his jacket, he headed toward the door. It was about 8:15 p.m. He opened the door and reached for the light, as he was about to step into the hallway. But before he could close the office door, he felt a powerful shove pushing him back into the office.

"What the hell?" he shouted as he turned around to see what was going on. As he did, he noticed two fairly large black males whom had shown themselves in and were locking the door behind them.

"Who the hell are you guys?" the dean said as he re-adjusted his suit jacket trying to convince himself that he wasn't afraid. Just then, one of the guys walked over to him in a calm and collected fashion. He stood in front of Phillips for a second before he drew back and sent the back of his rough hand sailing across the face of the much short-er man.

"Listen, you little pudgy bastard, there's only one thing I want you to say and that's okay, you get it, o-fuck-ing -kay. And I don't want you to say that until I'm fin-ished talking," the guy concluded as he grabbed a near by chair and sat down in front of the dean who was now lean-ing on the huge oak finished desk in his office. He was rubbing his face where he had felt the blow.

"Now, let's say that my name is Mr. X and that's Z," the guy said as he introduced the giant over in the corner who was standing guard. The guy continued.

"Word has it that you like sticking your dick in places where it doesn't belong. You get what um saying? Now I was thinking, you have something in common with Z over here because he does that too. But instead of fuckin the people who work under him, like yo' punk ass, he likes fucking cows." Phillips looked over at Z as this was said. From just looking at the rough demeanor of the man, he had no reason to disregard what he had just been told. Z himself didn't dispute it and even supported the statement with a smirk filled with evil intentions. At this point, the dean knew he had to act surprised. For the most part he was because he had never heard anyone refer to his carryings on with Abigail before.

"What are you talking about, I've been happily married for the last 18 years," he shouted. Mr. X looked up at the ceiling as the right corner of his mouth drew tight and he sucked his teeth.

"Z, could you come over here and show this prick how you approach cows when you're horny," X said. That's when the dark skinned, poorly groomed giant made his way over to the dean. Mr. X continued to speak.

"First of all, I told you what I wanted you to say and when I wanted you to say it. Ya' see, we have a long drive back to Carolina and we really don't have time to listen to your bullshit." The dean's facial expression grew into one of worry, as Z was about to reach him. He squinted his eyes as the massive hand of Z wrapped around his neck. The other hand went to the back of his trousers. Soon Phillips found himself being hoisted in the air and he heard his clothing starting to rip. The poor man looked like a piñata as he dangled in the air. He began swinging his fists wildly just hoping to make contact with the monster that was responsible for him being airborne. His eyes began to water form the helplessness of the situation. At that moment, one of the dean's flailing fists landed against the hairy cheek of Mr. Z. This caused him to fall to the carpet as Z became enraged.

"Fuck that, this bastard hit me. Um 'bout to rape his ass for real," he bellowed. With that, Z reached toward the floor where the dean was now laying and crying for mercy. Z ripped the trousers from his body with one swoop. By this time, Mr. X had jumped from his chair and started wrestling his huge friend from the dean.

"Wait outside man," he yelled at Z after finally pulling him away from his prey. Z agreed and walked over to the door with a huge smirk on his face. After closing the door behind him, the last thing he heard was his partner speaking to the man lying on the floor.

"Alright you lil' bitch, this is what's happening. I have a friend who needs a job and you're gonna make it happen."

The next day over at her cozy apartment, Kia walked back into her bedroom with a huge bowl of her favorite ice cream. She plopped on the bed next to a half naked Davis whom had just gotten out of the shower and had a towel wrapped around his waist. He was exhausted. They had made love for a greater part of the morning and afternoon. They both called in sick from work that morning and would do the same tomorrow because of their exhaustion. It wasn't a big deal for Davis since his internship ended the following week. But it was kind of careless on Kia's behalf since she was dealing with her career. She didn't care though. She had made up her mind to give her heart to him and as much time as she could spare.

On the third day of their little rendezvous, Davis had to convince her to work. Normally he wouldn't have minded her not working to spend time with him but he needed a break from her. He was fatigued and his back ached. Besides, he had to check on Abigail. He hadn't talked to her for three days. Usually this would not have happened considering that she was depressed about her unemployment, but if things had gone the way he planned, she would have been too busy trying to adjust to her new job.

Once he got home that Thursday evening, he heard a spirited message from Gail on his machine. She was ecstatic about the new job she had received from the school's radio station. He also heard two messages from Lisa.

After showering and ironing, he climbed under his quilt and picked up the phone to call Lisa back. The two talked for an hour before he finally fell asleep.

That Friday at work, his co-workers threw him a party since he only had three days left on his assignment. No one got much work done which was just fine with Davis considering he hadn't totally recuperated from his little escapade with Kia. At the end of the day he walked out with his supervisor. Today he was forced to catch a ride home since he had so much food and gifts. However Gail whom was waiting for him in the parking lot surprised him. He graciously took her up on an offer for a ride home.

In the car, she provided much of the conversation. She was ecstatic about her new job and couldn't help but tell him about it. That's exactly what she did. She glowed as she talked about every detail and all of the possibilities. She also talked about her salary which turned out to be much more than Davis expected. He was genuinely happy for her.

Gail continued on with her conversation but it took somewhat of a turn. She started to tell him about how much she appreciated everything he had done for her, Helping with her self-confidence, letting her cry on his shoulder, and all of the times that he made her feel extreme physical pleasure. She went on and on singing his praises. This eventually caused a dip in emotions for him.

As she talked and talked, he compared her conversation with the praises that Kia had bestowed upon him earlier that week. Now he started to feel bad. They were two women who had tough exteriors when he first met them. Fortunately or unfortunately, he managed to find the one weakness in both of them. Gail's weakness was her promiscuity with men of power and her false hopes of marrying one of those very low lives that would put her through such a thing. And then there was Kia. She wore her success and independence as if it were a shield, protecting her from all of the dishonest and unreliable men in her world. This same shield also prevented suitable mates from entering that same world and she never even thought about such a thing. But in six months time, he had witnessed both of these women confront their weaknesses and each came out richer for the experience.

On the surface, that was great but the thing that was

eating away at him was that he was receiving credit for it.

"I'm nothing but a lying asswhole. I've been deceiving these women from the beginning. I've become just like one of those sorry bastards from the projects. The very men, whom I said I would never be like and now I'm nothing but a spitting image of them," he cursed himself.

"Then on top of everything, both of them think I'm some type of Second Coming when in actuality, I'm nothing but an embarrassment to my mother."

He regretted the fact that he hadn't told Gail about Kia earlier. If anybody, he felt that she would understand. For a quick second, he even contemplated telling her. But he didn't entertain that thought for too long. He definitely didn't want to take a chance at crushing her after all she had been through.

She continued to drive on as she got caught up in her own conversation. At one point she came to a red light and finally had the chance to look over at him as she continued her conversation. As she turned her head in his direction, she saw something that shocked her. Davis was sitting there motionless with tears running down his cheeks. She attempted to understand why. Maybe he was joyful for her. She had never seen a man cry for her before but she had never been through so much with a man before as she had been through with him either. She had been doing all of the talking. Maybe something dramatic happened at work and she hadn't even bothered to ask him how his day went. He was starting to cry copiously and didn't even notice her looking at him. She still had a few seconds at the light so she decided to touch his cheek in a soft manner and inquire what was wrong with him. She would later learn that that was not a good idea.

As her cold hand touched the warm wet tears on his face, it bought him back to reality. He had been in another world and had forgotten that she was even there. It was better in his world for those few lonely seconds. The only person he had to contend with was himself. At the exact moment that she touched him, he was whizzed back to a world where other people could be hurt besides himself. As soon as the back of her soft hand grazed one of his tears, he realized exactly that and it caused him to explode into even more tears. His head slowly lunged forward and his crying was no longer silent. He buried his head in both of his hands as the floodgates opened.

Poor Gail, who had no idea what was going on, was nearly hysterical. She immediately thought that she was the cause of what was happening since he got more animated the minute she touched him. After the light turned green, she decided to drive through it and pull over at the next available curb. After doing exactly that and putting the car in park, she turned to Davis to investigate the cause of his tears. It was a fruitless effort though. Three times she asked him what was wrong and attempted to touch him differently to comfort him and each time he started whaling even louder.

Meanwhile, back at the dormitory, Holly and Mary were busy collecting his dirty clothes and were a few minutes from walking out of the door. They usually made a Friday night of doing laundry over at her house while making dinner and this Friday was no exception. Holly was still a little uncomfortable about any woman besides his mother handling his underwear. As he tried to gather all of his boxers inconspicuously, the ringing of the phone interrupted him. Mary smiled at him as she continued to pick up his boxers knowing that he was trapped by his obligation of answering the phone. She thought the entire thing was too precious.

Holly didn't say much on the phone. Mary could tell that there was something-serious going on by looking at his quarter-sized eyes.

"Bring him here right now," Holly said in a deliberate tone that was totally foreign to Mary. Afterwards he hung up the phone and gave her orders to follow him down stairs. She knew that whatever it was, it was extremely serious so she didn't bother asking any questions. She just followed.

After six minutes of waiting in silence outside of the dorm, Holly and Mary watched as a frantic Gail pulled up in their presence. She was crying herself by now and Davis was still doubled over in the passenger seat. His condition hadn't changed. From the moment that they pulled up, Holly took control. He instructed both of the ladies not to waste anytime asking questions. He comforted them as Mary began to shed tears as well at the sight of a broken Davis. Holly nearly cried as well but he knew he had to be the strong one in this situation. This was more than his roommate it was his friend someone who had put his life on the line for him. The truest friend he had ever known outside of his family and every second was crucial to this friend.

He instructed both of the women to help him get Davis' large frame to the back seat and they did exactly as they were told.

"Ms. Upshaw, we're going to Crawford Long Hospital. We're taking eighty-five north and getting off at Tenth Street. I want you to turn on your hazard lights and drive as fast and as safely as you can," Holly said in a polite yet commanding voice. Gail didn't hesitate. She nodded her head in compliance and got the car rolling. Mary looked over the back of the passenger seat to see her man comforting his friend by embracing him with both arms while Davis was trembling and crying simultaneously. There was no time for macho bullshit. Holly had a firm grip on his roommate and was intent on letting him know that he loved him through his grip. Mary was so proud to witness how Holly took control of the situation. She then turned back around in the passenger seat and grabbed Gail's hand, which was now a clinched fist on the armrest. She was still hysterical and Mary knew she had to be comforted as well.

Soon the white sedan was pulling up at the emergency entrance of the hospital. They all got out and escorted Davis inside. A nearby nurse, who saw the three of them dragging the large individual in, quickly grabbed a gurney and met them. After the four of them got Davis situated on the gurney, the nurse asked what had happened to him. At this point Holly told the two ladies to go back outside and park the car.

"No no, I can't go anywhere," Gail spouted.

"Gail," Holly yelled in an attempt to let her know that there was no time for discussion, "I know exactly what is wrong with him. I'm going to the back so I can help the doctor deal with him. The best thing you and Mary can do is move your car and have a seat in the waiting room, okay." Gail looked at the nurse's face as Holly's words sank in. The nurse gave a nod that suggested Holly was right. Mary saw the nod as well and wrapped her arm around Gail to lead her outside.

Once the two ladies had walked out of the door, Holly turned to deal with the nurse.

"Ma'am, my friend is having a nervous breakdown. We need to get him a sedative and an examination real fast," Holly said in a deliberate tone. The nurse wanted to ask him how he was so sure but she didn't bother. She had seen nervous breakdowns before and she agreed with Holly's diagnosis. He helped the nurse push Davis back to exam room eight and closed the door.

An hour and twenty minutes had passed when the doctor entered the room for the third time. He was a tall thin white man with gray hair. He had just come from the waiting room where he updated Gail and Mary on Davis' condition. At Holly's request, he only told the ladies that Davis had been sedated and was talking and coherent. This made both of them feel a lot better. When they asked for a diagnosis, he told them that they were still awaiting tests.

The doctor himself was now searching for the entire

truth from Holly. He sat down to question him. Holly held Davis' hand as he began to tell the story. Davis listened on in embarrassment as Holly explained how the situation with Gail and Kia had taken its toll on Davis. Holly also spoke of Davis being under pressure since he was a first generation college student. By the time Holly finished, a technician had opened the door to hand the doctor some test results. After going over the results the doctor looked at a nearly delirious Davis and started talking.

"Well son your blood work seems to all be in order which means you don't have any chemical imbalances in your brain. I hope you realize how lucky you are and I also hope that you will take care of your dilemma before things become a whole lot worse." The doctor removed a small package from his coat pocket.

"Now here's two more sedatives. Take them tonight after you have eaten something and go to bed. I suggest you spend tomorrow in bed," the doctor said as he turned to walk away.

"Oh.. and son don't try to be something you're not. Believe me when I tell you, I've seen a lot of people do a lot worse than have a nervous relapse when I was in medical school. Be truthful to yourself and let your God handle the rest." With that, the doctor vanished.

The ride back to the dorm was a slow and quiet one. Both ladies were content with the silence as long as Davis was okay. They were extremely curious as to the nature of the problem but they were willing to be patient as long as Davis was better. Holly would spend the night and the following day making sure his roommate got some uninterrupted rest.

26

Holly did a good job of watching over his roommate the next couple of days. He didn't allow any calls to get to Davis. He only talked to Ms. Virginia when she called. Holly found it odd that the news of her son's break down didn't upset her much. She just proceeded to ask him questions about the women in her son's life.

Davis slept very soundly. Holly only woke him to take sedatives that the doctor had prescribed. After two days of sleep, Holly thought it was time to get him up and out of the room. After all, Davis was twenty years old today. It was only right that he celebrated in some type of way. A celebration was exactly what Gail had in mind when she called. She could use this as an excuse to finally talk to him since the incident occurred. She couldn't do that over the past few days since Holly had been playing the junk yard dog and not letting any of her calls get through. She had attempted to talk to Davis twice over the phone but it was easy for Holly to deny access since Davis was sleeping extremely well. He was about to deny access again but Davis walked in from the shower and inquired as to whom was calling. Holly reluctantly passed the receiver to him. He truly felt that Gail was being selfish.

After assuring Gail that he was okay and back to normal, the two made plans to have a birthday lunch for him downtown. Davis proceeded to iron and get dressed. He could tell his roommate was upset with his plans and he understood why. He was happy he had someone besides his mother who would look out for him in a situation like that. Davis had promised to spend the evening with him and Mary after celebrating later that night. He could use the two of them to wiggle out of any sexual fantasies that Gail may have had.

Davis and Gail walked into Rah–Rah's at about 1:30 in the afternoon. It was a popular spot in Midtown that he had heard much about. Gail had done well in the car. She never said anything about the hospital incident even though it scared her tremendously. She was also curious about what type of stress he had been under since he didn't have to worry about classes. She concluded that she would learn in due time. She was exactly right.

"I took the liberty of ordering one of your favorite dishes," she said.

"Which one?" he asked curiously.

"Chicken Parmesan and besides that, I have a big surprise for you that should be here shortly," she concluded. She knew he loved surprises. He deduced that he would just have to wait as the waiter took their drink order. He found it strange that she didn't order a drop of alcohol.

The two started to talk about her last few days at work at his request. She was more than happy to oblige since she was still loving her job. Midway through their conversation, his face grew confused and he put down the glass of water that he had been preparing to sip from. Gail cautiously stopped talking to check to see if he was okay. She couldn't bare the thought of something else happening to him.

"Davis are you okay?" she asked in a panic stricken voice. His eyes were focused on someone or something across the room.

"Yeah, I'm fine. It's just that there's this woman sitting at the bar who looks exactly like my Godmother," he commented. Gail's face suddenly wore a mischievous grin.

"Oh you can't really tell with all of the dim lighting in this place, she said in an attempt to get his mind off of it. Afterwards he focused in on her conversation again. She was now trying to get him to talk so she could have a chance to marvel at how handsome he looked in his semi-casual attire. She started with a simple question.

"Well, school starts next week, are you ready?"

"Am I!" he retorted. "After this summer I can't wait" He suddenly stopped speaking and buttering the bread that he had in front of him. When she focused in on his face to search for the reason of the abrupt stop, she could see that his eyes were focused on something over her shoulder again just like last time. However this time his stare was much more intense. It forced her to turn around and look for herself. The only thing Gail noticed was middle aged woman walking in their direction. As the woman stopped almost directly in front of Davis, his face was now wearing a look of total confusion.

"Dee, what are you doing here?" he managed to say.

"Well baby ain't ya' gonna introduce me to your lady friend?" she asked.

"Yeah, Gail, this is my mother Delois Virginia," he said without taking his eyes off of his mother. He was still wearing a look of bewilderment.

Gail was smiling by now. She knew exactly what was going on. Little did he know that this was the surprise that Gail had mentioned. Gail told him exactly that with a huge smile on her face.

"Oh this isn't the only surprise," Dee said as she took a seat beside her son.

"Oh, Gail she's talking about my Godmother over at the bar," he said with confidence as if he had already figured out the second surprise.

"Dee you want me to go and get her?" he asked.

"No baby, that's not the surprise. Don't worry it'll be

here shortly," his mother said as she placed a napkin in her lap and reached for the bread and butter.

"So you're Gail. It's so nice to finally put a face with the voice," Dee said as she smiled enthusiastically at Gail. Davis nearly lost his breath after hearing the last statement. He looked over at Gail who returned a smile. This caused his eyes to roll towards the ceiling as he could all but imagine how many conversations the two had had. All he could think of at the moment was that Dee knew what was going on between he and the much older Gail. But his mother's actions didn't support that theory. She was too jovial. At that moment he looked at the bar again and this time he caught the eyes of his Godmother. She was mouthing the words;

" I love you." Then she held her wine up in a toasting fashion. Since the two ladies at his table were so busy conversating, he saw no harm in toasting. He reached for his tea that the waiter had brought moments ago and held it up in the same fashion as the woman at the bar. The two dipped their glasses from across the room and they both took a drink. Davis looked back at the bar once he lowered his glass in an effort to find the woman he had just toasted with but someone who was now walking in his direction drew his attention. His neck lunged forward in an attempt to give his eyes more focus power. Instantly after confirming what he thought he saw the first time, his head turned to the side and towards the grounds. His mouth then expelled all of the fluid that he had just taken in. It rushed out of his mouth in a misty like spray for almost a full second. Coughing followed this. As he lifted his head back to its original position he was surprised to find his mother waiting with the coldest stare and a towel for him to dry his mouth. Gail was quite worried.

By this time the person whom he thought he had seen had made their way over to the table. Dee looked up at her.

"Oh, you must be Kia," she said to the woman. Kia greeted Dee with a very warm smile. Dee proceeded to invite her to join them. Davis was still coughing at this point. Gail and Kia both looked worried but Dee was still very much calm. As he continued to clear his throat of the tea, he looked over at his mother with an expression that asked, "how could you?" "Excuse me ladies as I escort my son to the rest room. Davis couldn't believe what had just happened. He didn't stop coughing until he and his mother had reached his Godmother at the bar. Julia could only shake her head as she looked at her Godson.

"I asked your mother not to do this baby," she said.

"Hush Julia and let me talk to my son please," Dee said in a non-serious tone. Davis dropped the towel from his face and looked at his mother.

"I can't believe it. My own mother busted me out," he said.

"You can't believe it? Let me tell you what the fuck I can't believe," Dee, said in a much more serious voice now. I can't believe my son has had a nervous breakdown trying to be some kinda' Romeo. Ya' hear that Julia, he's trying to be a playboy. He ain't homesick. He ain't trying to be a good student but a playboy," Dee said as she grabbed him under the chin and turned his head in the direction of the two ladies at the table.

"Look at that. There are two loving and probably innocent ladies who have no idea about each other. Not to even mention the young lady who attempted suicide." She then positioned his head so he would be looking directly at her as she used her other hand to point towards the table.

"Now, you have two choices. You can go over there and end this shit like the man I know you can be or you can stay here and let me go over there and end this. Either way baby, it ends today. Like I told you, I'm not loosing you to no bullshit." After listening to the conviction in his mother's voice, he turned to go and do what had to be done.

As the two ladies watched their beloved Davis walk towards the table, they began talking.

"So Dee, how did you reach these ladies and how did you get each of them here today," Julia asked. Davis made it back to the table as they looked on.

"Well I had his roommate get their phone numbers out of his phone book which he keeps hidden."

"If he keeps it hidden, how did the boy find it," Julia asked.

"Well one Saturday morning, I kept the poor baby on the phone and talked him through all of the logical hiding places," Dee answered.

"I knew both of the ladies would want to celebrate his birthday if they cared for him not to mention the chance to meet me."

"So now there's going to be friction between him and his roommate," Julia concluded. By this time Davis was well into his conversation with the two ladies. Dee corrected Julia as they continued to watch the table.

"I can't see Holly telling him how it happened," Dee went on.

"You're not going to tell him either," Julia asked.

"Hell no, he needs to always wonder about me and how I stay on top of him. It gives me an edge. And as far as that little book, he'll probably never guess that it has been tampered with and so he'll always wonder how I found out." They both noticed that Kia had started crying as they looked on from the other end of the room. Gail had dropped her head in disbelief but unlike Kia she wore a weird little smile that suggested she couldn't believe she had been had.

Julia continued with the interrogation.

"So why did you give him a choice just now? Why didn't you just get it over with while you were at the table?"

"Julia," Dee said, as she looked her old friend directly in the eye, "you always have to give them the opportunity to be men. He took the right step and in spite of all he has done, I'm proud of him," she finished. As Dee turned to look at the table again, she was just in time to see Kia's hand land across Davis' face before she stormed out of the restaurant. Gail was next but she handled it differently. She casually got up and gave him a patronizing kiss on the forehead and strolled off. Dee walked over to the table to collect her son. As she reached down for his hand, he looked up with tears in both eyes.

"I guess I needed that." His mother nodded in agreement.

14 MONTHS LATER

It was a slow-moving Saturday night as Davis lay in reclined position with his head on his girlfriend's stomach. The movie they had been watching was just ending and Davis reached for the phone to call Holly and tell him he was on his way home. Once he got off the phone, the young lady embraced him with a hug.

"I don't want you to leave me tonight," she moaned. C'mon baby we've been through this. It wouldn't be right for me to spend the night," he said as he kissed her nose. With that he headed for the door. Just as he was about to turn the knob, she shouted his name. He turned to see that she had disrobed. He was now looking at a magnificent naked female body. This caused him to turn completely around and walked towards her. He reached her and planted a kiss on her lips followed by a huge hug. Then he stood back to look in her face.

"Good night Lisa," he said. The young lady attempted to speak under her now obvious tears. "I just can't understand why you're not attracted to me," she muttered. Then he grabbed her by the back of the head and pulled her toward him.

"Not attracted to you, please. Lisa, you're beautiful inside and out. I pray for strength to resist temptations of the flesh every night before I enter your apartment.

Remember that Lisa. I can still remember the Bible study we had about that very topic. Now let me tell you something, I've been in sexual experiences that a lot of men would beg for. This would happen time and time again. The only thing about flesh is that it only feels good while you're touching it. The minute you stop touching or the second you climax, I dare you to remember anything about it the next day unless you had more than a physical attachment to that person. Now I know that you have never been sexually active and I have and at the risk of sounding selfish, I don't want to engage in intercourse again until there is no question whatsoever about the love. I've done it that way before and let me tell you, there's no sweeter feeling," he concluded. With that he turned and opened the door.

"I'll call you when I get home," he said as he walked out. He was right and she knew it.

On his drive home, he listened to the jazz station as he often did. He loved listening during this time slot because he knew the DJ personally. It was Gail and he loved to listen to her sexy voice. It had been eleven months since he had heard it personally.

While waiting at a red light close to campus, he listened as Gail came back form commercial.

"Welcome back to WCLK, the jazz of the city where we give you all jazz all the time. This is wailing Gail Upshaw and I want to do something a little out of the ordinary right now. I would like to dedicate this next compilation featuring Miles Davis live in Philadelphia to a very special young man out there. This guy has taught me a lot about life in the short time that I've known him and I just want to say Davis, if you're listening, give me a call at 880-8901," she concluded.

He couldn't believe what he had just heard. He rushed the 1988 Maxima up Fairs Street so he could run into the dorm before he forgot the phone number. The phone rang five times before Davis heard Gail's lovely voice answer. She was delighted to hear from him and they immediately started reminiscing. They talked for about three minutes before Gail noticed the record coming to an end.

"Davis I have to go but listen, I have someone here who wants to say something to you, okay."

"Sure," he responded as he wondered who in the hell else at the radio station would be waiting to talk to him especially at this time of night.

"Hello, Davis," a voice came over the phone. He sat quietly for a second in disbelief.

"Kia?" he asked. After confirming it was her, the two started talking. He learned that her and Gail had grown to be close friends ever since that day in the restaurant. The two were going out after Gail's shift to celebrate a promotion Kia had just received. Davis was truly happy for them both. They sounded like they were enjoying life.

As the conversation drew to a close, Kia had something she wanted to get off her chest.

"Davis, I want to say that I have never felt worse than I felt that day at Rah-Rah's. You really hurt me and I thought you should know that before you did it to anyone else. On the other hand, you forced me to evaluate myself and eventually start enjoying my life. I thought you should know that too. I just want to say you have taught me a thing or two about myself. I wanted to say thank you. Good bye Davis. The phone went dead as he stared at the receiver.

"You guys taught me a whole lot more Kia...a whole lot more."

www.CarlRomeoJackson.com

ORDER FORM

Use this order form to order other Bestselling titles.

Name:_____

Company _____

Address: _____

_____

City: _____ State_____ Zip_____

Phone: (_____)_____ Fax: (_____)_____

E-mail: _____

Credit Card: ☐Visa ☐ MC ☐ Amex ☐Discover

Number _____

Exp Date: _____Signature: _____

DESCRIPTION	PRICE	QTY

...SHIPPING CHARGES		
Ground	one book	$ 4.50
each additional book		$ 1.00

Subtotal
shipping
8.5% tax (NY/NJ)
Total

Make checks or money orders payable to
A&B Distributors 1000 Atlantic Avenue,
Brooklyn, New York, 11238